C0-CFJ-261

The Hanging Tree

'The original crossroads used to run by here,' Sam told Rafferty. 'Legend has it that this was the old Hanging Tree ...'

When Inspector Rafferty first hears the report that a bound and hooded body has been seen hanging from a tree in Dedman Wood, he dismisses it as a schoolboy hoax, especially when police at the scene find nothing out of the ordinary.

But his anxiety rises sharply when the witness turns out to be a respectable local magistrate, who identifies the corpse as Maurice Smith, a man once accused of four child rapes. Thrown out on a legal technicality, Smith's case had become a *cause célèbre* which generated much ill-feeling within the community.

Rafferty and Sergeant Llewellyn visit Smith's home – to discover he has mysteriously disappeared. And in his flat they find a threatening letter, and fresh bloodstains ...

Then the body turns up again in the woods. Could there be a self-appointed executioner at work, meting out his own form of justice on the legendary Hanging Tree?

By the same author

DEAD BEFORE MORNING
DOWN AMONG THE DEAD MEN
DEATH LINE

The Hanging Tree

Geraldine Evans

MACMILLAN

First published 1996 by Macmillan

an imprint of Macmillan General Books
25 Eccleston Place London SW1W 9NF

Associated companies throughout the world

ISBN 0 333 653394

Copyright © Geraldine Evans 1996

The right of Geraldine Evans to be identified as the author of this
work has been asserted by her in accordance with the Copyright,
Designs and Patents Act 1988.

All rights reserved. No reproduction, copy or transmission of this
publication may be made without written permission. No paragraph
of this publication may be reproduced, copied or transmitted save
with written permission or in accordance with the provisions of the
Copyright Act 1956 (as amended). Any person who does any
unauthorized act in relation to this publication may be liable to
criminal prosecution and civil claims for damages.

9 8 7 6 5 4 3 2 1

A CIP catalogue record for this book is available from the British
Library.

Phototypeset by Intype, London
Printed by Mackays of Chatham PLC, Chatham, Kent

To all TOGGs – you know who you are!

Chapter One

It was 10 p.m. and Inspector Rafferty was thankful to be going home. The week before Christmas was not the best time of year from a policeman's point of view; Essex, in common with the other densely populated southern counties, had too many criminals with shopping lists of luxury items and a matching reluctance to pay for them. The combination had made his day long and tiring. So he was inclined to snap when Constable Smales burst into his office, crashed the door back against the wall and melodramatically exclaimed, 'It's gone, sir. *Vanished.* Lilley says—'

'Can't you open a door without smashing it off its hinges, man?' Rafferty demanded. 'What's the matter with you?'

Crestfallen, Smales said, 'Sorry, sir.'

'What's gone, anyway?' Rafferty asked as he shrugged into his coat.

'I thought you'd have heard by now, sir.' Smales' fallen crest was now on the rise again and he came forward excitedly. 'A body was reported hanging in Dedman Wood. Only, as I said, when Lilley got there it had vanished, so—'

Rafferty was dismissive. 'Is that all?' Smales' schoolboy enthusiasm for corpses killed his small stock of common sense and Rafferty made a mental note to put the young constable down for a few more post-mortems as a cure for the condition. 'Hardly reason to take the paint off my wall. It's another hoax, man. Have you forgotten it's the school holidays? Last week it was armed robberies – this week it's corpses. With a bit of luck, by next week the bored local teenagers will be tormenting the fire brigade instead of us.'

Smales flushed but continued doggedly. 'It wasn't a kid that reported it, sir. It was a woman. According to Beard, a posh-sounding woman. Very adamant, she was. And she was there waiting for Lilley. Said she almost burned his ears off when he finally got to the scene. And another thing, Lilley said there were definite indications that a body *had* been hanging where she said.'

Rafferty, still keen to get home and put his feet up, wasn't easily moved from his opinion that the call had been a hoax. The world was full of attention-seekers who had forgotten to take their medication; a posh voice and a bossy manner didn't make his conclusions any less likely. Still, he reminded himself, callers intent on wasting police time didn't usually hang around for the police to arrive.

'Lilley said there were what looked like rope marks on one of the more sturdy boughs,' Smales went on. 'And the grass was flattened directly underneath it. A small tuft of rope was still clinging to the bough itself.'

'Could have been made by children with a tyre swing.' Rafferty still felt their witness would turn out to be less impressive in the flesh. But maybe he ought to look into it. Resignedly, he removed his coat and indicated that Smales should continue.

'Beard said the woman who reported it told him she was a magistrate from Burleigh.' Burleigh was in the north of the county, while Elmhurst was in the south, near the coast. 'A Mrs ffinch-Robinson. I can believe the magistrate bit and all, because Lilley said that when he got there and the body had gone, she didn't half give him a ticking-off. Seemed to think he should have got there sooner. Anyway, she said she'd be in to make a formal statement. She hadn't been drinking, either,' Smales added. 'Lilley made sure of that.'

2

Rafferty frowned. ffinch-Robinson. The name rang a bell. And from what Smales said she sounded both sane and sober. But if so, and she was telling the truth, what the devil had become of the body? And if the cadaver was a suicide, as seemed likely, what reason would a third party have for removing it?

Having come up with no answers, he said, 'I want to see Lilley the second he gets back. And warn him he'd better make sure he can read his own writing, because I shall want to know exactly what this Mrs ffinch-Robinson said to him. I'll need chapter and verse, because, by the sound of her, nothing but another corpse will satisfy her.' Pity we can't provide her with one, he muttered to himself.

Mrs ffinch-Robinson arrived at the Elmhurst police station twenty minutes later and was shown into Rafferty's office. She proved not only entirely sober and respectable, but less than understanding of the slow police response.

Rafferty did his best to soothe her ruffled magistrate's feathers. 'It's nearly Christmas, Mrs ffinch-Robinson. A very busy time for us. And—'

'I understand that, Inspector. But I would have thought a report of a man's body hanging in the woods would take precedence over public-house brawls.'

'Normally it would, of course. Unfortunately all the uniformed officers were out or otherwise engaged when your call came through. All I can say is that an officer was despatched in response to your call as soon as possible.'

Thankfully, Mrs ffinch-Robinson didn't pursue the complaint. But she had another that was equally sensitive.

'I suggest you speak to the young officer who finally arrived in response to my call, Inspector. I found his manner offensive. He not only had the effrontery to smell my breath as though he believed me to be drunk . . .' Briefly, Rafferty closed his eyes, surprised at Lilley's clumsiness; it was more the behaviour he had come to expect from young Smales. '. . . but he also warned me of

3

the penalties for wasting police time – hardly conducive to good police–public relations, you must agree.'

As he gazed at Mrs ffinch-Robinson, perched, with all her ruffled magisterial dignity in his visitor's chair, Rafferty wished he hadn't sent Sergeant Dafyd Llewellyn out to soothe the latest victim of Elmhurst's Christmas-shopping criminal fraternity. He could do with Llewellyn's diplomatic skills here. He marvelled at Lilley's nerve. Pity his judgement wasn't so hot, because, from the top of her rather stylish Lincoln green deerstalker hat, to her no-time-to-waste French-pleated hair, through to her firmly corseted figure and practically shod feet in their brilliantly burnished tan boots, Mrs ffinch-Robinson proclaimed authority, sobriety and a total lack of hysteria. Her voice, as crisp as a Cox's Orange Pippin, was clear, precise, and as demanding of a policeman's respect as the rest of her. Hardly surprising, of course. As she had been at pains to explain, she *was* a magistrate.

Rafferty, earlier inclined to scoff at tales of vanishing cadavers, didn't doubt that she was telling the truth about the missing body. Apart from anything else, her statement hadn't varied by as much as a word from that taken down by Lilley. She had told them she was staying with her daughter and had taken the daughter's dog for a walk. It had been the dog who had led her to the corpse. All that was simple enough. But what she had to tell him next was even more worrying and did little to reassure him that the next few days would be anything but difficult.

'I didn't say anything to that young officer,' she told Rafferty, 'as he didn't exactly inspire confidence that one would be believed, but I'm certain the corpse was that of a chap called Maurice Smith.'

Rafferty frowned as another bell rang. Now why did he recognize *that* name?

Mrs ffinch-Robinson's intelligent grey gaze noted his dilemma. 'His was something of a *cause célèbre* about ten years ago. Maurice Smith was charged with raping four young girls. The case was dismissed on a legal technicality on the first day of the trial.' Her firmly chiselled nostrils expressed her disdain for such legal bumbling. 'One of his victims killed herself when Smith was released. As you can imagine, the victims' families were outraged and made various threats against Smith.'

Rafferty nodded. Details of the case were slowly coming back. He seemed to remember that, of the families that Mrs ffinch-Robinson mentioned, one had done more than threaten. The father had waylaid Smith and given him one hell of a beating, receiving a prison sentence for his pains. 'Excuse me, Mrs ffinch-Robinson, but how did you recognize him? After all, it's ten years since—'

Mrs ffinch-Robinson interrupted him. 'Smith used to live in Burleigh, which is where I sit on the bench, and he had come up before me in the Magistrates' Court on several occasions in his teens. His front teeth protruded quite dreadfully. Extraordinary the parents didn't get them seen to, though, of course, the mother was one of those spiritless women you could advise till you were blue in the face. Anyway, the teeth of the corpse were exactly the same. That's how I recognized him. He'd changed very little in other respects, too. There is no doubt in my mind that it was Smith. None at all.'

Reluctant to appear to doubt her, Rafferty had, nevertheless, to question her further. 'Pardon me, but I thought you said he had a hood over his head when you found him, Mrs ffinch-Robinson?'

Although she looked a little put out that he had detected a flaw in her statement, she answered promptly enough. 'So he did. I didn't touch anything, if that's what you're implying. I didn't have to as the wind must have got under the hood and it was half off. Naturally, I shone my torch on his face. You should be grateful I did, Inspector.' The Cox's Orange Pippin in her voice became crisper than ever. 'At least you know the body's identity.' She gave him a stern, magisterial smile. 'Now all you have to do is find it.' She paused. 'And his murderer, of course.'

After Mrs ffinch-Robinson left, Rafferty checked Smith's history. A colleague at Burleigh, as long on the job as himself, was able to confirm all that Mrs ffinch-Robinson had said and more, and it was a pensive Rafferty who called Llewellyn in on his return and briefly explained what had happened.

'You believe her?' Llewellyn asked.

With a wry smile, Rafferty nodded. 'I think we can take it that Mrs ffinch-Robinson wasn't hallucinating. She's a magistrate, no less, and the type to take Harrods trips, not LSD ones.'

'No chance it might be a suicide? After the shock of finding a body, even magistrates can get their facts wrong. It was dark, remember.'

'No chance at all, I should think,' Rafferty told him. Of course, Llewellyn hadn't met Mrs ffinch-Robinson, he reminded himself. 'According to the witness, the body not only had that hood over his head, but his hands were also bound behind his back. No, I'm convinced she was telling the plain, unvarnished truth.' He wished he could say otherwise. Mrs ffinch-Robinson would make a wonderful showing in the witness box – confident, firm, and not to be swayed by the defence counsel's tricks. But first, as she had mentioned, they had not only to find the body, they had also to catch the murderer – without him, their star turn would remain off-stage, probably giving the producer hell from the wings.

After speaking to his Burleigh colleague, Rafferty had done some more digging and now he filled Llewellyn in on the rest. 'Smith moved from Burleigh to Rawston after the aborted rape trial. From there, after a new neighbour recognized him, he moved here, where I gather he's lived for two years. If this missing cadaver *does* turn out to be Maurice Smith, I very much fear someone's been acting as judge, jury and Albert Pierrepoint.'

6

Was there anything more worrying to a policeman than the public taking the law into its own hands? Rafferty mused. Yet at the same time he was aware of a degree of sympathy with such action. Particularly in cases like Smith's, where justice was not only not done, but *seen* not to be done.

Becoming aware of Llewellyn's expectant gaze, he straightened his shoulders, firmed up his spine, and said, 'First, we'd better check that he *is* missing. Send Smales round to his home, Dafyd. Here's the address. And for God's sake tell him to be discreet. Smith's living under the name of Martin Smithson. Tell Smales to make sure he asks for him under that name. When you've done that, I want you to contact Smith's family. Find out when they last saw him or heard from him. I'm sure I don't need to tell *you* to be discreet. As for me and Lilley, we're going to Dedman Wood to take a look at the scene.'

Llewellyn nodded and departed. Rafferty opened his door and shouted for Lilley and when the young officer appeared, told him, 'We're going out to Dedman Wood. I want to have a look for myself.'

It was now getting on for 11 o'clock and Rafferty, cheated of his early night, was in just the right mood for issuing Mrs ffinch-Robinson's advised rebuke. After shrugging into his coat, he said tersely, 'And next time an obviously sober citizen like Mrs ffinch-Robinson reports finding a body, please try not to get their back up. Apart from anything else, it offends against Superintendent Bradley's favourite pet project, *Politeness in Interaction with Members of the Public.*' Rafferty always made sure to mention it whenever one of the younger officers offended against the programme. He felt he had to do his bit to keep it alive. 'You know how fond of it he is. You wouldn't like him to get to hear of your doings, I'm sure.'

Lilley's blond complexion went a little paler and he shook his head. It was well known that Bradley threw himself into a towering rage whenever anyone breached his *Politeness* programme, though few realized the reason why. As, by now, Lilley was staring at his boots, he didn't notice Rafferty's lips twitch. 'Sorry, sir. Won't happen again, sir.'

'See that it doesn't. Admittedly, you're not likely to have too many truly disappearing cadavers in your career. But if you treat important witnesses like Mrs ffinch-Robinson in such a cavalier fashion, your career's likely to be short. Remember that.'

Rebuke over, Rafferty shut his door behind them, hiding the tiny smile as he did so. Even at the end of a long day that promised to wipe the smile off his face, reference to PIMP had the power to amuse. Several months ago, he had got away with supplying the apt acronym for 'Long-Pockets' Bradley's latest attempt to enhance his status at Region with the immoral, penny-pinching, 'Politeness costs nothing' scam. When Bradley had finally woken up to it, Rafferty had succeeded in convincing him that, not only had his suggestion been made in all innocence, but that Region would be less than impressed if he dropped his wool-over-the-public's-eyes wheeze when he had spent so much time and money on its promotion. Warmed by the memory, Rafferty's step, as he followed Lilley to the car park, was more jaunty than it had any right to be.

'Maurice Smith's family say they haven't seen him since yesterday evening,' Llewellyn reported, when Rafferty got back to the station after examining the scene. It had been as Lilley had described, even down to the rope tuft. Rafferty nodded glumly, doubts and amusement both already fading.

'And, as far as they know, he had no travel plans. From what they say, he's something of a loner, and rarely went out or socialized. He had no friends, as far as they're aware. They said they don't see much of him themselves, though I got the impression they don't exactly extend a hearty welcome when he does visit.'

8

'Understandable,' Rafferty commented. 'He must have put them through hell one way and another. Still,' he continued, uneasily, 'if Mrs ffinch-Robinson is right, and it *was* Maurice Smith's body she saw, then this case could have some very awkward connotations. If he's been killed by the family of one of his victims, then public sympathy for them will make our job extremely difficult. *Nobody*'ll co-operate. Nobody'll answer our questions and our chances of catching his killer could be zilch.'

Rafferty, his attitude towards the victim still ambivalent, wasn't sure that wouldn't be the best result. From his understanding of the case, Smith had ruined enough lives; dead, he wouldn't have the chance to ruin more. But, aware that the high-moral-ground Welshman would be unlikely to share his opinion, he kept it to himself. Llewellyn believed that, whatever the provocation, no one had the right to take the law into their own hands. Increasingly these days, Rafferty found his own beliefs wavering. The man, rather than the policeman, thought that, ultimately, every human being was responsible for their own survival and that of their family. If Parliament and the courts, who were supposed to protect the honest citizen, failed in their responsibilities, what was the law-abiding citizen to do? Cower in a corner and let the barbarians do what they liked?

Society had been overwhelmed by crime in recent years; like a flood tide, it poured over their homes, their schools, their neighbourhoods, tainting every aspect of life. The courts issued what he and many other people considered to be futile punishments to the perpetrators, when they punished them at all. Young criminals, in particular, laughed at the law. Without majesty, dignity and a strong right arm, the law *deserved* to be laughed at for the joke it had become. Lately, he had often thought that the Old Bailey, the Central Criminal Court and the prime upholder of the law, should be crowned with *Crime Rools OK* graffiti, rather than the bronze *Justice* statue.

With a sigh, he forced such thoughts to the back of his mind and asked how Smales had got on.

'He was unable to get a reply from either Smith or his landlady,' Llewellyn told him. 'And as he was anxious about your warning on discretion, he thought better of asking amongst the neighbours. I told him to return to the station. I hope that's all right.'

'Yes. It's getting late, too late for banging on doors and disturbing people. We'll go ourselves in the morning. For the moment, I want to keep this low-key. I know Mrs ffinch-Robinson was convinced it was Smith, but it's possible she made a mistake. Time enough to turn up the volume if Smith *has* vanished.'

In spite of his forced optimism, Rafferty wished he could get out of his mind the conviction that the Mrs ffinch-Robinsons of this world were pretty well infallible. Such thoughts were, he felt sure, guaranteed to give him a sleepless night.

Chapter Two

On Friday morning Rafferty and Llewellyn drove to Maurice Smith's flat. He lived in an Edwardian terraced house, once a family home, that had seen better days and had long been converted to separate dwellings. Smith's home was on the first floor, above the landlady, Mrs Penny's, flat. There was an unlocked outside door, and inside this the two flats each had their own doors with letter boxes and secondary bells. Rafferty noticed that Smith's door had a spyhole, an amateur effort that he had probably made himself.

After getting no answer from Smith, Rafferty tried the landlady's bell. But there was no answer there either and he suggested they have a look round the back.

A six-foot double wooden gate concealed concrete hardstanding. Rafferty frowned as he saw the lock on the gate had been forced. 'Looks very recent,' he observed as he examined the bright wood around the lock. As well as the broken gate lock, when they walked up the back path they found a few threads of navy cotton clinging to the fire escape. According to Mrs ffinch-Robinson, the corpse she had found had been wearing a navy and maroon tracksuit. After drawing Llewellyn's attention to the threads, Rafferty sealed them in a plastic bag without further comment.

He was beginning to feel he should have posted an officer in Dedman Wood last night to secure the scene. But it was too late for that now and he consoled himself with the thought that there could be few enough people choosing to walk in the woods after dark, particularly in the depths of winter. Anyway, on the way out this morning he had instructed Lilley to stand guard duty at the scene and with such a belated effort he had to be content. After all, with no corpse they couldn't be sure they had a murder on their hands and, until they *were* sure, he didn't want to alert the press by putting a uniform on guard duty.

They found nothing else and came back to the front of the property. Mrs Penny had still not returned, but, determined to get some answers, Rafferty decided they would wait. There was a baker's on the corner and he sent Llewellyn over to get coffee, which they drank sitting in the car.

The baker's had a three-tiered wedding cake in the window. It turned Rafferty's mind to things other than Smith. Llewellyn had been courting Rafferty's second cousin, Maureen, since the previous April, and, from various remarks that Llewellyn had made, Rafferty had got the impression that a wedding was imminent. But several months had gone by and no announcement had been made. Now, glancing at Llewellyn, he asked, 'So, how's the love life? Popped the question yet?'

Beside him, Llewellyn stiffened. 'We *have* only known one another for a little over eight months, you know. Matrimony is too important a step to rush into.'

'And faint hearts never won fair lady,' Rafferty reminded him. 'What's the matter? Getting cold feet?'

Llewellyn said nothing and Rafferty, who would himself like nothing more than a spot of connubial bliss, commented tartly, 'If I know you, you'll be saying the same in eight *years*. You *do* love each other, I take it?' They'd certainly looked moony-eyed enough to Rafferty on the occasions he'd seen them together.

Llewellyn forced out a 'yes'.

'There you are, then.'

Of course, the Welshman couldn't help being the way he was, Rafferty reminded himself. His background as a Welsh Methodist minister's only son was hardly guaranteed to turn him into a young Lochinvar. What Llewellyn needed was an agony uncle. Or a boot up the backside. Or both.

He plumped for the gentle approach. 'So, what seems to be the problem?' Rafferty now asked, in his best bedside manner. 'You've got heaps in common, you love each other fit to bust. What's holding you up?'

Llewellyn hesitated, then confided, 'I want her to go up to Wales with me to meet my mother. Just a short visit, over a weekend.'

'And Maureen won't go, I take it?'

Llewellyn nodded glumly. 'She said she has no intention of being paraded around my home village like a prize cow.'

Rafferty spluttered into his coffee and muttered to himself, 'That sounds like Maureen.' He thought for a moment, then said brightly, 'So, if the prize cow won't go to the cattle show, what you've got to do is hold the show down here and let Daisy parade only for the prospective purchaser rather than the non-spending gawpers.'

'I wish you wouldn't refer to her as—'

Rafferty held up his hands. 'All right. Sorry. It's a good idea, though, isn't it? Isn't it?' he repeated, when Llewellyn failed to respond.

'It would be if it didn't have several drawbacks, which was the reason *I* didn't suggest it. For one, my flat's too small. Of course she could stay with Maureen's mother, but—'

'Exactly – *but*.'

Maureen's mother was a difficult woman. No, Rafferty thought, scrub that. She was bloody impossible; all airs and graces and condescension; starched tablecloths and starched pillowcases. Starched knickers, too, probably. 'She wouldn't stay in a hotel, I suppose?'

13

'I wouldn't ask it of her. Hotels can be very lonely places. And she's lived a very quiet life.' He glanced quickly at Rafferty. 'You'll probably find this amusing, but she still hasn't got a television set.'

Rafferty didn't find it funny at all. In a sudden burst of generosity, he found himself saying, 'She could stay with Ma. She's got plenty of room.'

Rafferty, always convinced his ideas were excellent until events proved otherwise, pushed this one with his usual enthusiasm. Ignoring the doubtful look in Llewellyn's eye, he said, 'It's the perfect solution, Daff. They're both widows, both alone, it'd be company for both of them. At least let me put it to Ma.'

Llewellyn's old-fashioned look made Rafferty re-examine his initial enthusiasm. Perhaps volunteering Ma and her best spare room wasn't such an inspired notion, after all. If Llewellyn's childhood had been even half as dreary as Rafferty suspected, his mother must be a dour old biddy, as narrow in outlook as his ma was broad.

But he realized he had talked Llewellyn into it when the Welshman suddenly asked, 'You're sure Mrs Rafferty won't mind?'

'Sure I'm sure.' Rafferty swallowed hard and added, 'She'll love it.'

Rafferty's ma had taken even more of a proprietary interest in the romance than Rafferty and was well on the way to persuading Llewellyn to convert to Catholicism. Rafferty consoled himself with the thought that it would only be for a week or so. Just while Mrs Llewellyn looked 'Daisy' over. He'd have to ensure he made that clear. 'I'll ask her tonight,' he told Llewellyn. 'And then you can sort the details out between yourselves.'

It seemed Llewellyn, too, had a few reservations, for he said quickly, 'Perhaps it would be best to make the invitation for *after* Christmas? I'm sure your mother will be far too busy to want to entertain strangers then.'

'Good idea.' Christmas at Ma's house was normally riotous. Not suitable for an old-fashioned Methodist matron, who was likely to be long on sin and short on forgiveness. Not suitable at all. Though the more Rafferty thought about it the more he realized there were few periods in the year when the visit *wouldn't* turn out to be an unmitigated disaster. Why don't I keep my big mouth shut? he asked morosely. It'll all end in tears, I know it will. Probably mine.

He pushed his gloomy conclusions aside as he saw a comfortably built woman in her seventies walking towards them, a well-filled shopping trolley pushed before her. 'Want to bet that's Smith's landlady?'

Not being a betting man, Llewellyn didn't take him up on his offer. But Rafferty's guess was borne out when she stopped at the front door and pulled out a key.

They got out of the car. Rafferty, careful not to startle her, took his warrant card from his pocket and softly called her name. As she turned, he held the card up and slowly approached.

'We're police officers. You *are* Mrs Penny?' She nodded and Rafferty introduced himself and Llewellyn. 'I wonder, could we have a word? It's about your lodger.'

'About Ma-Martin?' She studied them anxiously before asking, 'Why? Whatever has he done?'

'He hasn't done anything,' Rafferty hastened to reassure her. At least not lately, he silently amended. 'We just need to speak to him, but as he isn't home . . .'

Mrs Penny hesitated, then said, 'You'd better come in.'

Mrs Penny's living room was homely; comfortable, if over-furnished, with masses of family photographs dotted about. Her face creased in anxiety as, after she had sat them down, she said, 'You're sure he's not in any sort of trouble?'

'No.' Rafferty paused and added, 'That is, not exactly. As I said, we just wanted to speak to him. Actually, one of my officers called round yesterday evening, but he could get no reply at either Mr Smithson's flat or yours. Of course, it *was* rather late.'

In spite of her obvious anxiety about her lodger, Mrs

Penny managed a tiny smile. 'Isn't that always the way? Last night was the first evening I've been out in four months. Went to a WRAF's reunion at a local hotel. It was after midnight before I got home. Haven't had such a good time since I don't know when.'

The houses on either side were also multi-occupancy, she told them, but their landlords, unlike her, didn't live on the premises and the tenants were mostly young and tended to come and go. She had been widowed two years earlier and nowadays she rarely saw anyone unless she went out and, apart from shopping, that happened seldom. 'But here am I forgetting my manners. Let me make some tea.'

She bustled into the kitchen and was soon plying them with such quantities of tea, home-made sponge and biscuits that it wasn't hard to guess the extent of her loneliness.

As she sat down, Rafferty explained that her lodger had been reported missing. He judged that was the safest way to describe the peculiar events of yesterday. 'There are certain – aspects, shall we say, that warrant further investigation.'

Her wide brow creased as she returned to his previous answer. 'But who would report him missing? He has no friends, and although he saw his family on Wednesday evening, that's the first time he's seen them in weeks.' Her warm gaze was sad. 'His mother died some years ago and he doesn't really get on with his stepfather and half-brother. From odd things he's said, I gather they don't encourage his visits. I don't know why he bothers. Still, I suppose they're the only family he's got. But in reality I'm probably the nearest thing he's got to true friend and family both, and I certainly haven't reported him missing.' She eyed them shrewdly. 'So who has?'

'I'm afraid I can't tell you that, Mrs Penny,' Rafferty replied. 'I can only say again that the person who did so is very respectable, very responsible, and wouldn't make such a report without being pretty sure of the facts.'

Her expression anxious, she told them, 'You know, now you mention it I haven't heard him at all this morning and he's generally an early riser. Usually, I hear him moving about. Wednesday evening he was pacing up and down as though he had something on his mind; it went on till the early hours. Yesterday evening was the same – at least until I went out. It worried me to leave him all alone when he was so obviously troubled. I had half a mind to stay home after all, but Martin wouldn't hear of it. He wouldn't tell me what the matter was and I couldn't force him.'

She sighed heavily. 'And now you tell me he's missing. I do hope he hasn't done anything silly.' Her warm brown gaze rested steadily on Rafferty's face. 'You know his real identity, I take it?'

Rafferty nodded, surprised that she should be aware of it and still let Smith remain in her home.

She explained. 'He told me who he was a couple of months after he moved in. He knew from the Social that I was on the list of those prepared to offer a home to men like him. I suppose he felt he could confide in me.' She sighed again. 'I do wish he'd told me what's been worrying him this last day or two.'

'You weren't concerned when he told you of his background?' Rafferty asked.

'I'm seventy-six, Inspector,' she told him calmly. 'An age I thought unlikely to rouse Maurice's anti-social urges. I felt sorry for him. He was – is,' determinedly she corrected herself, as though unwilling to accept the possibility that her lodger might be dead, 'a pretty sad young man; plain, awkward, lacking any social graces. He desperately needed someone to talk to, someone to take an interest in him. I don't think anyone else ever did. Of course with most people his appearance and diffident manner went against him.'

She studied them for a moment, as though weighing

17

them up, before confiding, 'My son had a similar problem to Maurice. My Alan committed suicide when he was twenty-eight because he hated himself so much. No one seemed able to help him. He served a prison sentence for assaulting one young girl. He had an awful time there and was terrified he would weaken, attack another young girl and get sent back. He was ashamed of what he'd done, but he told me when he got these urges they seemed to take him over.' In her lap, her hands gripped each other tightly. 'I think in the end, he felt he could no longer cope with the emotions raging inside him, so – he destroyed himself. He felt it was his only choice. I thought . . .' She bit her lip. 'I thought I might be able to help Maurice, where I'd failed to help my son, prevent the same thing happening to him as happened to my boy. They can control that sort of sexual compulsion nowadays, can't they? Only—' She faltered. 'Only nobody seems terribly bothered to do so. I knew Maurice confessed to the police. He expected to be put away, to get help. Only he wasn't and he didn't.' Abruptly, she got up. Rafferty guessed the memories of her son were too painful, too full of self-blame and thoughts of *if only* for her to wish to dwell on them. 'You'll want the key to his room.'

'Thank you.' Rafferty paused. 'I gather Maurice Smith's been here about two years now?'

She nodded and handed over the key. 'You'll not disturb things too much, will you?' she asked. 'Only he'll be upset if I have to tell him you've been going through his things. He can be very secretive.'

Rafferty reassured her. 'I wonder, have you any idea what he was wearing yesterday evening? It would help our enquiries to know.'

She nodded. 'He was wearing a navy and maroon tracksuit.'

Rafferty and Llewellyn exchanged glances.

Mrs Penny hadn't missed the exchange. In a shaky voice she added, 'He was wearing it when I went up to say goodbye at seven-thirty.'

She hurried on as if reluctant to enquire further as to what significance they placed on the tracksuit. 'He preferred such clothes to shirts and proper trousers. Didn't show the dirt and saved ironing, he said, though I'd have willingly done his laundry for him, and his cleaning, if he'd let me. But, as I said, in many ways he was a very private person and he was wary about getting too close. He didn't like letting anyone in his room; he told me he'd had threats made against him in the past. He always kept his front door on a chain and never released it till he had checked his caller's identity through that spyhole he drilled in his door.'

She paused, and, eyes clouding with anxiety, she added, 'The jogging suit should be in his laundry basket. He always went to the laundry on Friday nights.' Obviously, even without their confirmation, she had concluded for herself that the tracksuit was important, for before turning away she added, 'I hope you find it.'

So did Rafferty.

Rafferty put the key in the lock and opened the door to Maurice Smith's flat. Though 'flat' was a grand name for what was little more than a large bedsit with cubbyhole kitchen and tiny bathroom. Bathroom was another misnomer as there was no bath, merely a shower cubicle and a grubby toilet. He wondered why Smith hadn't taken Mrs Penny up on her offer to do his cleaning, because it was obvious he didn't trouble with such chores himself. The place was filthy, with the sour smell of unwashed sheets, discarded food and rarely opened windows.

Rafferty was about to make a derogatory comment on Smith's slovenly housekeeping when a fleeting picture of his own bathroom with its less than sparkling white enamel made him think better of it. But, he persuaded himself, his bathroom did not the man make. Obviously other habits had far more bearing on character. He checked through the laundry basket. Though it had several items of dirty clothing, the navy and maroon track-suit wasn't amongst them.

With downturned lips, Llewellyn surveyed the room; from its leaning tower of yellowing newspapers, to the unmade bed with its soiled grey sheets, to the mis-matched crockery piled in the kitchen sink. 'Tidy chap, wasn't he?' he commented, his words revealing that he not only shared Rafferty's distaste for Smith's sluttish housewifery, but also the growing conviction that Smith *was* dead.

Rafferty smiled crookedly and advised, 'Just be grateful we remembered our Marigolds,' as he pulled the thin protective gloves from his pocket and put them on. 'And, although this is not yet an official murder investigation, that doesn't mean it mightn't be soon, so try not to move the dust around too much.'

They didn't know what they might find here, he reas-oned. If Smith was dead, as seemed increasingly likely given the build-up of evidence, it was possible the flat might yield valuable clues to his murderer's identity.

There was a battered sideboard against the far wall and Rafferty made for it, with the unkind thought that it would do his fussy Virgoan sergeant the world of good to plunge his suit and his sensibilities into the collection of Grub Street's outpourings that Smith seemed to have amassed. Besides, he added to himself in mitigation before his conscience could chime in, the sideboard seemed the most likely place for Smith to keep anything of a personal nature and was therefore the inspector's prerogative.

Behind him, Llewellyn sneezed as he began to dis-mantle the pile of newsprint. 'These are all about the court case,' Llewellyn told him shortly, as he held the yellowed ten-year-old Elmhurst *Evening Echo* at arm's length and began to read from its front page. '*Maurice Smith freed on legal technicality. The Court was in uproar after the Judge's decision to free self-confessed rapist, Maurice*

Smith. In the public gallery, the crowd were on their feet, shouting, screaming, demanding justice. Outraged, several of the victims' fathers yelled, "We'll get you, you b——" at the defendant.

'In the dock, the defendant's face, shocked when the judge declared the evidence inadmissible, now became positively ashen, his body visibly shaking. He looked terrified. As the police bustled twenty-year-old Smith out of the courtroom, several of the crowd managed to get in the odd punch, the odd kick. The police officers didn't appear to try too hard to stop them.'

'Maurice Smith's fifteen minutes of fame,' Rafferty commented when Llewellyn paused. 'Mrs Penny gave us the impression he wanted help, hated himself, yet the fact that he kept that pile of newsprint would seem to indicate that his notoriety had fed a fair-sized ego. Makes you wonder.'

Rafferty eased his back and bent again to his searches. Like the first, the second drawer was stuffed to overflowing with paper. Unsurprisingly, Maurice Smith's correspondents, in the main, seemed to have been the Social. From the time-scale of the correspondence, it was evident that Smith hadn't had a job since the court case, though, from what Rafferty had read about him recently, Smith had seldom held down a job before it either and was apparently inadequate in more ways than the obvious.

Incredibly, or perhaps not so incredibly given his amassing of newspapers giving details of the case, Smith had also kept the hate mail that had been directed to his original family home. There were about fifty in a bunch, held together by a thick elastic band. Rafferty flicked through them. In the way of such missives, they were unsigned and contained the usual badly spelled bile. They were well fingered, in some places split along the folds as though Smith had found a masochistic thrill in reading and re-reading the messages of hate he had spawned.

Rafferty put the letters to one side and was just about

to push the drawer back in when he noticed the corner of another piece of paper poking over the back edge of the wood. Pulling the drawer out completely, he put it on the floor before retrieving the paper. This one differed from the rest, he immediately saw. For one thing, the paper looked new, still crisp, still white.

His heart began to thump as he turned the paper over and saw that someone had taken the trouble to painstakingly cut out characters from a newspaper and stick them down on the sheet. The rest of Smith's hate mail had been either typed or handwritten.

'Dafyd,' he called. 'Come and take a look at this.'

Llewellyn abandoned his newspaper scavenging with alacrity and came over.

'*Your identity is known,*' Rafferty read. '*You can hide no longer, your evil deeds will soon be brought to public notice once again. Confess, confess, and admit your crimes. Beg your victims for forgiveness or further action will be taken against you. You have twenty-four hours.* Seems like he was threatened with "outing",' Rafferty commented.

'Outing', the practice originally directed by gay-and-proud-of-it activists at closet homosexuals in high-profile positions in society to force them to admit their sexual identity, had recently taken another turn. It was now used against rapists like Smith, who had got off on legal technicalities and who were either living under aliases for their own protection or whose names, to protect the identity of their victims, had never been released to the general public. It was suspected that the information about their victims' whereabouts was supplied by disgruntled police officers.

Although the more militant elements in women's groups were almost certainly the main proponents of 'outing', they were careful enough to cover their tracks and never admitted their involvement. Rafferty had often wondered what stopped them, as they would surely welcome the publicity a criminal prosecution would bring to their cause.

There was a Rape Support Group locally. Rafferty knew Mrs Nye, their spokeswoman, personally and he doubted she would be involved in 'outing' rapists or allow any of her members to do so. Still, *someone* had attempted it.

He pulled a plastic bag from his pocket and carefully slipped the missive inside. In view of the care the writer had taken to hinder handwriting identification he thought it unlikely they'd find any fingerprints on it, but if Smith didn't turn up soon he'd get it checked out by the Document Examiner. He hunted for the envelope the 'outing' letter might have come in and eventually found one that looked a possible. It was in the small wicker wastepaper basket. Plain white, with a first-class stamp, someone had taken the trouble to use a stencil set to write Smith's name and address. He checked the postmark: Tuesday morning, so it had presumably arrived some time on Wednesday. The letter had given Smith twenty-four hours to come clean about what he had done – no wonder he had spent that evening and the next pacing his floor; and now he was not only missing but reported dead. Ironic, really, Rafferty thought. After all, Smith *had* already confessed, all those years ago.

Rafferty found another couple of bags, one for the envelope and one for the hate mail, then carried on with the search. He was about to return downstairs to ask Mrs Penny if she had known of the letter or if she could tell them by which post it had arrived, when his mobile phone rang. It was Smales. And if Rafferty had ever heard of the warning to be careful for what you wished as your wish might come true, he had no premonition that he was about to learn the truth of the adage.

Chapter Three

'Sir? You know that body that was hanging in the woods?'

Rafferty, warned by the deliberate drama in Smales' voice, said sharply, 'What about it?'

'It's only turned up again, sir. Hanging in the woods, like before. Lilley is there now, guarding it in case it does another vanishing act.'

Just like a child on Christmas morning, when Santa had brought him *exactly* what he'd asked for, Smales could hardly contain his excitement. Rafferty smothered a sigh and reminded himself that Smales was still very young, very inexperienced, and looked even younger than his years, traits which caused some of the women officers, who found his boyish ways endearing, to make a bit of a pet of him. Rafferty, in an attempt to compensate for this smothering, found he had frequently to play the stern father role. It didn't come easily.

'Try to remember, Smales, that this cadaver – if it's not just a figment of Lilley's eager-beaver imagination – was somebody's loved one.' Unless it *was* Smith, of course, Rafferty reminded himself. Smith; unloved and sure to be unlamented by everyone except his landlady. 'If you concentrate on that thought, you'll find it takes the edge off the hormones.' Besides, Rafferty told himself, not very convincingly, the body mightn't even be Smith's. Though the chances of two different cadavers hanging in Dedman Wood in the space of twelve hours was pretty slim.

24

There was an embarrassed throat-clearing at the other end of the phone.

'So what makes you so sure this is the same body? Have you got a confirmed identity?'

'No doubt about it, guv.' Some of the earlier excitement edged its way back into Smales' voice. 'Lilley got Liz Green to take a copy of Smith's mugshot out to the woods when the warden told him he'd found a body. It's Maurice Smith, all right.'

Rafferty silently congratulated Lilley's initiative. Obviously, he had taken to heart his words of warning and was doing his best to impress. However, he changed his mind as Smales' voice ran breathlessly on, advising that the body was right by where Mrs ffinch-Robinson's cadaver had vanished.

'Is that so?' Rafferty frowned. 'Lilley was supposed to be guarding the scene of crime,' he snapped. 'So how come the warden, rather than Lilley, found the body?'

This time Smales wasn't quite so ready to push his opinions and a deathly silence wafted down the airwaves.

'Get a touch of the ghostly ghoulies, did he?' Rafferty asked. 'Sat his sentry-go duties out in his car, I suppose?' Rafferty couldn't altogether blame him, as he knew his own imagination would have gone into overdrive in the same situation. His gaze settled on Smith's armchair and his eyes narrowed. Was he seeing things, or did one of the stains on the back of the chair look fresher than the rest?

'. . . didn't seem likely there'd have been two different bodies hanging in the woods in such a short space of time, sir,' Smales gabbled in his ear, repeating his own earlier conclusion. 'Funny thing, though. Lilley told me that last time, the witness claimed the body was bound and had a hood over his head. He has neither this time, though he's still wearing the navy and maroon tracksuit and—'

Rafferty broke into Smales' rhetoric. 'Tell me, has he any injuries? A stab wound, for instance?'

25

'Funny you should say that, sir.' Rafferty smiled at the astonishment in Smales' voice, and guessed his detecting skills had gone up a notch in the young copper's estimation. 'He's been stabbed high in the back, according to Lilley. Slap bang through the heart.'

Rafferty nodded to himself. Although he had no reason to think Lilley an expert on forensic pathology, it was likely he was right. According to his record, Smith was a small, slight man. He couldn't be sure, of course, but it was his guess that the stain on the armchair was exactly where he'd expect to find it if a man of Smith's height had been sitting in it when stabbed through the heart.

Rafferty, remembering what Mrs Penny had said on the subject, found himself wondering who Smith would have trusted enough to let enter his room? Taking the 'outing' letter in conjunction with the earlier hate mail he had received after the case, he would surely have been even more wary than usual? According to Mrs Penny, his family didn't encourage Smith to visit *them*, so it was hardly likely they were in the habit of visiting him.

Swiftly, he gave his instructions to Smales. He wanted a team sent to Dedman Wood and another to Smith's room. 'You know what to do to get it organized. Sergeant Llewellyn will wait here for the arrival of the second team.'

Rafferty thought it probable that Smith had died in his flat, but the sooner they knew for certain the better. He decided to postpone questioning Mrs Penny again. For the moment he felt it was more urgent to confirm the cadaver's identity for himself. Besides, he reasoned, if it *was* Smith, he'd rather question her further when he broke the news to her. 'Has Dr Dally been contacted?'

'Not yet, sir. Lilley only just called in.'

'I'll give him the good news myself,' Rafferty decided. 'Off you go.'

He told Llewellyn what had happened, drew his attention to the armchair and told him to point it out to the forensic team when they arrived. Then he dialled Sam's number. Surprisingly, Sam Dally answered immediately the switchboard put him through. 'You're eager, Sam. Got nothing left to cut up?'

'Why?' Dally countered. 'Are you volunteering?'

Rafferty checked his heart. It was still ticking. 'Not yet. I'll get my GP to let you know when I'm ready for the slab.' He paused. 'Got a live one for you.'

'You mean you're letting me kill the customers as well as cutting 'em up, now? That should keep me in business till I collect my pension.'

'A live *dead* one,' Rafferty corrected himself. 'A swinger, though I doubt the rope killed him as, according to young Lilley, he was stabbed through the heart, and this is his second stringing up.' Quickly Rafferty explained about the earlier episode. 'The troops are on their way. I just thought I'd ring you myself and give you a chance to fill your flask with a warming nip of something. It's bitter out there.'

'What a thoughtful wee laddie y'are, Rafferty. So, where is it – this swinger?'

Rafferty told him. 'I'll see you there.'

The December morning was raw and overcast, and by the time Rafferty arrived the uniformed branch had stationed officers with torches at strategic points along the lonely, little-used lane. Rafferty turned the last corner and before he doused his headlights they picked out Lilley's fair hair and pale face.

The young officer, recognizing the car, hurried forward. 'It's Smith, sir, I'm sure of it,' he told Rafferty as the inspector climbed out of the car.

Rafferty nodded and got into his protective gear as Lilley repeated what Smales had already told him. 'Let's have the mugshot,' he said. Lilley gave it to him, and, after Rafferty had given his name to the officer recording each arrival, he guided him eagerly along the taped-off route.

As before, when Lilley had accompanied him to the

scene and shown where Mrs ffinch-Robinson had found the body, Rafferty saw that no attempt had been made to conceal it deeper in the wood. It hung from one of the lower branches of a sturdy oak tree, swinging to and fro on the end of the noose, the tracksuit rucked up, exposing the skinny, mottled torso.

Rafferty gazed at the body impassively for several minutes before he raised the photograph that Lilley had supplied. He switched on his torch and compared the two. As Mrs ffinch-Robinson had claimed, the teeth were certainly the same, prominent, yellow and protruding over the bottom lip, one with a little chip missing. The ears, as though designer-constructed to match the teeth, also stuck out.

Not a face to inspire love, Rafferty concluded. Nor one likely to incline its owner towards a confident, outgoing nature. With a pang of unexpected sympathy, Rafferty felt that in a society obsessed with good looks such a face was more likely to belong to an introverted misfit; one of society's rejects. Smith had certainly been that, he felt, and as he switched off the torch he immediately asked himself if he wasn't being too simplistic? There were, after all, few enough beauties in the world of either sex, yet most people, the bat-eared and the goofy included, managed to pair up.

What was it they said? he asked himself. That emotional involvement was the murderer of good police work. They were right, he knew that. Even so, he still couldn't help feeling sorry for the poor little bastard. Of all the corpses he had seen – and he'd seen a few – he felt this one was in many ways the most pitiful. He could sense, just by looking at him, that Maurice Smith's life had contained little, if any, joy; restriction and misery and frustration had undoubtedly been his usual companions; no caring family, no girlfriends, not even money to pay prostitutes; an existence, nothing more. Maybe if someone had done something years earlier, straightened his teeth out, had his ears pinned back, *loved* him, he might never have done what he did.

Rafferty realized he was doing it again – letting his emotions get too strong a grip. He reminded himself that Smith had raped little girls. What excuse could there be for that?

It was eerie in the wood. The trees seemed to loom threateningly and Rafferty told himself not to be ridiculous. The torches gave only a sparse half-light, faintly assisting the grey day, and, above the murmured voices of his colleagues, he could still hear the creaking of the branch under its unaccustomed weight. Although in the gloom, with his own torch switched off, he was unable to make out more than a pale blur where Smith's face was, he could still see it clearly in his mind's eye; the rabbit teeth, the weak chin, the bat ears, the pathetic skinniness of the flesh where the tracksuit had parted. He shivered and turned away to let the photographer get on with his work.

Even the usually black-humoured Sam Dally, the police surgeon *cum* pathologist, was affected by the scene when he arrived five minutes later. His first comment as he took in the dangling corpse only served to increase the sense of doom and gloom.

'*Though every prospect pleases, and only man is vile.*'

'I suppose that's one of Llewellyn's borrowed homilies,' Rafferty said.

Sam nodded. 'Some eighteenth-century bishop, if I remember correctly. Must be a sixties child,' he said briefly, as he studied the corpse, explaining for the benefit of those too young or too slow to appreciate the allusion, 'still swinging'. Nobody laughed.

After Lance, the photographer, had finished filming the body *in situ*, a shivering Sam Dally quickly confirmed both stab wound and the extinction of life, and the body was cut down.

He went through his usual checks with even more

speed. As Rafferty had remarked, it was a freezing day, the sky heavy and threatening snow, and none were keen to linger longer than necessary; the pathetic cadaver, its flesh having already been exposed to the elements for some time, had such a chilling effect, physically, mentally, emotionally, that Rafferty felt he would never get warm again, never get that sad, plain face out of his mind, and as soon as Sam had finished ministering to the corpse he relieved him of his flask and took a reviving nip. Strictly against regulations, of course, but now was not the time to worry about such things.

He stared hard at the body and thought about the 'outing' threat: although the first finding of the body, with its macabre accoutrements, might be explained as the threat being carried to its ultimate conclusion, it didn't explain its removal and second appearance. He and Lilley had examined the surrounding area the day before, and checked missing persons in case the identification had been wrong. And although the branch *had* shown signs of damage, with a rope tuft still clinging determinedly to it, the body had certainly gone. Now here it was again; as large as life. Or death.

Rafferty shivered again and turned to Lilley. 'I gather the warden found him?'

Lilley nodded. 'That's him, guv.' He pointed to a middle-aged man sitting in one the police cars. The warden had a sour face, the disapproval on the countenance set in concrete, as though he felt the whole scene, corpse, bustling coppers and all, had been organized solely to discommode him.

Rafferty sighed and tried to make allowances. The man had had a shock after all. He was bound to look a bit grim. Even so, he thought, he still looks a miserable b—.

Sam Dally interrupted him before his charitable impulse was totally eroded. 'I'd say he's been dead something like twelve hours, which would fit in with what you told me.'

'Reckon whoever strung him up the second time was hoping to pass it off as a suicide?' Rafferty asked.

'Need more than hope to bring it off, seeing as he had a bloody great stab wound in his back.' Sam pulled back the wrist cuffs on the tracksuit to expose weals on both wrists. 'A suicide who ties his own wrists?' he went on. 'You'd have to be one of life's eternal optimists to think you could convince anyone it was a DIY job.

'Almost certainly died from the stab wound,' Sam added, 'as there are no petechiae in the conjunctiva, which I'd expect from death by hanging, though confirmation of that will have to wait till I've done the post-mortem. We're a bit slack at the moment. The usual winter rush of customers hasn't materialized – must be waiting to see what Father Christmas brings them – so I'll fit him in straight after lunch.'

Rafferty grimaced. That meant no lunch for him. Post-mortems made his stomach churn enough when it was empty. It had been touch and go at the last autopsy he had attended and he didn't want to risk it again. Sometimes, he suspected Sam deliberately timed the post-mortems on his cases for just after meals. He wouldn't put it past him.

'You said on the phone that this is the second time he's been strung up,' Sam commented.

Rafferty nodded. 'Same body, different tree. The first time, according to the witness, a Mrs ffinch-Robinson, who's a magistrate from Burleigh, no less, and a very reliable witness, it was hanging from that tree over there.' Rafferty pointed to a venerable oak; huge and gnarled, it looked like it had been around since the beginning of time. 'Only by the time Lilley got here to investigate, the body had gone.'

Rafferty told Sam the corpse's identity and about the 'outing' letter they had found. 'It looks very much as if someone's been playing Judge Jeffreys and Lord High Executioner combined. I don't like it.'

An odd expression danced its way across Sam Dally's face as Rafferty finished his explanation. 'The original crossroads used to run by here,' Sam told him, ominously adding, 'Legend has it that this,' he pointed to the gigantic oak, 'was the old Hanging Tree. One of them, anyway – in medieval times they generally put a beam across the branches of two trees and kicked away the ladder when the condemned was aloft.'

Rafferty gazed at the tree with quickened interest. Oak trees always reminded him of elephants; he supposed it was the coarse, scored look of them. This one, even in the gloomy half-light under the branches, looked like the oldest elephant who had ever lived, a real Methuselah of an elephant, all criss-crossed skin, the individual diamond shapes standing out half an inch and more from the flesh. It was an easy step to convince himself that it had a matching elephantine memory and, hidden deep in its trunk, it would have stored the name, face and emotions of every one of the hundreds of poor wretches it had helped despatch to the next world.

'Used to string up witches, heretics and other individualists,' Sam continued. 'Though, as I said—'

'Witches?' Rafferty interrupted. 'I thought they were always burned?'

'Read your history books, laddie,' Sam advised. 'That was always more of a Scottish custom. It became popular down here when Scottish Jimmy inherited the English throne in the early seventeenth century. A man with a mighty big fear of witches was old Jimmy One. Last century, by comparison, they were much less obsessed with punishing supposed witches and more into doing the dreaded deed to anyone who struck a Privy Councillor, damaged Westminster Bridge, or impersonated a Chelsea Pensioner. The list of punishments for which you could be hanged in the earlier part of the nineteenth century was long and merciless, I tell you.'

The latter description was much like Sam Dally,

Rafferty reflected, as Sam, who always seemed to get great pleasure out of encouraging others' worst fears, added, 'For once, it looks as if your theory is bang on target. When it comes to your murderer, Lord High Executioner seems about the size of it. For your sake, I hope your killer isn't as determined to rid the country of rapists as James I was to rid it of witches, and later monarchs of Chelsea Pensioner impersonators.'

Such a possibility had already occurred to Rafferty, but he hadn't been willing to dwell on it. Now, though, hearing it put into words by the far-from-fanciful Dally, he felt as though an icy hand had gripped his stomach and twisted it. His own unspoken concerns, taken together with Sam's robust observation, forced him to consider the worst-case scenario in earnest: what if this killing wasn't simply a one-off act of revenge but the beginning of a determined campaign? An 'outing' campaign with a vengeance? One that didn't stop at threats of exposure and their follow-through.

As Rafferty's guts practised reef knots, the tubby little doctor tortured him further. 'I know this looks like an unimportant little lane now, but at one time this was an ideal place to dangle corpses, educationally speaking. Before they built the modern highway across the fields, this was the main thoroughfare; one arm led, ultimately, to London, the opposite one to the port of Harwich, one to Elmhurst and its ancient Priory, the other to Colchester. It was a pretty busy road, too, by the standards of the time, with Walsingham pilgrims; merchants' carts with wool or woven cloth bound for continental markets, even royalty often travelled this way; Henry VIII's blonde-bombshell younger sister, Mary, had a home at Woodbridge.'

'What a mine of information you are today, Sam,' Rafferty commented morosely. 'What did you do, swallow an encyclopedia for breakfast?'

'Not me; the wife's the one who swears by roughage.

She's also the history buff. She's recently joined the Local History Society and she dragged me along to their last outing – said it should interest me as it was my line of country. Their treasurer, who has a rather suspect fascination with the more ghoulish side of history, brought us out this way. Anyway, he told us all the pretty little tales I've just told you; presumably on the principle of give 'em plenty of fascinatingly grisly stuff from the off and they'll stay and pay more subs. Play your cards right, Rafferty, and I might be able to wangle you an invite to their annual Iceni versus the Romans war games.'

'Sounds just my kind of thing,' Rafferty murmured, wishing Sam had taken longer to recover his equilibrium. To his relief, the Coroner's Officer finally gave permission for the body to be moved and the Scene of Crime team began to wrap it in its protective covering. He stamped his frozen feet in an attempt to encourage some life into them and wished the SOCOs would get a move on.

Never one to waste a captive audience, Dally went on. 'Interesting chap, this treasurer wallah. Did you know that hanging, as an instrument of judicial execution, came to England by way of the Anglo-Saxons?'

By now numbed in mind and body, Rafferty merely shook his head.

'Who, in turn, got it from their German ancestors. According to this lecturer, hanging became the established punishment for many crimes in the twelfth century when Henry II instituted trial by jury and assize courts. You and I, Rafferty, have both cut down enough suicides to know it's not the swift, painless death most people imagine it to be. Hanging is a very difficult thing to carry out efficiently. It takes precision, expertise and plenty of practice to get all the variables correct; the length of rope, the weight and drop ratio, et cetera. Get 'em wrong and instead of breaking the bones of the cervical vertebrae, crushing the spinal cord and paralysing the body, the poor wretch strangles to death.'

Rafferty, who always tried to avoid thinking about the more upsetting details of death, made to interrupt, but Sam was well into his stride and not to be put off.

'No, not a pleasant death. Many executions were botched jobs, of course. Some poor souls lingered for ages, slowly strangling. Ghastly business. Though I suppose that was the whole point; make it as ghastly a spectacle as possible and you'll keep far more of the populace on the straight and narrow.' He rubbed his hand round his short neck feelingly and grinned. 'It would certainly have kept me a Simon pure.'

'You were never a Simon pure,' Rafferty told him gruffly.

'How little you know of your sainted man of medicine.' Sam's smile was benign, his tongue anything but, as he continued in the same sadistic vein. 'Sometimes, if the executioner was unusually kind or the family had the wisdom to bribe him well, he'd allow a member of the condemned's family to pull on the victim's legs to hasten the end. Not very popular with the crowd, that, of course, they'd come to be entertained. Must have got their money's worth when the poor blighters were hanged, drawn and quartered.' His smile twisted slightly as he went on. 'I remember this chap told us of one particular execution where—'

'*Thank* you, Sam.' Rafferty broke in forcefully before Sam launched into some other grisly anecdote. 'I think I've learned all I want to know about hanging for one day.' In his opinion, the sainted man of medicine was as much of a ghoul as the treasurer of the History Society. 'Anyway, according to you, this chap almost certainly *didn't* die by hanging. So—'

'What's that got to do with it?' Sam demanded. 'You were the one who dragged executions into the conversation. And as the murderer seems to share your strange interest in hanging, I merely filled you in from my own extensive knowledge.'

'Very good of you, I'm sure.'

Thankfully, the corpse, now wrapped in his temporary modern winding sheet, was ready for the off. Rafferty spoke to the warden who had found the body, who seemed more concerned with sounding off about poachers and could tell them little more than when he'd found the cadaver, so Rafferty, having suffered more than enough lectures for one day, got in his car and bumped his way behind the Coroner's van back down the narrow lane.

Chapter Four

'*Another triumph for British justice*', the yellowing editorial of the Elmhurst *Evening Echo* that had appeared the day after Smith's trial proclaimed on the front page, outrage from the previous day understandably undiminished. Because Maurice Smith, self-confessed multiple rapist, had been freed on a legal technicality, in spite of his confession, in spite of testimony from his young victims, in spite of months of police work.

How could it happen? everyone had asked. The victims' families, their MPs, all demanded an enquiry. But no matter how many voices were raised in a clamour of justice, *this* case was over. Maurice Smith was free to rape again.

'And now he's dead, murdered.' Rafferty flung the newspaper he had brought from Smith's flat on to the table in the newly set-up Incident Room and sat down heavily. 'And he had to die on our patch.'

Lilley's identification had been correct; any doubt had soon been banished with the fingerprint evidence, which, as Smith had been in trouble before the failed rape trial, was still on file.

Thank God we weren't the officers to make a botch of Smith's confession, Rafferty thought as he stared at the expectant faces in front of him. His mind turned back to that morning, when Maurice Smith's body had been discovered for the second time, and he had to force it back, force himself to concentrate on the here and now.

*

It was some time later, with the team briefed and most dismissed to their house-to-house investigations, that Rafferty studied the remaining faces, before handing Hanks the list he'd obtained from the police at Maurice Smith's old stamping ground of Burleigh.

'These are the names and addresses of Smith's victims and their families. It's ten years old, so there may be divorces, house moves, remarriages. I want you to check out their current whereabouts. But be discreet. When you've confirmed their current addresses come back here. I don't want them questioned yet. Have you got that?' Hanks nodded and left the office.

Rafferty turned his attention to Lilley and Lizzie Green. 'I want you two to go and ask around Smith's present neighbourhood. See if there's been any strangers hanging around, *anything*, in fact, that's out of the ordinary. His landlady was out that night. She was too upset when I broke the news to her earlier to be able to tell me much, so speak to her as well. She might have remembered something more now she's had a little time to get over the shock of Smith's death.'

He handed over the plastic-enclosed envelope with its stencilled address. 'We know Maurice Smith was sent an "outing" letter and according to Mrs Penny, Smith's landlady, the postman brought this envelope on the Wednesday morning before he died. She was able to identify the envelope and, as whoever sent it went to the extraordinary trouble of stencilling the address, it seems a likely supposition that it contained the "outing" letter.'

'But I thought Mrs Penny and Smith had separate letterboxes,' said Lilley. 'At least, that's what Smales—'

'They do. But she said she generally waited for the postman.' Milkman, baker and candlestick maker, too, probably, Rafferty added silently to himself as he remembered how, on their first visit, she had continued to press more tea and buns on them in an attempt to extend their stay. 'She told me she took the post for both of them most days and was able to tell us that Smith never received handwritten letters – the hate mail ceased long ago, as we know from the postmarks. All he ever received were bills or official, typed letters from one government department or another. Anyway, on Wednesday, when she took the letter into her flat with her own post, she said she forgot all about it till Smith came in some time after eight that evening.'

Smales grinned. 'That's her story and she's sticking to it, hey, guv? Bet she tried to steam the envelope open.'

'That's what you'd do, is it?' Rafferty asked drily. 'What a pity for the investigation that not everyone shares your lack of scruples, Smales. And, for your information, an envelope that's been steamed open has a bumpy, bubbly look to it when you reseal it and this one hasn't.'

Thankfully, Smales didn't think to enquire how Rafferty had come by such knowledge and Rafferty hurried on before it occurred to him to do so. 'You might also ask Mrs Penny's near neighbours if they know when her back gate was damaged. Mrs Penny herself has no idea and, as it seems likely the damage could be tied to Smith's murder, I'd like to know for sure. Right, that's enough for you to make a start. Off you go.'

Once the room had cleared, Rafferty turned to Llewellyn. 'As for you and me, we're going to see Smith's family.'

In view of what they had already learned concerning the family's relationship with Smith, even Llewellyn, who abhorred the job of breaking news of death, approached the meeting with little trepidation. As he had told Rafferty, he doubted Smith's relatives would be too heart-broken.

It wasn't as if they were even what most people would regard as family proper, as Smith's father and mother had divorced when he was two, his father had disappeared into the wide blue yonder, and his mother had married again when Smith was four, producing a half-brother eighteen months later. The mother had died shortly before the rape case had come to court, and now the only 'family' Maurice Smith had left was his stepfather and half-brother.

The Bullocks, father and son, lived in a flat near the bus station, in conditions of squalor only too typical of an all-male household; discarded chip wrappings and other takeaway containers sharing the decorative honours with crushed lager cans and choked ashtrays.

According to what Llewellyn had discovered during his last conversation with them, neither had a job. The television was on, the over-excited voice of a race commentator screamed at them. Rafferty asked for it to be turned off and without awaiting permission pressed the on–off button, and the maniacal voice was thankfully silenced. The son scowled at this interference, but Bullock said nothing and simply sat back in his well-squashed armchair and awaited developments.

Jes Bullock was a well-built man of fifty-seven and suited his name. His youthful muscles had turned to fat and now overhung his trousers. A thin veneer of politeness covered his natural aggression but it failed to mask the bully beneath. Rafferty took against him on sight; the thick sensual lips, the fingers like pork sausages, the slow, unhurried movements, all spoke of a man with tastes more physical than intellectual. Strangely, when Rafferty broke the news of his stepson's death, he seemed over-anxious to lay claim to a grief Rafferty judged him unlikely to be capable of. According to Smith's newspaper collection of that time, after the trial Bullock's voice had frequently been raised against his stepson, and sprinkled through the anger had been the resentment that he was being blamed for the inadequacies of another man's son, insisting that Smith was 'no blood of mine'. It was obviously a grievance he still felt, but the circumstances and his own claim to the role of grief-stricken stepfather appeared to inhibit his previous free expression of it.

He had little to say when Rafferty told him his stepson had died in less than natural circumstances. It was almost as if, beyond the insincere mouthings of loss, he was keeping a guard on his tongue. Rafferty wondered why he should feel it necessary.

'Mr Bullock, you told my sergeant here that your stepson didn't visit regularly and that you last saw him on the Wednesday before his death.' He paused for Bullock's nod. It was slow in coming. 'I gather you didn't seem very sure of the times involved in his last visit and I wondered if you'd thought any more about that?'

Jes Bullock licked his lips and darted a glance at his son. 'What do you reckon, Kevin?'

Kevin didn't have the winning personality of his father. He was sullen, and, unlike his father, made no attempt to pretend to a grief he didn't feel. Clearly he had resented his half-brother. Although he didn't utter the words, his curled lip said 'good riddance' as clearly as words. Rafferty found this lack of hypocrisy more refreshing than his father's pretence. It was understandable, too. He and his father must have gone through many difficult times because of Smith, who had still been living at home at the time of his arrest. His family would have drawn nearly as much bile as Smith himself. It must have been especially hard on his younger brother, who could only have been in his early teens at the time. Such experiences would hardly endear Smith to either man.

Kevin's mouth was a thin, tight line, as though he was reluctant to tell them anything. But finally he admitted, 'He was here for only half an hour on Wednesday. Left around seven-fifteen. That's the last we saw of him.'

His father gave a quick nod. Rafferty thought he seemed relieved, as though uncertain his son would answer their questions at all, and as he spoke his voice grew increasingly confident. 'Kevin's right. I remember now. We'd been out since lunchtime, celebrating my birthday, and we left the pub when the chippie opened around five.'

41

Llewellyn broke in to enquire which pub he meant and with an evident reluctance Jes Bullock told them it had been the one on the corner, the Pig and Whistle. 'We'd hired a couple of videos for the evening and Maurice arrived partway through the first one.'

'Yeah,' Kevin chipped in. 'Right when it was getting exciting.'

His father shrugged his meaty shoulders as if to say what else could you expect? 'He brought my birthday present over.'

Rafferty found it hard to believe that unloved and unloving loner, Maurice Smith, would waste a chunk of his Giro on buying such a stepfather birthday presents. However, he made no comment.

Although he chose not to question him further about times at the moment, Rafferty was surprised also that Kevin should be so precise. He would have thought the earlier birthday celebrations likely to render time-keeping uncertain. For the moment, he didn't challenge this statement either, but turned to another matter. 'You must remember the hate mail and threats he received after the trial. Were you aware of any more recent threats? Serious threats?'

Kevin shook his head. 'No. Occasionally the lads around the flats here would chase him and rough him up a bit, but that's been going on for ages and was only because he was such a dipstick. Nothing to do with the court case, if that's what you think – nobody around here knows anything about that.' He scowled as he remembered the reason for Rafferty's visit. 'Bloody well will now, though, won't they? Sod Maurice. If we have to bloody move again . . .'

Rafferty turned to the father. 'What about you, Mr Bullock?'

Jes Bullock shook his heavy head ponderously. 'He never said nothing to me.'

'And you're quite sure you've not seen him since Wednesday evening?'

'That's right.' Kevin glowered, as if challenging them to make something of it. His father chipped in.

'Not one for visiting, wasn't Maurice. We'd see him half-a-dozen times a year. Kept himself to himself.'

'So you definitely didn't see him the next evening? The Thursday?'

'Haven't I just said?' Kevin demanded, the heavy jaw that was so like his father's thrust forward. 'We went out the next night. Up the pub. Maurice wasn't invited.'

'Not a pub man, Maurice wasn't, Inspector,' Jes Bullock informed them cryptically, as if trying to imply that if he *had* been, he, as his stepfather, would have been the first to extend an invitation.

They left soon after. The Bullocks lived on the second floor, and as they reached the car Rafferty glanced up to see Jes Bullock watching them from the balcony. As he caught Rafferty's eye, he backed hurriedly away and re-entered his flat.

Rafferty again had the impression that Jes had something on his mind. And he was willing to bet a month's salary that it wasn't grief. The man reminded him of someone, he realized. He wrinkled his brow, but he couldn't remember who. He was certain it was no one connected with the case and knew it would drive him mad till he remembered.

As they got in the car, he mentioned his suspicions to Llewellyn. 'The Bullocks have every reason to dislike Smith. Every reason to wish him dead. Think they could have done it?'

Llewellyn thought it unlikely. 'Why would they wait till now to kill him? Unlike the families of the victims, or whoever sent that "outing" letter, they've known where to find him all the time. Besides, if their alibis check out, they were in the public house all evening, presumably with plenty of witnesses.'

Rafferty started the car. 'Maybe they're trusting in their bereaved status and imagine their story won't be checked out.'

However, Llewellyn was right about one thing; they *had* known where Smith lived and, as far as they had yet discovered, they had less reason to wish to be rid of him now than they'd had ten years ago when the fury over the case was at its height.

'But Jes Bullock's worried about something,' Rafferty insisted. 'I intend to find out what it is. Kevin's information was very precise – too precise for my liking. Get on the radio and get Hanks – no, he's busy – Andrews, then – to ask around the flats. Tell him to find out if anyone saw Smith arrive and leave. They said they went to the pub on the Thursday night. Get him to ask the landlord what time the Bullocks got there that night and if anyone saw Smith pay a second visit to his family on the Thursday night.'

While Llewellyn contacted the station Rafferty consulted his watch. It was nearly time for the post-mortem. 'We've just got time to grab a sandwich if you want one.' Rafferty's stomach rumbled, but he ignored it; there'd be no lunch for him. 'I hope Sam can narrow the time down, as I've got a feeling time might be very important in this case.'

Sam Dally was waiting for them, freshly scrubbed and gowned, a cherubic smile on his face. 'Lunched well, I trust?' he asked Rafferty. 'Don't want you fainting away from hunger, do we?'

'Get on with it, you old sadist,' Rafferty muttered.

After another even more cherubic smile, Sam did so. He confirmed that Smith had been strung up *after* death. He also confirmed that the cause of death was the stab wound to the heart and that he had, in all likelihood, died immediately, thus confirming Rafferty's suspicions that he had not only died in his own flat, but in his own armchair.

Although Smith's armchair had fresh stains, they had been few enough. Sam explained why. 'Unlike incised knife wounds where the edge of the blade makes cutting gashes, stab wounds, where the point of the knife enters the body followed by the rest of the blade, generally cause *internal* bleeding. The wound has one acute angle cut and one blunt, indicating that the knife used had only one sharp edge.'

Rafferty nodded. The weapon had yet to be found. It hadn't been left at the scene. He was still musing on this some time later as the attendant with the power saw cut through the top of Smith's skull.

Swallowing hard, Rafferty hastily dragged his gaze from Smith's face to his torso. As this had already suffered the usual indignities his gaze didn't linger long. But it was long enough for him to comment, 'He seems to have a lot of bruises.'

'Nothing gets past you, does it, Rafferty?' Sam taunted. 'It's only taken your rapier-like gaze the best part of two hours to notice the blindingly obvious. How does he do it?' he demanded of the room at large.

'It's your fault.' Rafferty, a firm believer in the notion of attack being the best form of defence, immediately went on the offensive, and under the noise of the saw murmured, 'You shouldn't have such stunners as assistants, Sam. Can't take my eyes off them.'

As each of Sam's female assistants bore a striking resemblance to Eeyore, the only strategy Sam judged necessary was a loud snort. Ignoring this as well as Llewellyn's pained sigh at such blatant political incorrectness, Rafferty asked, 'Reckon someone beat him up before knifing him?'

'If you paid more attention to my pearls of wisdom, Rafferty, and less to controlling your lusts and the rumbling of your empty stomach, you'd know contusions can occur post-mortem as well as ante-mortem. And, as you've already said, he was moved, not once, but thrice after death; once when he was taken to the woods, once when he was removed from thence and once when he

45

was strung up again, so bruising is to be expected. But, rest assured, *my* rapier-gaze is well ahead of you. I noted each of them before you even got here.'

Pausing to admire his gleaming array of silverware, Sam gave a happy sigh. 'He was probably concealed in the boot of a car each time, so his body would have been thrown around a fair bit, rupturing blood vessels, particularly those areas engorged with post-mortem hypostasis, causing them to ooze blood into the tissues. As you can see,' Sam pointed his blade at the cadaver, 'such contusions look just like bruising to living flesh.'

Sam broke off again to make more comments into the microphone, then continued. 'But I'll of course test the injury sites for leucocytes – white cells to you – the things that rush to the site of an injury to begin the healing process. An abnormally high number of white cells would indicate some of the damage happened before death. It'll take a bit of time, though; the contusions are quite extensive.'

Rafferty nodded and managed to keep his end up pretty well through the rest of the post-mortem by musing on Sam's conclusions about the bruises. Although, as Sam had remarked, Smith had been transported about sufficiently after death to suffer extensive bruising, he couldn't help but wonder, if some of the bruises *had* been inflicted before death, who was the most likely person to administer a beating. It didn't take long for Jes Bullock's face to float into his consciousness.

Chapter Five

It was already getting dark by the time they came out of the mortuary.

Rafferty turned the car round and drove towards Habberstone, the busy market town about four miles west of Elmhurst, where ex-Inspector Stubbs had settled on retirement.

Before he did anything else, like interviewing Smith's victims, their families, and Mrs Nye of the Rape Support Group, Rafferty wanted to speak to the inspector who had been in charge of the Smith case. He wanted his opinion of Smith's victims' families, to gain his impression of them as people – and as possible murderers.

His flimsy recollection of the case had been well bolstered by Smith's newspaper collection. One man interested him greatly – Frank Massey, the father of one of Smith's victims who had beaten Smith up and served a term in jail for it. Of course, that had been before Smith and his family had moved to a secret address, but even after such an event there were ways and means of finding out someone's whereabouts if you were determined enough or rich enough. Was he the only one amongst the four families capable of vengeful violence? Rafferty wanted to know. Or were others equally capable, given the opportunity? One of his victims, the young Walker girl, had killed herself when Smith was freed. Her family had even stronger reasons than Massey still to wish him dead.

Innocent or guilty, Rafferty was determined to handle them all with kid gloves, and as the law had already failed them once, he was all the more anxious to prove to them and any other doubters that the law could be efficient, caring, *just*. It would be bad enough for them having all that emotion stirred up again, but to know that for the second time in their lives Maurice Smith was the cause, would, for some of them, be almost too much to bear.

Rafferty took a deep breath. First things first, he reminded himself. Let's get *this* interview over with before you start worrying about the next ones. God knew, from what he'd learned on the phone when speaking to some of Inspector Stubbs' old colleagues, this one was likely to be difficult enough.

Archie Stubbs was reckoned to be a lonely and bitter man. It was odds on that he'd resent their questions, their prying into his conduct of the Smith case, the implication that if it hadn't been botched the victims and their families would have suffered much less. Certainly, Massey would probably never have tried to extract his own justice; never have gone to jail, lost his job, had his marriage torn apart. The Walker girl would likely still be alive. Uneasily, Rafferty realized he had yet to discover what other tragedies might have sprung from Smith's release. Who amongst them had additional reasons to hate Smith?

Stubbs: Rafferty repeated the name of his next interviewee uneasily to himself. In a way, Stubbs had become another of Smith's victims. He had lost his career, been pushed into early retirement from the force, he'd even lost his wife shortly after. Yet if Stubbs had wanted revenge he could have extracted it long before this, as easily as the Bullocks; with his contacts he could have found out Smith's whereabouts with little difficulty.

Maybe he had done so but had until now been satisfied simply to keep tabs on the man. *Until now*, Rafferty repeated to himself and wished he could ignore the fact that an ex-copper like Stubbs would have the knowledge and experience to commit murder and get away with it. That he hadn't done so ten years ago was no reason to discount him as a suspect now.

Rafferty pulled up in front of the grim, grey-painted bungalow that was Stubbs' home. He had only to compare the difference between Stubbs' property and those of his neighbours' to know that the years had done little to diminish Stubbs' bitterness.

Although it was December, the front gardens of the other bungalows in the row were still gay and colourful, the plants obviously chosen specially to withstand winter's blasts. Rafferty, who had recently taken over the care of his mother's garden, which task was beginning to get beyond her, immediately recognized the cheery yellow of the winter jasmine, the equally bright and sunshine-flowered witch hazel, the pink and white flowered viburnums bright against the glossy evergreen leaves of the Mexican orange blossom; all defied the chill and proclaimed not only their owners' contentment with their lot, but a certain quiet happiness. Archie Stubbs' garden displayed no such emotion; in his, every season was the same; from fence to wall and back to fence the rich soil supported only a tough, black tarmac.

Stubbs appeared as uncompromising and as unwelcoming as his home. He was fairly short, certainly at the lower levels of the old height requirements. Short, and grey of face and manner, being monosyllabic to the point of rudeness, and so obviously reluctant to talk to them that Rafferty thought they were going to have to conduct their conversation on the doorstep. But he suddenly relented when one of his neighbours, a gnomelike little man of cheery red face and genial air, shouted across to him that it was nice to see he had visitors.

Archie Stubbs scowled and told them, 'You'd best come in, before Happy Harry comes across to join us.'

Although spotlessly clean, the inside of Stubbs' home was a repetition of the outside; drab, grey and depressing. Rafferty and Llewellyn exchanged a glance as, through the partly open door of the dining room, they both glimpsed the yellowing piles of newspapers stacked on the table. Before Stubbs noticed their interest and shut the door, Rafferty had read the headline on the uppermost, and guessed the rest, too, were about the Smith case.

As they followed Stubbs to the living room and sat down, Rafferty wondered how Stubbs would react if he told him that he and Smith had shared an obsession. His earlier anxieties returned as he realized that, if anything, Stubbs' old colleagues had minimized the extent to which the professional failure had affected him. He knew that Stubbs' wife had died soon after the move from Burleigh; from what he'd learned, she'd never been strong, and the strain of coping with her husband's bitterness had taken its toll. They'd had no children, and even though his colleagues had made an effort to keep in touch, gradually Stubbs had cut off contact with all but one of them.

Rafferty found it easy to understand how, alone in this lonely little grey box, the man's bitterness could fester till it became consuming. Once again he reminded himself that, as an ex-copper, Stubbs had had the contacts to discover Smith's current whereabouts. Had he done so and brought about what he must consider a belated justice?

In the force, Stubbs had been a thirty-year man, and Rafferty, over twenty years on the force himself, desperately wanted to be able to scratch his name off the suspect list. But this ambition, he now realized, might not be as quickly accomplished as he had hoped. He was wondering how best to continue the interview when Stubbs ended his self-imposed monosyllabism with a gruff comment.

'You said on the phone you wanted to speak to me about the Smith case. I wish you'd get on with it and go.'

'Very well.' Rafferty paused, then asked, 'How do you feel about his death?'

'How do I feel?' Stubbs' forehead wrinkled, then he admitted, 'I'd be a liar if I said I wasn't glad. For his victims more than for me. Perhaps, now the bastard's dead, they can finally put the past behind them and make something of their lives.' The words *It's too late for me* were implied by Stubbs' whole demeanour.

Rafferty nodded. 'You mentioned Smith's victims – I wanted to talk to you about them and their families. You must have come to know them all well.' Rafferty had explained over the phone the manner of Smith's death and what had followed, and now he went on, 'Although his death was pretty certainly caused by stabbing, his stringing-up afterwards had all the hallmarks of a ritual execution, a punishment. Would you say any one of them in particular would be capable of such an act?'

Rafferty's prophecy that few people would be willing to help them catch Smith's killer seemed to be borne out by Stubbs' reaction. He seemed determined to assist them as little as possible, as his answer made clear.

'How should I know? Apart from Frank Massey, I haven't seen any of them for ten years.'

'Ah, yes, Massey.' Rafferty paused. 'I understand you stood as a character witness at his trial?'

Stubbs bristled. 'What of it? Least I could do for him. He wasn't a violent man. I was surprised he had it in him to attack Smith; he was an academic, a man who worked with his mind rather than his body.' Stubbs' face, inclined to broadness, now took on an aspect like a pugnacious bulldog. 'Of course it wasn't surprising that the court ruling at Smith's trial changed all that. It ruined his previous rather naïve belief in British justice. He seemed bewildered at first, then that bewilderment turned to rage. For the first time in his life he used his fists instead of his head and look where it got him. If you think he's likely to have had another go at Smith I should forget it. He had a terrible time in prison. He's not likely to want to repeat the experience.'

'Not likely, I grant you,' Rafferty agreed. 'But he may

51

still have decided to risk it. After all, he had *two* wrongs to right, not just one. And, as you say, no one could claim he got justice from the courts.'

' "Revenge is a kind of wild justice," ' Llewellyn quoted softly, adding, 'at least, according to Francis Bacon. Perhaps Mr Massey still feels wild justice is the only kind available to him.'

Stubbs stared at him for a moment and then retorted, 'That's as maybe, but he'd had his try for revenge once. You're barking up the wrong tree if you think he could gird himself up a second time. He's not the same man at all. He wouldn't have it in him.'

'You thought that once before,' Rafferty reminded him, but he didn't pursue the point. For the moment he was prepared to accept what Stubbs told them. 'Tell me – did *you* believe Smith was guilty?'

'Damn right I did. He was guilty as hell. Although I was beginning to have doubts we'd get a conviction as proof rested on the evidence of the victims and Smith's confession, I had no doubt at all that he raped those young girls. He even admitted to Thommo and me when we went to see him after the judge acquitted him that he'd raped another young girl; an attack we knew nothing about and which had never even been reported.

'Oh, I know we shouldn't have gone!' he burst out, as he caught Rafferty's surprised glance. 'Been warned off, hadn't we? But we went just the same. Smith said he'd picked this other young girl up in broad daylight. Wanted us to find her so he could apologize for smashing her violin!'

He shrugged. 'I suppose the parents must have thought she would get over it more quickly without the trauma of a court case. Turns out they were right, doesn't it? Can't blame 'em, I suppose. Smith's other victims were all very young, none older than ten, and Alice Massey was only eight. Smith said this other girl was no older. That was the way he liked them, young and gullible.'

Stubbs rubbed the flat of his hands on the rough material of his trousers as if he felt he could rub away the stain of his own guilt over the case. Rafferty got the impression Stubbs found it as hard to forgive himself for his failure as he found it to forgive Smith for his perversion.

'Even though, in his chambers, the judge accepted Smith's confession as true, he rejected it as evidence because he thought the prosecution would have a hard time proving it hadn't been obtained by oppression. Said something about me and Thommo not saying "please" and "thank you" often enough, à la the decrees of PACE. So that was that.'

Rafferty understood Stubbs' bitterness only too well. How often had he himself experienced that hollow feeling of despair, all too familiar nowadays to crime-wearied policemen? It wasn't that he didn't agree with aspects of the Police and Criminal Evidence Act – he did, many of them were needed, certainly for first-time offenders. But it was a different matter altogether for practised criminals. In their case, it made the pursuit of justice more of a lottery than it should ever be. Naturally, the practised criminals and their lawyers took such advantage of a legal system so weighted in their favour that, to the law-abiding public, it seemed that the very service set up to prosecute offenders more often acted as their accomplices.

The trouble, as Rafferty had frequently pointed out when an excess of Jameson's had made him unwisely vocal on the subject, was that so much of the legal process and its administration was in the hands of icy-veined intellectuals, who seemed to think the law was more about arguing legal points than securing justice.

They were so far removed from the mass of the population in their thoughts on the subject that they might as well have been visiting Martians for all the confidence they inspired. And when they were paired with the bleeding-heart social workers who thought Johnny could

53

do no wrong, who would never accept that Johnny might just naturally be a nasty, evil little bastard, who liked hurting those weaker than himself, such despair was unsurprising. *It's his lack of education, it's his background, he's from a one-parent family, it's because he can't get a job*, they cried.

Rafferty, secondary-school educated and from a one-parent family himself, knew damn well that often Johnny didn't *want* a job. Why should he, he reasoned? He got far more rewards from mugging old ladies or selling drugs than he'd ever get filling shelves in the local Sainsbury or working in a Woolies' storeroom, which was all his limited education had equipped him for. It was no wonder ordinary people, coppers included, raged, then despaired. No wonder, either, if some of them took to dispensing their own justice.

Rafferty, suddenly aware that his heart was hammering wildly, took a deep breath and forced himself to calm down. Llewellyn was right, he realized; thinking along those lines just led to frustration, indigestion and coronaries. Worse, it clouded his brain with negative emotions and ruined his judgement.

He forced his mind back to the current problem. 'As you said, the Smith case was thrown out because the judge ruled that his confession was inadmissible. But why did it ever get as far as the Crown Court?'

Stubbs sighed heavily. 'I suppose good old human error was at the root of it. But, in mitigation, you must remember the Smith case was brought at a very difficult time. It was 1986; at the beginning of the year PACE was implemented throughout England and Wales, and by October of the same year the bloody Crown Prosecution Service or as I call it the Criminals' Pals Society, took over the prosecution of offenders from the police.

'It was change, disruption, difficulties at every turn. As I said, the whole legal process was in a state of flux; endless new rules to remember and bumptious young prosecution briefs getting up everyone's noses. There was no DNA evidence to help us then; it was another year till the courts started to accept such evidence. Not that we had a blood sample. We didn't even have a semen sample. Crafty sod had used rubbers; all he had was Smith's confession and the testimony of the girls.'

Stubbs scowled again as, probably for the thousandth time, he relived his bitter memories. 'I'd worked long and hard on the Smith case – we all had. Most of the team had daughters round that age or younger. And by the time we caught him we were all exhausted. I,' he paused, then went on, 'I just about cracked up.'

From his rigid posture, Rafferty could see how much it cost him to admit this. He already knew, of course. Stubbs' old colleagues had said as much and more.

'But we got the confession out of him before my GP had me hospitalized. As I said, the whole team was exhausted by the time we finally nailed him, and although I had my doubts as to whether his confession might contravene the new PACE rules, the Prosecutor appointed was so young and eager to get her teeth into a rape case that she just charged ahead with it. Got through the Committal Proceedings with no trouble, but then we both know magistrates are often glad to pass the buck upwards to the Crown Courts when it comes to ruling on a point of law, such as admissibility.

'Anyway, I'll tell you plain, we were both humiliated when it got to the Crown Court. Especially Ms Osbourne, the prosecuting counsel. Not too keen on women, old Judge Jordan; hated having them in his court and always gave them a hard time. He called Ms Osbourne into his chambers and told her she wasn't fit to iron his robes.' Stubbs gave a sour grin. 'I only learned about it later. Like most coppers, I'd never been keen on the introduction of the CPS and Ms Osbourne had me convinced I was right. As I said, she was arrogant and flaunted her college education as if she thought we were a bunch of dinosaurs and that experience counted for nothing. It was the only bit of satisfaction I got when I heard that old Jordan had wiped the floor with her.'

The light faded from his eye. 'Still, it was a difficult time to be a policeman.' Rafferty nodded. 'I tell you, if I could have ended my career any other way I'd have been glad to retire then.'

'But surely, sir,' Llewellyn spoke up, 'the Chief Prosecutor would have overseen—'

'Old Stimpson? Don't make me laugh. He was near retirement himself. He only took the job as a favour to the new Regional Director, he didn't intend to work *too* hard, I can tell you, and he gave a pretty free rein to the young bloods in his traces. Spent as much time on the golf course as he did in his office. Besides, although it was never admitted officially, it was accepted that there would be a fair few balls-ups during the changeover period. And there were.'

Rafferty nodded again. He remembered some of them.

'Not, from my understanding, that things are any better today; the CPS is still largely staffed by inexperienced, not-so-bright graduates. The clever ones mostly go into private chambers. Can't blame them, I suppose, it's much better paid.

'The CPS still tends to get either the idealistic ones like Ms Osbourne, or the ones who couldn't get accepted in chambers. Admittedly, this was a completely new service with many jobs to fill, and they perhaps couldn't afford to be too particular if they wanted to get the show on the road.' He directed a sour grin at Rafferty. 'Much like the police force in the seventies, when they accepted anyone who could walk and talk.'

Rafferty flushed. He had joined in the seventies and he wondered whether Stubbs was having a dig at him. However, as Stubbs showed no inclination to dwell on the subject, he decided he wasn't.

'Anyway, they managed to make me the fall guy. I'd made too many waves over too many years, made it obvious too often how I felt about my superiors. I was five years off retirement, I was expendable. Not Ms Osbourne, though. She's gone from strength to strength. I often wondered if she'd been warming old Stimpson's arthritic bones. She's Chief Crown Prosecutor on your manor now,' he told Rafferty. 'Who'd have thought she'd rise so high from such beginnings?'

Rafferty stared. 'You mean your Ms Osbourne and Elizabeth Probyn are one and the same?' My God, he thought, just managing to bite back the sardonic grin; she must have put her back into the job of keeping *that* quiet.

Stubbs nodded. 'I've kept tabs on her. Masochistic, I know, but . . .'

Rafferty said nothing, but he found himself wondering again who else Stubbs had kept tabs on from that time? The name of Maurice Smith came to mind.

'Changed her name when she got married, though she stuck to the Ms bit.' Stubbs gave them another sour grin. 'You ask her about the Smith case and watch her squirm.'

Stubbs stood at his doorway and watched them walk away as though he wanted to be sure they left. Rafferty glanced at Llewellyn as they turned the corner to where they had parked the car. 'You realize we'll have to check his movements, ex-copper or no ex-copper?'

Llewellyn nodded.

'God knows, he had motive enough. He had the means to find out Smith's address. If we discover he also had the opportunity . . .' Rafferty didn't finish the sentence. Llewellyn knew as well as he how difficult it would be to get evidence against an experienced ex-copper. If Stubbs had killed Smith he'd have been well able to cover his tracks. He'd made no attempt to hide his bitterness. He'd seemed almost to flaunt it, challenging them to make a case against him.

'What about the other officers on the case? Thompson, for instance?'

'They'll have to be checked out, too.'

The prospect of investigating fellow officers was a depressing one for both of them and silence fell until they had reached the Elmhurst road and Rafferty stopped at a red light.

'Let's disregard the police suspects for the moment,' he said. 'What if Smith was killed by one of the victims or their parents? It might have taken them this long to track him down, especially as he not only changed his name but also moved twice since he left Burleigh. Hiring an investigator costs money, and for an ordinary person finding Smith would be like looking for a needle in a haystack.' But not for a policeman, he thought again.

'True,' said Llewellyn. 'But I feel even his victims and their families would surely need some other spur to act after all this time. Heightened emotions don't stay heightened indefinitely; like the passions of love, the passions of hate have a course to run. The first flickers, the growing heat, the all-engulfing flames, the dying embers, and finally cold ashes.'

Astonished by his sergeant's sudden and poetical verbosity, Rafferty felt compelled to remark, 'I'm not sure Stubbs, for one, would agree with you. And even if his emotions had reached the cold ashes stage, he's got all the time in the world to rake them over. And as for the victims and their families, who knows if some new tragedy affected one of them? Something related to the original crime, something they might consider directly attributable to Smith; then the flames of passion might rise from the ashes. Events like rape do tend to bring on other tragedies in a family – sometimes years after the event – look at Frank Massey, for one.'

Tragedies like nervous collapse, and divorce – broken families and broken lives. Rape often cast a long, lingering painful shadow among the victims and their families, as Rafferty knew. Particularly when the victim was a child. Particularly when, as in the Smith case, the physical rape had been followed by judicial rape.

58

Rafferty squinted at his watch as the car passed under a street lamp. It was after six. No wonder he was hungry; he hadn't eaten since breakfast.

'Get on to the station, will you, Dafyd? Get Beard to make an appointment for tomorrow for us to see Mrs Nye of the Rape Support Group. He's likely to find her at that refuge she founded in St Boniface Road. If any of her group sent that "outing" letter, she might be willing to drop a hint as to which of her group could be responsible.'

Although the names of the more militant feminists in the Rape Support Group and similar organizations were well known to the police, Rafferty felt he had to tread cautiously, wary of accusations of police harassment. He had no proof that any members of the local RSG were responsible for the 'outing' threats that had occurred recently in the town. But he'd always found Mrs Nye a reasonable woman. He didn't believe she would condone 'outing'. If she harboured any suspicions against her more hot-headed colleagues, he felt he would be able to persuade her to reveal them.

He broke into Llewellyn's transmission. 'Get Beard to make an appointment with Elizabeth Probyn while he's at it. I'd be interested to see what she remembers of the case. Tomorrow's Saturday, so she won't be able to fob us off with excuses about being in court. Oh, and ask him to get me a couple of rolls from the canteen before the lovely Opal goes home.' Llewellyn gave the message and replaced the microphone.

Rafferty had no doubt that fobbing them off would be Elizabeth Probyn's first instinct. She wouldn't enjoy discussing her early, spectacular failure; particularly with him. She was one of those coolly distant prosecutors with whom he could find no common ground. He had little doubt she would find the interview humiliating.

And you, Rafferty? his conscience prodded. *What will you find it? Enjoyable? Maybe you'll crow a little? Rub her nose in it, will you?*

Rafferty denied it. Unfortunately, his lapsed Catholic conscience, privy to his every thought, word and deed, was well aware that Elizabeth Probyn was not his favourite person. She had subjected him to several humiliations over the years. She must have learned quickly from that early failure, he now surmised, because *he*'d never had cause to rein her back in a case. On the contrary, unlike Stubbs' experience of her, with him she seemed to delight in refusing to take on the prosecution of cases for which she felt the police had provided insufficient evidence. *Going to take the opportunity to get your own back?* his conscience probed again.

'Oh, shut up!' Rafferty growled.

'Sir?' Llewellyn's head jerked towards him, bewilderment on his face. Hardly surprising, of course, as the Welshman had been innocently gazing out of the window when Rafferty made his outburst.

'Nothing,' Rafferty mumbled. 'I'm just having an internal argument. Take no notice.'

Chapter Six

Rafferty found Mrs ffinch-Robinson waiting for him when he got back to the station. She wore an air of vindicated self-righteousness – everything she had said having proved true – and seemed to have taken up occupation of his visitor's chair as though she intended a lengthy stay.

Rafferty, hungry and looking forward to breaking his post-mortem fast, gave a long-suffering sigh. Unfortunately, she was just the sort of person he found it most difficult to deal with; not only serious-minded and unlikely to appreciate his jokes but also self-assured, strong-willed and convinced she knew best. But as his conscience didn't fail to remind him that he had a lot to thank her for, he did his best to look pleased to see her.

As soon as he sat down, she began to criticize, the cut-glass tones and authoritative magistrate's manner combining to make him feel as though he was some ne'er-do-well she was lecturing from the bench. As in his youth he hadn't exactly been the best-behaved boy on the block, the analogy didn't make him feel any easier.

'I hope, Inspector, that you've reprimanded that young officer as I suggested.'

To Rafferty, her suggestion had sounded more like an order, but, as she didn't pause long enough to give him a chance to confirm he'd obeyed her, he was saved the indignity of a reply.

'It's officers of his type who create a barrier between police and public. I've often said that . . .'

With difficulty, Rafferty tuned her out. He remembered how her lips had thinned when she had entered his office the previous evening and taken in his unruly auburn hair, his limp brown suit and his inadequately cleaned black shoes and knew that any attempt to defend Lilley would be a waste of breath. He doubted she had any interest in excuses, be they his own or anyone else's.

Vowing to make sure to tell the desk staff that he was out – permanently, should she decide to make visits to the police station a regular event – he sat back and as far as he was able let her crisp tones float over his head. He was becoming convinced she intended to haunt him.

Her voice rose, as if she suspected he had stopped listening, and he breathed a sigh of relief as he tuned in again and learned she would be returning to Burleigh the next day.

'That's why I felt I had to come in,' she explained. 'I imagine, now that you *have* found the body, you'll want to go through my statement again.' Mrs ffinch-Robinson didn't wait for his agreement to this any more than she had for his confirmation that he had chastised Lilley, and proceeded to go over not only her statement but her view of the murder, what she had deduced, and her recommendations as to how he should proceed, apparently of the opinion he'd need all the help he could get.

Maybe she's right at that, Rafferty thought grimly and he attempted to butt in, but she obviously had huge experience in quelling mutinous males be they felons or middle-ranking police officers, and his attempt to board the debate dinghy was ruthlessly crushed.

'Obviously, Smith's body must have been left in the woods during darkness on both occasions,' she told him. 'Even in winter there are too many people about during daylight hours. That being the case, you'll certainly want to have a word with the local poachers. I've spoken to my opposite numbers on the Bench in Elmhurst and they've supplied me with the details of those who come up before them most often.' She rustled in a large, businesslike leather handbag and produced her list, which she placed under his nose.

'If one or two of them were about their usual nocturnal activities they may have seen something of that car I heard in the lane before I found the body. If you remember, I told you it never passed me and next I heard an engine revving and a car drove off and a few moments later I found the body. The two things must be connected. And another thing . . .'

Worn down by her determined vigour, Rafferty reflected weakly that the Age of Empire might have died, but its natural inheritors were still alive and kicking. No longer, like their forebears, in a position to boss half the world, latter-day memsahibs had simply lowered their sights to Mother England's more limited shores. Magistrate's Benches, Council Committees, and Police Authorities up and down the country were littered with clones of Mrs ffinch-Robinson, dispensing justice, Council Tax spending allocations and strongly worded directives about where the police force was going wrong.

In many ways he admired such women. If only they weren't so exhausting to the rest of us, he wryly mused. Still, he shouldn't complain, he reminded himself again. Her information at least had helped them to pinpoint the time of death more accurately, and if, as seemed likely, a ten-year-old vengeance had finally caught up with Maurice Smith, this information could be vital.

When he'd finally convinced Mrs ffinch-Robinson that he had taken her advice to heart and that she could go home with a clear conscience, he walked along to the canteen. After collecting tea and the spicy and delicious if now cold sausage rolls, that Opal, the cook, made to her own recipe, he rounded up the officers he had earlier despatched on special duties and brought the lot back to his office.

'Right,' he said. 'You first, Andrews. What did you find

out about the Bullocks' and Smith's visit to them?'

Andrews pulled a face. 'Not a lot. Couldn't get anybody to confirm or deny what time Smith arrived and left the Bullocks' place on Wednesday. And if he was at the flats at all on Thursday evening I couldn't find anyone who'd seen him. 'Course, it was bitter weather both nights, so everyone would have been indoors. I checked in the pub on the corner and both the Bullocks were in there on the Thursday night. The son, Kevin, from about seven and Bullock himself from about nine-thirty, though according to the landlord it was unusual for Bullock senior to arrive so late.'

'Mmm. Interesting, especially when you consider I was given the impression that they went to the pub together.'

'Do you want me to go back and question them further?'

'No. I'll do that. I'd like to hear what Jes Bullock has to say for himself. He's not the sort to be late for his pint . . . not unless he has something important on. I'll give him a day or so to stew first, though. Let him get nicely softened up.' Rafferty paused and, turning to Llewellyn, he changed the subject. 'Has the rest of the paperwork arrived from Burleigh yet?'

Llewellyn picked up the phone. 'I'll check.'

'What about you and Liz?' Rafferty asked Lilley, as Llewellyn spoke quietly into the phone. 'Manage to find out anything new?'

Lilley nodded. 'We spoke with Smith's neighbours as you told us, guv,' Lilley reported. 'You wanted to know if anyone had been hanging around recently. Well, someone had. Several someones, in fact. This little old lady, by the name of Miss Primrose Partington, who lives on the corner of the next street to Smith's, says that a stranger's car was parked outside her house from Wednesday morning to Thursday evening, when it left suddenly. She's not seen it since. Said she doubted she could recognize them again, but she did say they were females, three of them, and that they seemed to be taking turns at some sort of guard duty. All they did was sit there, though – at least that was all they were doing each time she looked. I checked, and from where they were parked they'd have had a good view of both the front and back of Smith's home. They could have seen anyone entering or leaving from either the front door or the fire escape.'

'Does she know the exact time this car left?'

'Afraid not. But it was gone when she looked out at ten o'clock before going to bed.'

'I suppose it's too much to hope that she took the registration number?'

Lizzie Green answered. 'Wrong angle. But she recognized the make – an old Zephyr. Said her uncle used to have the same car.'

'You've checked they're not our own officers on surveillance for some drugs bust?'

Lilley nodded. 'The station knows nothing about them. It's odd, though, don't you think, guv, that the car should have left the spot on the Thursday evening, the night Smith died yet before his identity was disclosed. They've not been back since, though they'd not moved before that. It's almost as if they'd been watching him for some reason and, knowing he was dead, called a halt.'

Knowing he was dead. Rafferty repeated Lilley's words silently to himself as he recalled the threat contained in the 'outing' letter. Who would have known he was dead but his killer or killers, or the person or persons who were responsible for moving his body?

Llewellyn interrupted his train of thought to advise that the Burleigh papers had arrived. Constable Beard was bringing them up.

Rafferty nodded and turned back to Lilley. 'You said Miss Partington wasn't able to give you a description of these women, but surely she must have noted something to know there *were* three of them.'

Lilley pulled a face. 'Afraid not, guv. She said it was

65

more impressions – of hairstyles and so on – rather than individual features that made her think there were three of them.'

'So, it could just as easily have been *one* with three different hairstyles,' Rafferty muttered.

Liz Green seemed to find it necessary to make excuses for the old lady. 'She *has* got a long front garden, sir. It's got a lot of bushes in it, so it would have been difficult for her to see plainly. And she doesn't go out as she can't walk far.' With a toss of her dark curls she added provocatively, 'She did say that if it had been men rather than women parked there she would have phoned us without question.'

Rafferty snorted. 'Sure to be up to no good, men. Not like the girls – they're made of sugar and spice and everything nice. Everyone knows that.' He took a huge bite of his sausage roll before continuing. 'What about the gate? Manage to find out when it was damaged?'

Liz Green told him, 'Several of Mrs Penny's neighbours seem to think it can't have happened before Thursday. A wind got up on both that night and the Wednesday night but they only heard the gate banging on the Thursday night. Complained it kept them awake. If it had done the same the previous night they'd have remembered.'

Rafferty nodded. 'Well done. Right. I want you two to go back to that street and keep knocking on doors till you get some more answers. The old lady can't be the only one to remember the car, seeing as it was parked there for the best part of two days. It's the sort of thing people notice; very territorial, the human animal. Don't like strangers parking on their street. Seem to think they own it.'

He knew the station received plenty of complaints from irate householders on the subject. Many times, when he'd been in uniform and on desk duty, he'd had to bite his tongue to stop some sharp retort and explain politely that the driver had a perfect right to park his car where he liked as long as he wasn't on a yellow line or in some other restricted area. It was possible another of Smith's neighbours had been annoyed enough about the interloper to note down the number and to ask the police to tell the occupants to shift it. It was something of a longshot, but worth checking.

Rafferty turned to Hanks. 'How did you get on? Did you manage to track down the current addresses of Smith's victims and their families?'

Hanks nodded. 'Of the four families two have moved from Burleigh – the Walkers and the Masseys. The Walkers, the family of the young girl who killed herself, emigrated to Australia six years ago.'

'What? The whole family?'

Hanks nodded again.

'Get on to our Aussie opposite numbers, will you? Ask them to check that none of the family was missing from home during the relevant period, though it seems unlikely. If you're intent on revenge you don't move to the other side of the world. What about the other families?'

'The Dennington father's dead; died of a heart attack shortly after Smith was released. The girl's two brothers are in the army in Cyprus.'

'Should be easy enough to check they were with their units. You can do that when you're finished here. What about the daughter?'

'The girl – Sally – is now twenty. She still lives with her mother in their old home in Burleigh.' Hanks consulted his notes. 'The Masseys moved to London eight years ago when Frank, the father, was released from prison after his attack on Smith. The daughter, Alice, is now eighteen. She was – is – an only child.'

Hanks cast a speculative glance at Rafferty as he laid his papers on the desk. 'I know you told me to be discreet, but it seemed a waste of time not to dig a little when their old neighbours were so chatty, so I thought—'

Rafferty nodded and gestured him to go on.

'I gather from their old neighbours that Massey had a breakdown and was still a mass of neuroses when they moved. One particular set of neighbours still keeps in touch with Christmas cards and the like and told me the parents have since split up.

'As for the Figg family, they stayed in their old home – it's their business as well. They're scrap metal dealers, bit of a rough and ready crowd, well known at Burleigh nick, apparently. If anyone was going to kill Smith, they'd be the most likely ones to try it. From what I heard, you don't cross the Figg family; not if you've got any sense. The two eldest boys have put several people in hospital. And they don't just use their fists, a knife's their favourite weapon.'

Rafferty congratulated them all. 'You've done well. Keep it up and we might have this case over before Christmas. Is that your report, Hanks?'

Hanks nodded and picked up the sheaf of typed papers from the desk beside him and handed them over.

'What about the rest of you?' Rafferty asked. 'Where are your reports?'

A chorus of excuses followed and Rafferty held up his hands. 'All right, all right. Just don't forget to get them written up. When they're done, I'll get Sergeant Llewellyn here to check your spelling. You know how much he enjoys a good laugh.'

They grinned at this and filed out.

Llewellyn's lugubriousness was becoming as much a byword at the nick as his cautious driving, earning him the title of Dashing Daffy, the Tittering Taffy or 'DDT' for short, the short form encompassing also his deadly way of dealing with the more pestilential form of policeman that hung round the canteen. This last trait had ensured the station wits took care to keep him in ignorance of his new name. But at least the fact that they had given him a nickname indicated to Rafferty that the intellectual Welshman was starting to gain acceptance at the station. He was pleased to discover it.

Rafferty and Llewellyn settled down to read the rest of the reports that had accumulated in their absence from the station. Rafferty broke off when Constable Beard brought the papers from Burleigh, to ask him to fetch coffee, strong, black and plentiful, from the canteen. It was going to be a long night.

Rafferty finally called a halt at ten o'clock. He was nearly home before he remembered his promise to Llewellyn. He'd have rung his ma and asked her about accommodating Llewellyn's mother, but, even if he'd thought of it, he'd had no chance during the day and he knew his ma hated getting telephone calls late at night; she always expected disaster. But a promise was a promise. She'd still be up, he knew, as she rarely went to bed before midnight. With a tired sigh, he turned the car and made for her home.

He opened the door with his key, shouting, 'It's only me,' as he shut the front door and opened the one to the living room.

His ma was sitting in her armchair, staring into space, at her feet the box containing the Christmas decorations and in her hand the baby Jesus from the manger scene she always set up in the corner.

He remembered most of the decorations from childhood; the paper bells and lanterns that hung from the ceiling, the cheap balls with the chips of colour missing that hung from the tree. They were all pretty tatty by now, but as they held years of memories in their every chip and tear, his ma refused to throw them out. Every Christmas, when she dug them out, she'd smile and say the same thing, 'Do you remember—?'

Strangely, this time, she said nothing at all.

'Ma?' Rafferty finally gained her attention. 'What's the matter? You look a bit down.'

Kitty Rafferty sighed and told him, 'I've had some bad news, son. It's Gemma. She's pregnant.'

Rafferty stifled a groan of dismay. Gemma was his

eldest niece, the daughter of his second sister, Katy. Gemma was sixteen and looked even younger. He searched the mass of family photographs on the wall for the latest one of her; his ma had so many of them all – angelic babies, grubby-faced toddlers, cheekily grinning schoolkids, serious at First Communion and Confirmation ceremonies. He finally found the photo he was looking for; it could only have been taken a few months ago and, from the happy smile, had been before she had known she was pregnant. She had a dimple in the chin like him. Dimple in chin, devil within, his gran had always said. She'd certainly been a little devil when she was younger and was always the first to lead the rest into mischief. He supposed that was why she was his favourite.

Rafferty hunkered down beside his ma's chair and gave her a hug. 'It's not the end of the world.' He paused and tried to cheer her up. 'You wait – in another few days you'll be looking forward to the birth and knitting like a demon. *And* you'll be the first great-grandma on the street. It's one in the eye for her next door, hey?'

Kitty Rafferty gave a watery smile. 'I suppose so.'

'So, when's it due?'

'She's only two months gone. That worried me, too. It's bad enough that she's pregnant but today, when Katy told me, she said Gemma's daddy was pushing for her to have an abortion. Just like a man, looking for a short-term solution and creating a long-term problem.'

Rafferty knew an abortion would upset his ma even more than the pregnancy. Unlike him, she was a staunch Catholic, and although she had her little idiosyncrasies and didn't blindly follow the Vatican line on everything, abortion was a subject on which she felt very strongly.

'What about Gemma? What does she want?'

This time the smile was more definite. 'She told her father she was going to make him a grandad whether he liked it or not.'

'That's our Gemma. And what about after? Will she keep it or have it adopted?'

'Adopted? My first great-grandchild?' Ma's voice was indignant. 'She'll not have it adopted, not if I've got anything to do with it.' She got up and made for the adjoining kitchen, adding, in a firmer voice, 'It's early days yet for such decisions. Wait till the baby's in her arms and then let her see if she could let him go to strangers.'

He heard the kettle filled with water and plonked on the gas stove, her voice raised to be heard above the kitchen noises. 'It's not as if young Gemma has no one to turn to; she's got a large family. She'd never forgive herself if she gave the baby up; she'd always be wondering what he was like, whether the new parents were kind to him or whether he had been shunted aside by the arrival of a natural child. I knew a girl when I was young who gave her baby up. She never got over it. I don't want that to happen to Gemma.'

Rafferty propped himself against the kitchen door. 'What about the father?'

His ma sniffed. 'He's no more than a kid himself. Same age as Gemma. What sort of a father would he make?'

The kettle boiled and she made the tea, automatically buttering bread while she waited for the tea to brew. The scratch meal was soon ready and Rafferty carried it into the living room.

'So,' his ma began. 'You never said. What brings you here so late?' Rafferty told her. The idea of Mrs Llewellyn's visit seemed to cheer her up immensely. 'Of course, she'll come for Christmas,' she decided. Rafferty tried to dissuade her but she was adamant. 'It'll give her a chance to meet all the family.'

'Are you sure that's a good idea?' Rafferty asked.

'And why wouldn't it be?' she bridled. 'Admittedly, Maureen's mum's likely to be a bit of a starchy-arse, her and her lah-di-dah notions, but I can always give her a jollop of something to loosen her up a bit.'

71

'That wasn't quite what—'

Ma waved him to silence. 'Dafyd's mum must take us as she finds us. If she turns her nose up, it's better for Maureen to know it now than after the wedding.' Her face softened, even her tight Christmas perm seemed to loosen a bit as she added, 'You must remember, Joseph, she's only got the one chick. She's entitled to give us all the once-over. She wants her boy to be happy, same as any mother would. Should I begrudge her the chance to make sure he's marrying the right girl? Talking of weddings,' she went on, 'that reminds me. I've picked up a new suit that would fit you a treat. Come and have a look.'

Following her into the bedroom, Rafferty picked up the local paper and glanced at its headlines while she rummaged in the wardrobe. Not surprisingly, they were still leading with Smith's murder. Determinedly, he turned the page. A small paragraph caught his eye. *Wedding outfitters robbed.* It was certainly one way to cut the costs of the average wedding, he mused. He wondered if Llewellyn had considered it?

He glanced again at the paragraph as his ma held up a smart grey suit of far better quality than the ones he usually bought.

'What do you think? Reckon it's about time you gave that tired brown suit a holiday.' She held the jacket out to him. 'Feel the quality of that. Lovely bit of cloth. Real bargain, it was.'

Rafferty's gaze narrowed. Ma and her 'bargains' were a by-word for trouble. 'Why are there no labels on it?' he demanded. 'Suit's got to be a bit iffy if it hasn't got any labels. So where did you get it? It says here in the paper that—'

She raised her eyes to the ceiling and complained, 'The man's offered a quality suit at a bargain price and he worries about a little thing like labels. I'll put a blessed label in if you're that fussy.'

'Not if it's bent gear. You know—'

'Bent? What kind of language is that? Slightly out of kilter it may be, but that's all. The man I got it from said he was doing a favour for a friend. Some poor devil of a tailor down on his luck, he said.'

'You mean an insurance fiddle? A put-up job?'

'Sure, and I didn't ask the man his private business. You know me, I've never been one to pry. Anyway, even if what you say is true, nobody's lost anything. Only the insurance company and as everybody knows they're the biggest bunch of crooks this side of prison bars; you couldn't really call it a crime at all. More an act of mercy. Like Robin Hood.'

'I doubt the force would agree with you, Ma,' he said as he followed her back to the living room. 'Perhaps you should come and defend me when I'm hauled in front of the Super for not only receiving stolen goods but *wearing* the blessed things. Get rid of it, Ma. Please. For all our sakes.'

Chapter Seven

Rafferty gave a low whistle as he pulled up in the short drive of Elizabeth Probyn's house on Saturday morning. 'She's spent a few bob on security here.' He grinned. 'Wonder who else she's managed to rub up the wrong way? One of those criminals she feels so impartial about, perhaps?'

The burglar alarm squatted like a square red carbuncle on the white-painted face of the house; the front door had a spyhole, and the ground-floor windows all had dark green metal shutters that could be rolled down at night.

Although Rafferty had only once before, some five months previously, had occasion to visit the house, he knew none of these precautions had been in evidence then. He grinned again. He couldn't help it.

Of course Llewellyn had to speak up for her. 'I think you misjudge her. She does her job well; but she does it within the limits of the law. If one were to listen solely to your opinion of her, one could be forgiven for thinking she wasn't successful. But she is – frequently. As for the security, I imagine she receives the usual threats when one of the more vindictive amongst the criminal fraternity gets sent down. Why make it easy for any who decide to carry out their threats?' He rang the bell.

Rafferty's lip curled. His sergeant was of as cool and impartial a turn of mind as Elizabeth Probyn and could be relied upon to stand up for her. Of course, Llewellyn hadn't experienced the shouting matches that he had with her. Or rather, ruefully he corrected himself, *he* had been the one to do the shouting. Typically, Elizabeth Probyn had responded in that cool manner of hers that always infuriated him even more.

Unlike several other CPS lawyers with whom Rafferty had worked in the past, Elizabeth Probyn made no attempt to pretend she was there to help the police nail villains. On the contrary, she insisted that the role of the prosecutor was an objective, impartial one; to lay before the court both the facts for the accused as well as those against. As she had crisply informed Rafferty on more than one occasion, the Prosecution Service was a representative, not of the police but of the public, on whose behalf cases were brought. Winning or losing didn't come into it.

Rafferty had no patience with such legalese; it invariably rendered him incoherent with rage. Older and wiser after their first few confrontations, he had with difficulty learned to control his feelings when they met and, while simmering underneath, on top he was all unnatural politeness like a reluctant dancing partner.

The door was eventually answered by a dumpy middle-aged woman in a dingy grey overall, who through lips that held a dangling cigarette told them she was Mrs Chadden, and that she 'did' for the prosecutor. She was new, too, Rafferty realized. He remembered the previous cleaner had been thin, elderly and tending to sniffiness when Rafferty had introduced himself. He had concluded that, out of the courtroom at least, Elizabeth Probyn dropped a large chunk of her prized impartiality. No doubt the other cleaner had retired.

They were expected and Mrs Chadden let them in with all the chatty enthusiasm of one whose main occupation was finding excuses to stop work. The state of the kitchen confirmed that she had little trouble in finding such excuses. It was barely superficially clean. It was obvious that as a 'treasure' she had limited worth. Rafferty was surprised Elizabeth Probyn didn't get rid of her and hire a more competent model.

'Madam said she'd been delayed and I was to look after you,' she told them when her first rapid flow of chat was finally used up. 'I don't normally work weekends, but she rang and asked me to come in special this morning.' She left them in no doubt that she regarded this as a major concession.

'I suppose you want tea?' Not pausing for their response, she filled the electric kettle and plonked it down on its base on the worktop and switched on, before reaching into a cupboard for mugs. ''Course, what with that high-powered job of hers and now with her daughter being in hospital, she seems to spend all her time running from pillar to post. And then her previous lady retired suddenly. She was lucky I was available at such short notice.'

Which explained her employment of Mrs Chadden, Rafferty reflected. 'I didn't know she had a daughter,' he remarked. It was hardly surprising. Their stilted working relationship scarcely encouraged the bringing out of the family albums. Rafferty, who liked to get to know colleagues on a more personal level, found her standoffish attitude even more constraining.

'Been abroad at school, I imagine. Not met her meself. As I said, it was the hospital visiting on top of her work that got me the job. Some sort of women's trouble, the daughter has, I gather,' Mrs Chadden confided, in delicately lowered tones. 'Must admit, she does look terribly peaky in the latest photos the Missis took of her. So, as I say, what with the long hours the Missis works and then the hospital visiting, she needed a decent woman to look after her, and I was happy to oblige. Recommended, I was.' The idea appeared as startling to her as it did to Rafferty.

Must have been a disgruntled copper who had made the recommendation, Rafferty thought. He watched, fascinated, as the cigarette, in apparent defiance of the laws of gravity, remained perched on the edge of her lower lip as she chattered on.

'Best little job I've had for a long time, I don't mind telling you. 'Course, I've only worked here a few weeks, and she might be being on her best behaviour, like. Some do. But then,' she gazed round the barely clean kitchen with a proprietary air. 'You can see she's used to having things nice.'

She glanced at the clock and frowned. 'I hope she's not going to be much longer, only I've got to get to the chemist in town and it's their early closing day. Promised my old mum I'd pick up some snaps of her and some other old biddies she was in the forces with. I don't like to leave you here on your own. Hardly hospitable.'

Rafferty's glance caught her straw basket, through the holes of which a bag of sugar was visible, and it occurred to him that it wasn't politeness that was making her anxious so much as concern that, left on their own, the law's finest might half-inch stores that she regarded as her prerogative. Judging from the other holes, the sugar had company. Careful to keep the amusement from his voice, Rafferty attempted to reassure her, but she showed no inclination to trust them and depart.

'Two hours a day I put in here, Monday to Friday,' she told them. 'From eight to ten in the morning.' It was now 10.10 a.m. on a Saturday and she was obviously getting restive. She slopped water into the cups, gave the teabags a dunk or two and tipped the milk in. 'Help yourselves to sugar,' she invited, as she dumped the cups before them and sat down. She gazed with a pained expression as Rafferty helped himself to three sugars and took a tentative sip.

Thankfully, they weren't to be subjected to Mrs Chadden's runaway tongue beyond bearing, as, after another couple of minutes, she cocked her head on one side and announced, 'Here she is now,' before rearranging the folds

77

of a cardigan more discreetly over the basket and getting into her coat. 'I'll be off, then,' she told Ms Probyn, as she came into the kitchen.

Elizabeth Probyn was a tall woman, and although she was undoubtedly a little overweight Rafferty noted once again that she carried both height and weight well. She was, he knew, thirty-six, two years younger than him, though from her poised, confident air she always seemed much older. In a burst of honesty, Rafferty acknowledged that if he hadn't lacked these qualities himself he wouldn't feel nearly so irritated by her possession of them. Unconsciously, he straightened his shoulders, commenting, 'Charming woman,' when Mrs Chadden had left.

If she suspected that Rafferty was making a sly dig about her poor choice of cleaner, Elizabeth Probyn didn't let it show. 'Can't say I've noticed myself,' she briefly commented, adding, 'Shall we go through to the lounge?'

The lounge was a spacious, comfortable room, though as in the kitchen the air of neglect was evident. Rafferty had learned on the police grapevine that Elizabeth Probyn was divorced. Grudgingly he admitted she had her work cut out keeping up a house of this size if the only help she had was the slapdash Mrs Chadden. She certainly looked tired; the mauve shadows under her eyes were beginning to deepen to purple and gave her an air of fragility he had never noticed before.

Determined to start the interview off on the right foot for once, as they sat down, Rafferty forced a sympathetic comment. 'I gather Mrs Chadden's something of a stop-gap while your daughter's in hospital?' She stared at him as if she resented his familiarity, and he said quickly, 'It must be a worrying time for you.' The frown told him she suspected he had deliberately encouraged her gossiping treasure.

She gave a sharp nod and abruptly changed the subject. 'You wanted to speak to me about the Maurice Smith case?'

His friendly overtures rebuffed, Rafferty now became equally abrupt. 'Yes.' Curiosity compelled him to let his gaze travel surreptitiously round the room, as he gestured to Llewellyn to take out his notebook. The only other time he'd been here he'd got no further than the hall, and now he noticed lots of framed photographs, presumably of the daughter, as a tiny baby and young woman, resting on top of the piano in the window alcove. She was an attractive girl, or could be if she took some trouble. But she dressed drably, as so many young women did now-adays, and she gazed out at the world with wary eyes from beneath an unkempt mop of dark hair.

'I wanted your general recollections, if any,' Rafferty continued, forcing a calmness he was far from feeling. Keep it light, Rafferty, he advised himself. Don't let her get to you. She's bound to be uptight about her ancient failure, especially as it's *you* asking the questions. 'For instance, you were the prosecutor in the case. Did you believe him to be guilty?'

As though explaining something to a tiresome child, her voice was measured as she said, 'Come, Inspector, you know I don't make such judgements.'

'But you did that time,' he came back at her. 'In fact, from what I understand it was you who insisted there was sufficient evidence to press ahead with the case, even though—' He broke off and tried again as he saw her lips grow thin. 'We've spoken to ex-Inspector Stubbs, the officer in charge,' he added, 'and he was helpful. And as it was his last case before he retired, he remembered it well, even though it was ten years ago.'

'I'm sure.' Ms Probyn gave them a taut smile. 'So do I. It was his last big case and my first, as I've no doubt he told you. And, if it gives you any satisfaction, Inspector, yes, I did believe Smith to be guilty. He was as guilty as hell.' For a moment the idealist that she must have been in her youth showed through the calm façade. Rafferty had always suspected that, underneath, she was a passionate woman and was glad to see his own judgement vindicated. He still couldn't warm to her, but at least it made her seem more human.

She flushed, no doubt embarrassed by her outburst. 'Of course, Chief Inspector Stubbs resented us.' She glanced coolly at him. 'Most of the police did.' She shrugged. 'It was a natural enough reaction, I suppose. There we were, a newly hatched Crown Prosecution Service taking the decision-making power about who to prosecute out of police hands, and with all us fluffy little chicks eager to stretch our wings. And then there was Inspector Stubbs, the rooster of the coop, wishing us all in perdition. I didn't deal with it very well,' she admitted. It was plain she found the admission difficult.

'Thankfully, experience has brought a measure of self-control, but at the time his attitude made me stubborn, and when he said he had doubts that we'd get a conviction and wanted more time I lost my temper and insisted that the prosecution went ahead. Foolishly, as it turned out. But then I was young, eager to prove myself. No doubt my head was filled with dreams of glory.' She gave a sudden, harsh laugh. 'As you can imagine, the Maurice Smith case brought me down to earth with a bump. I learned a hard lesson that day.'

Rafferty nodded, for the first time getting a glimmer of understanding of what had helped shape her outlook. The young Elizabeth Osbourne must have felt her career over before it had really begun and that, ever afterwards, her name would be associated with the Maurice Smith fiasco. She'd done well to put it behind her. She'd shed her idealism a touch quicker than most, and acquired a useful maturity; shame it wasn't matched by an equal compassion for the victims of crimes, he thought. But, whatever his private opinions, she *had* gone on to become one of the youngest Chief Crown Prosecutors in the country; not a bad achievement from such inauspicious beginnings. It must make it even more galling to be quizzed on her early days.

80

'I really don't see what I can say that Archibald Stubbs hasn't already told you,' she said with a return to her earlier brusqueness, as if anxious to get rid of them. 'It's all ancient history now. Do you really think—'

'It might be ancient history to you, Ms Probyn,' Rafferty told her sharply, pleased to be in the right for once. 'But I doubt the Walkers, the Masseys, the Denningtons and the Figgs feel the same.' He had the satisfaction of seeing he had discomfited her. But, as always, she had a tart remark ready to put him in his place.

'You'll have plenty of suspects, then. I hope—'

Convinced by her cool gaze that she was mocking him, Rafferty broke in. 'That's right.' It had been one of her most frequent criticisms in the past that he threw his net too wide, employing little logic and less finesse in his conduct of cases, wasting precious resources in the process. 'The little girls Smith assaulted and their devastated parents for a start.' She had the grace to flush and drop her gaze.

'We've also got another angle.' He told her about the 'outing' letter Smith had been sent. 'Probably from a bunch of local feminists, but we've yet to look into that.'

Her interest was piqued when he told her that. She offered no more taunts, intended or otherwise, answering the rest of his questions without another clash. But, as he had expected, he learned nothing new. He stood up to go. 'If you remember anything else that might help, anything at all, we'd be grateful.'

'Of course.' Her gaze was steady, unblinking, but Rafferty felt he could read a message in the grey depths. It was the same as the one that Mrs ffinch-Robinson had less subtly passed: You'll need all the help you can get.

With a brief nod he made ungraciously for the door, leaving Llewellyn to observe the civilities.

As Llewellyn climbed into the car beside him he placed a couple of tickets in Rafferty's lap. 'Ms Probyn gave me these for a performance of the "Scottish play" she's been acting in for the last week, but I think your need is greater than mine. It might help you to see another side of her.'

'I've seen more than enough sides of her already, thanks.' Still, he took the tickets and stuffed them in his pocket. 'Took the wind out of her sails this time, at least. You could see she hated being questioned about the Smith case. I wonder how she *really* feels about it?'

He gave a cautious glance at Llewellyn before venturing a further comment. 'I know she could be said to have less reason to hold a grudge than Stubbs, Thompson or the victims and their families, but it *did* come right at the beginning of her career.' Ignoring Llewellyn's sceptical silence, he added, 'Maybe a person's first case, like the first love, stays in the memory.'

Llewellyn threw him a pitying look and Rafferty admitted, 'All right, maybe I'm indulging in a bout of wishful thinking. I agree the Smith case taught her a valuable lesson and could be said to have acted as a springboard to success, but—'

'Quite.'

'*But*,' Rafferty repeated determinedly, ignoring Llewellyn's tart rejoinder, 'you must admit she seemed pretty ill at ease discussing the matter.'

'I did notice. But then,' Llewellyn added drily, 'so would I be in her position, if *you* were the one doing the questioning. You really must be the proverbial red rag to a bull as far as Ms Probyn's concerned.' He started the car. 'Lucky for you she's tethered by such admirable self-control.'

Rafferty subsided, muttering, 'Leave a bloke his fantasies, at least. They're all that keeps me warm these cold nights.' Especially the one where he banged her up in a cell for the night with a couple of the more downmarket toms for company. He bet that would make her lose that cool, legal manner that got up his nose so much.

As though determined to make Rafferty admit that there *was* another side to Elizabeth Probyn as he waited in the driveway for a break in the traffic – always a long-winded business with Llewellyn – the Welshman commented, 'Did you notice that wonderful piano?'

Rafferty refused to be drawn. 'You mean that big polished brown thing by the window? No. Can't say I did.'

'It was a Steinway, that's all. Beautiful thing. The Rolls-Royce of pianos.'

'Only the best for Ms Probyn. What did you expect her to have? An out-of-tune, second-hand job with yellow keys and wonky pedals?'

The image put him in mind of his own youth and, softer-voiced, he added, 'Funny, you rarely see one now, but everyone used to have a piano when I was a kid. We even had one. God knows why, as none of us could play it, though my old man used to do a bit of a turn on his fiddle when he was merry.' He sighed. 'Happy days. Simpler, kinder, too, in many ways. We all used to play out till all hours, especially in the summer holidays. Who would let their kids do that now? Everyone used to be able to leave their front door key hanging from a length of string behind the letterbox. Try doing *that* now. You'd think prosecutors like Elizabeth Probyn would have a bit more sympathy with the public's anxieties.'

Wisely, Llewellyn said nothing and, now that the road was clear for well over a hundred yards in either direction, he pulled out and turned in the direction of the refuge and Mrs Nye.

Fortunately Mrs Nye was a woman unlikely to set Rafferty's teeth on edge. He had always found her sympathetic, understanding and willing to help. He hoped this occasion wouldn't prove an exception. She was a widow, well set up financially, with time on her hands, and she used her money and her time in a variety of benevolent works.

She welcomed them in her usual friendly manner and led them to her office. 'How can I help you, Inspector?' she asked as they all sat down.

As the women he thought the most likely senders of the 'outing' letter were colleagues of Mrs Nye, Rafferty eased gradually round to the reason for their visit. 'We're investigating the murder of Maurice Smith,' he told her. 'I imagine you've read about the case?'

She nodded and clasped her hands firmly together, resting them on the cheap deal table she used as a desk. 'Forgive me for being blunt, but I don't see how I can help you. The women who come here are victims of violence, not its perpetrators.'

Rafferty paused before he answered. He admired Mrs Nye, respected her. He didn't want to antagonize her. He hadn't wanted to antagonize Elizabeth Probyn, either, he reflected, but he had still managed it. He reminded himself that Mrs Nye was not Elizabeth Probyn. Often, in the past, her persuasion had convinced a rape victim to make a statement, submit to a medical examination, and thus help the police get a conviction. He wanted her on his side. She was educated, fair-minded and, most of all, she believed in justice. He appealed to that last trait now.

'It wasn't actually the women of the refuge we wanted to speak to you about.' She raised an enquiring eyebrow and he continued with the point she had herself raised. 'You know, in many ways I think it's fair to say that Maurice Smith was also a victim – of his upbringing. Apart from being physically unprepossessing, he came from a broken home, had an inadequate mother, a bullying stepfather, little love of any description, according to his police record. Is it any wonder he became what he did?'

Rafferty had expressed his views on criminal matters often enough to feel like a hypocrite as he voiced their opposite. But it was true that Maurice Smith had had little enough going for him. One of the 'underclass' that politicians had taken to spouting about in recent years, Smith had undoubtedly been a victim of sorts. Thankfully, Mrs Nye was too polite to point out his volte-face. She pointed out something else instead.

'But he still had a *choice*, Inspector. To rape – or not to rape. Oh, I know the case was thrown out of court, but even his own family – if the papers are to be believed – were quick to disown him as if they, too, believed he was guilty. I'm not condoning his murder. Like you, I believe in the rule of law.' Rafferty wished his own belief in the law was as firm now as it had been twenty, even fifteen years earlier. 'If there's any way I can help you catch his killer, I'll do it gladly.'

Rafferty was relieved she had made the offer. It made it easier for him to broach the subject. 'As you know, there have recently been a spate of rapist or suspected rapist outing cases in various areas of the country.' She nodded. 'We've had one or two locally. Maurice Smith was a victim.' He watched her. She didn't seem surprised at the news.

'Outing a rapist is a long way from killing him, Inspector.'

Rafferty nodded. He dug in his pocket and laid a photocopy of the letter Smith had received on the table. 'You said you wanted to help us catch Smith's killer. Quite possibly the people who sent him this had nothing to do with his murder, but I'm sure you appreciate that they need to be questioned. If you suspect any of your Rape Support Group members might have anything to do with outing threats, I hope you'd tell us.'

Mrs Nye's expression was unhappy. 'Even if this,' she tapped a fingernail on the letter, 'has any connection with my members, it's a long way from murder,' she repeated. 'Outing, as I understand it, is to alert residents to potential dangers, to deter the rapist himself from further rape and, hopefully, encourage him to seek help.'

'And is it not also to terrorize him a little?' Rafferty added softly. 'To give him a taste of what it feels to be a victim?'

'I'm sure the motives are mixed.' She handed back the photocopy. 'The people who carry out such acts are misguided, of course, but understandably so in view of the many lenient sentences handed out by the courts. I don't agree with such actions, but many people do.'

Rafferty felt she was getting away from him, was losing her sympathy, and he was about to insist she give him some names, some indication if she suspected the involvement of any of her members, when from beside him Llewellyn intoned softly, ' "For evil to triumph, all it takes is for good men to do nothing." '

There was a long pause, then Mrs Nye said, 'Point taken, Sergeant.' Firmly, she added, 'Firstly, I have to say that I don't *know* anything, not for certain, but I'll tell you who I suspect.' She paused again. 'Three members broke away from my group several weeks ago, and I'm ashamed to say that these three *did* push for an official outing policy. I believe they had gained the secret support and confidence of several disgruntled policemen in the area, so they had no difficulty in learning of the whereabouts of such men as Smith. They left to form their own group when I told them that, with or without the connivance of maverick policemen, I couldn't condone them breaking the law.'

Mrs Nye must have noticed their quickly exchanged glances at this, for before Rafferty could ask her she added, 'Oh, I don't know the names of the officers concerned. If I did, I'd give them to you. I approve of policemen taking the law into their own hands even less than I do of anyone else doing so.'

Because policemen usually had the necessary knowledge to get away with it, Rafferty guessed she meant.

That was another area of concern for him in this case; the possibility that Smith had been murdered by a copper gone wrong. Because if a professional, experienced copper like Stubbs had killed Smith, he stood a good chance of getting away with it. It was disconcerting that the thought didn't trouble him more.

Although one half of his troublesome Libran personality pulled him towards the underdog, which was undoubtedly what Smith was, the other half had an even stronger pull towards natural justice – in whatever guise it appeared. Between the two viewpoints, the policeman element came a poor third. God help him and his career if Superintendent Bradley ever suspected it, for Bradley's zeal for convictions was nearly as strong as his interest in policing on the cheap.

Unfortunately, the information Mrs Nye gave them was not conclusive. Although she had confirmed that her ex-colleagues had pushed for an official 'outing' policy, she had no proof that they had actually gone ahead with it on their own. But she had given him their names, and at least Rafferty now had evidence of intention with which to confront them.

Their leading light was one Sinead Fay. 'Let's get round to her house,' Rafferty said. 'Mrs Nye seemed to think she'd be at home. I'll be interested to discover what cars Ms Fay and her friends drive and whether we can get them to let anything slip over this outing business. I'm more and more convinced they're involved.'

They got in the car and Llewellyn consulted his street atlas before pulling away from the kerb.

'When we've seen Ms Fay and her friends we'd better make a start on interviewing Smith's victims and their families,' Rafferty told him. 'The sooner we do that the sooner we should be able to remove a few names from the list.'

'What about Stubbs and Thompson?' Llewellyn asked.

'Don't worry, I haven't forgotten them. Actually,' Rafferty glanced across, 'I'd like you to check out their movements.'

As far as he could tell from Llewellyn's poker-face, the Welshman welcomed this difficult task. 'I'll have to drive up to London to speak to Frank Massey, his daughter and ex-wife as soon as I can fit it in; maybe you could check out the policeman angle then?' Llewellyn nodded. 'Only try to find out what we need to know by roundabout means if you can. I doubt Archie Stubbs would bother to thank me for it, but I feel we owe him and Thompson a bit of discretion. If they're innocent and word got out that they had been suspects in a murder case it could cause Thompson, as a serving copper, problems. We all know mud sticks and coppers are even more vulnerable to such taints.'

An alleyway gave access to residents' parking behind Sinead Fay's house. Rafferty stopped Llewellyn before he made for the gate, reminded him of their interesting discoveries at the rear of Smith's flat, and said, 'Let's take a look round the back. We may just learn something to our advantage.'

Rafferty wasn't totally surprised to find a Zephyr, the same car that Lilley had described as being seen parked near Smith's flat on the night he had been reported missing. How many of these old cars could still be running? he wondered, and made a mental note to check it out. He doubted there would be more than a dozen in the whole area.

He was surprised an educated feminist like Sinead Fay – if she *had* been involved in Smith's death – should be so careless, should have so little idea how to protect herself. Of course, leaving aside the matter of the 'outing' letter for the moment, it might indicate her innocence of Smith's murder. Equally, she might simply be displaying her contempt for males, in particular males in positions of authority, like policemen.

Another possibility occurred to him. Did she subconsciously *want* to get caught? Using such an old and easily recognizable car when she was involved in dubious enterprises was certainly one way of drawing police attention to your activities.

He quickly noted the registration number before peering in the driver's window. But there was nothing to see and it was unlikely he'd be able to persuade a magistrate to issue a search warrant when their evidence was merely circumstantial. He tried the boot but it was locked. Had Smith's body been transported in this? he wondered. Like a fox scenting a rabbit, he felt his pulse quicken and the adrenalin start to flow.

Chapter Eight

For the moment, however, the car wasn't going to tell them anything more and Rafferty and Llewellyn walked round to the front of the house. After radioing through to the station to check that the car *was* Sinead Fay's, they walked up the path and knocked on the door.

Although Rafferty had never met Sinead Fay, he had heard of her and what had happened to her, so he knew what to expect. However, the reality was still shocking and he tried not to stare at the ruin of her face as he quickly made the introductions.

The doctors had done a pretty neat job of stitching up the knife slashes, but some of them had gone deep, to the dermis and beyond, to the layer of subcutaneous fat beneath. Eight years ago the techniques for repairing such facial injuries hadn't been as advanced as they were now, but surely, he thought, even now, *something* more could be done for her?

'Pretty, aren't they, Inspector?' she commented by way of greeting. 'I call them my feminist battle scars.' Although her voice was careless, matter of fact, even, the rage still came through in the aggressive line of the jaw and the resolute stare with which she met his gaze, daring him to show revulsion or pity.

Some of Rafferty's colleagues who had met her were of the opinion that Sinead Fay had left her scars as they were in order to make men feel guilty. Rafferty suspected they were right. It certainly worked on him. She would, he was sure, make good use of such a natural male reaction. It would be more effective to the feminist cause than any number of rallies and demonstrations.

She must have been an enchantingly pretty girl before the vicious assault on her, Rafferty decided. She shared the glorious Black Irish colouring of his sister, Maggie; hair as dark as a raven, skin creamy as Jersey milk and eyes the bright blue of lazy Caribbean skies fringed with lashes as lustrous as palm fronds.

'How did it happen?'

Rafferty was torn abruptly away from his poetical musings by Llewellyn's question and wished he'd thought to warn him what to expect. Of course, he hadn't anticipated the normally sensitive Llewellyn would voice such a question.

Sinead Fay smiled softly, as though pleased that another unsuspecting male had fallen so neatly into her trap. Rafferty wondered just how much of a kick she got out of telling each new man she met.

'I was attacked by a knife-wielding thug, Sergeant,' she told him. 'One who didn't seem to understand that I found him entirely resistible. I had already refused to go out with him several times. I gather he thought that, with my face carved up, I wouldn't be able to be so particular. Oh, and he raped me as well, just to thrust the message home, as it were.'

Llewellyn merely nodded. Rafferty guessed she had expected the usual male response; a shuffling of feet, the lowering of embarrassed eyes, the muttered apology, for when the Welshman failed to do any of these things her eyes narrowed, her provocative mouth thinned, so that, strangely, it became even more provocative, and she spun on her heel with the words, 'You wanted to speak to me about the death of Maurice Smith, I believe?'

'The *murder* of Maurice Smith, yes,' Rafferty corrected. She glanced fleetingly over her shoulder at his correction, then led the way into what he assumed was her living room, though it looked more like the headquarters of an anarchist group. The walls were covered with posters; some urging the empowerment of women, others featuring the uglier face of man in all its aggressive guises, warrior, rapist, mugger. Piles of leaflets littered every surface and he realized that it *was* their headquarters, their advice centre, their meeting point where they planned future campaigns. Was it here that the 'outing' campaign had been formulated?

There were two other women present. They were bent over a table piled high with letters which they were stuffing into envelopes. He guessed these were the other two women who formed the breakaway Rape Support Group.

The elder of the two stared at them boldly. She had the kind of dark, gypsyish good looks that had no need of make-up. Rafferty guessed it probably infuriated her that her own natural attractiveness would encourage men to indulge in the kind of meaningless flirtation she must despise. As though to counteract her own good looks, she wore a shapeless pair of khaki dungarees with a badge on the strap that said, '*Mother Nature Nurtures – What Does FATHER Nature Do?*'

She was about thirty-five, he guessed, and his assumption that she was Ellen Kemp was confirmed as Sinead Fay made the introductions. The strong chin and squared shoulders spoke of the confident woman that Mrs Nye had described. She had told them that Ellen Kemp ran her own very successful business as well as bringing up her daughter single-handedly. She had the air of quiet self-assurance about her that made him wonder why she hadn't assumed the mantle of leader. But presumably her business took up a lot of her time. And there was always the position of the power *behind* the throne. The other woman was about twenty-five and was introduced as Zonie Anderson. She nodded but said nothing.

Ellen Kemp held his gaze for several seconds before

she said, 'Gwen Nye rang and told us you were on your way, though really I can't imagine what—'

'We just want to ask a few questions, Ms Kemp, nothing to worry about. We're investigating the murder of Maurice Smith and—'

'Wow! Men!'

Astonished to hear a voice in this house enthuse over his sex, Rafferty's head swivelled. A teenage girl stood in the doorway behind Sinead Fay. She shared Ellen Kemp's bold stare, but the stare she directed at him and Llewellyn was much warmer, the smile so naturally flirtatious that Rafferty wondered what malign trick of the fates had placed her in a house where males were regarded as some kind of alien race. Behind him he heard Ellen Kemp give the briefest of sighs.

'This is my daughter, Jenny,' she told them shortly.

Rafferty almost laughed at the cruel irony of it. About eighteen, Jenny's similarity to her mother was striking, though it obviously extended no further than the physical.

As though to demonstrate this fact, Jenny, hips swaying, sashayed slowly across the room and sat on the arm of her mother's chair, where she commenced a provocative swinging of one bare and slender leg. 'What are they doing *here*?' she asked her mother, as she appraised Llewellyn with such a steady, under-the-lashes stare of admiration that his ears began to turn bright pink.

With a restraint obviously born from plenty of practice, Ellen Kemp merely commented, 'These are policemen, darling. I don't imagine they'll be here long.'

'Pity,' Jenny said, continuing to stare moony-eyed at the discomfited Welshman.

Across Ellen Kemp's face passed a succession of emotions; irritation, affectionate exasperation, resignation and, finally, determination. 'If you've got nothing better to do, why don't you take the post to the mailbox?'

'What's the rush?' Jenny countered. She removed her gaze from Llewellyn for long enough to assess and dismiss the table with its piles of leaflets and already filled envelopes and said, 'There's nothing there that can't wait.'

As Jenny showed no inclination to leave, her mother was forced to resort to bribery. She dug in her pocket and said, 'Here's fifteen pounds. Why don't you and Cindy go to the pictures? You said you wanted to see that new film.'

'Trying to get rid of me, Mum?' Jenny asked. However, the bribe worked, because she took the heavy-handed hint and the crisp notes, pushed herself up from her mother's chair and, after picking up the post, swayed her way back to the door. 'All right, I'll make myself scarce. Maybe I'll go to see Aunt Beth later. Her place can't be any more dreary than this house and maybe I might be able to cheer *her* up.'

'I don't think that's a good idea, Jenny. She could do without your particular brand of cheering at the moment.'

Jenny shrugged.

'And remember what I said about going with Cindy. I don't want you going on your own.'

Jenny pulled another face as she made for the door again. 'Honestly, Mum, the entire world isn't populated by dirty old men in raincoats, you know. Though to hear you—'

'Please, Jenny, just do as I ask.'

Jenny flounced her way out, though she paused for long enough as she passed Llewellyn to say '*Ciao*' and blow him a kiss. The front door slammed behind her, leaving a strained silence, which, after a moment, Rafferty broke.

He gestured at the unoccupied settee, and asked, 'OK if we sit down?' Sinead Fay nodded. 'As I said, we wanted to talk to you about the murder of Maurice Smith.'

Interestingly, none of the women made a comment about his death. Given their frequent outbursts in the press about the leniency of the courts in dealing with rapists and other violent criminals, he'd have expected a 'good riddance' at the very least, and it was revealing that they chose to remain silent. He guessed Jenny's behaviour had not only embarrassed them but had also to an extent taken the wind out of their sails. He decided to take advantage of it by launching a surprise attack.

'I wonder, Ms Fay, if you can tell me what your car was doing parked by the victim's flat from last Wednesday morning to Thursday evening?'

There was a moment's electrified silence. But something about Rafferty's body language or choice of words must have given him away, for Ellen Kemp told them calmly, 'You're mistaken, Inspector. Sinead's car was parked in my garage all last week.'

Rafferty admired her coolness. Assuming it *was* the same car and it had been parked there for the reason he suspected, she was taking a chance that nobody had noted the number. Still, it was a calculated risk and he doubted Ellen Kemp ever did anything without calculating the odds. It was probably the character trait that had made her a successful businesswoman. And she had had enough time since Smith's murder to plan her answers.

A small voice of caution whispered in his brain that they'd hardly have parked the car outside Smith's flat if they'd been planning to murder him, and he as quickly riposted that murder mightn't have been the plan, merely the result. Having witnessed the pragmatic means she had used to remove her wayward daughter from the room, he judged that Ellen Kemp was not fanatical enough to incriminate herself deliberately or to allow the other two to do so. A woman of her spirit would find the restrictions of a long prison sentence unendurable.

He questioned her further. 'You say Ms Fay's car was in your garage?' She nodded. 'Can you explain why?'

'It's simple enough. It was playing up. It's quite an old car and Sinead was tired of being ripped off by male mechanics and having to put up with their sexist comments. She knows I'm quite good with cars, so she asked me to have a look at it.'

'And you didn't take it out at all?'

'Well, of course I took it out. I had to give it a test run to make sure I'd cured the problem. But I only took it round the block. Nowhere near Smith's flat.'

'You know where he lived, then?' he quickly asked and she answered equally quickly.

'I should imagine the whole world knows by now. Or don't you read the papers, Inspector?' Rafferty began to see where Jenny got her pertness from; they took different directions, that was all. 'I had no idea where he lived before his death.' She met his eyes as though daring him to contradict her. 'I had no reason to. None of us did.'

Rafferty nodded. Hoping their investigations would reveal whether she was telling the truth or not, he gestured to Llewellyn to take over the questioning; possibly his more low-key technique would get through their defences. Besides, he wanted a few free moments to study their faces.

As though suspecting she might be a weak link, Llewellyn turned first to Sinead Fay. 'I understand you and Ms Kemp and Ms Anderson here have recently broken away from the main Rape Support Group organization,' he began. 'Can you tell me why that was?'

When she answered it was clear she had taken her guide from the older woman's responses. 'Are you saying you don't know?'

'We don't operate on hearsay, Ms Fay,' Llewellyn told her mildly. 'I'd like to hear it from you.'

She shrugged. 'They'd become a bunch of bleeding-heart liberals, writing polite little letters to their MPs, asking them to do something about the rising levels of rape.'

Llewellyn had been wise to put his questions to Sinead Fay, Rafferty realized. Because although she made an attempt to lose the 'rant' from her voice, as she continued she was unable to keep it up.

'Asking!' Her blue eyes were scornful. 'They should

have been *demanding*, not asking. Making the cause front-page news, not—'

'How?' Rafferty immediately asked. He was quickly interrupted.

'Sinead,' Ellen Kemp's voice held a warning note. 'I'm sure they don't want to listen to all this.'

'Oh, but we do,' Rafferty assured her. He turned back to Sinead Fay. 'How?' he asked again. From his pocket he pulled a photocopy of the threatening letter he had found in Smith's sideboard. Holding it in front of him, he leaned forward challengingly to encourage an incautious response. 'By outing the rapists? Was that how you planned to get banner headlines?'

Or had they planned an even more newsworthy publicity campaign? he wondered. Sinead Fay, for one, seemed fanatical enough for anything and Ellen Kemp might have been unable to restrain her. If so, Sinead must be very pleased with her efforts. The story of Maurice Smith's 'execution' had filled the front page of every newspaper in the country.

For a moment Sinead Fay's eyes glowed with something akin to triumph and Rafferty felt sure that she was going to confess to Smith's murder. But then, as Ellen Kemp frowned at her, the fanatical light faded and she drew back. He could almost see the shutters go down.

'I just told you how,' she said flatly. 'By hounding as many MPs as we could, by making their lives a misery until they agreed to take up our cause. As for that letter, it's nothing to do with us. I've never seen it before.' The other two echoed her statement.

With an apologetic shrug, Rafferty gestured to Llewellyn to resume the questioning.

'Yet I understood from Mrs Nye that all three of you proposed the idea of an outing campaign here in Elmhurst. Are you saying that's not the case?'

As though concerned that Sinead Fay might let herself be goaded into making further provocative statements,

Ellen Kemp answered. 'No. She's merely saying that we haven't organized such a campaign.' As though anxious to take their interest away from her outspoken friend, she continued, 'But maybe an outing campaign is what's needed to make the authorities sit up and take notice. Women have always been too quiet, too undemanding about the things that affect them. That's why their needs are so often ignored. They should take their cue from the AIDS lobby.'

The other two were nodding. Obviously, Rafferty reflected, this was a much-discussed issue.

Although she kept her voice level, her feelings in check, it was evident that Ellen Kemp felt every bit as strongly as the younger woman. 'Do you know how much money and help the AIDS campaigners have had showered on them?' she asked. 'All right,' she admitted, 'many people would say it's a worthy cause. But then so is helping the victims of rape. So is doing something about the level of sexual assault.'

She leant forward as though to convince them. 'Apart from financial input from the government, the AIDS campaign get film stars hosting charity dinners, rock stars throwing charity concerts. What do rape victims get? You know the answer yourself – pretty pastel rape suites in police stations if they're lucky; a few pot plants to give the impression that the powers that be give a damn about women's fears.'

Ellen Kemp rose, walked to the table and picked up a selection of the RSG leaflets and handed them to Rafferty. 'I suggest you read these; you'll find all the facts in there. Were you aware, for instance, that over twenty thousand women and girls are raped or sexually assaulted in this country every year? And that's just the tip of the iceberg. There are many more who never report it. A fifth of the victims are under sixteen; little girls, Inspector. Vulnerable little girls, just like Smith's victims. Easy prey for rapists, of course, that's why they target them. They can be pretty sure that the ordeal of testifying in court will deter most of them from seeking justice. Understandable, of course, when you know how their courage is rewarded by the – mostly male – legal system.'

She opened a leaflet and began to read, her voice matter of fact rather than ranting. 'Take just one year – 1991 – more than 4000 women and girls reported rape to the police and just 559 men were found guilty. Roughly one in eight. With time off for good behaviour, most of them were out in very few years. It's their victims who got the life sentence.'

Rafferty knew what she said was true. It often angered him; he had a mother, sisters, nieces. Maybe one day he'd even have daughters . . . He knew the terrible, life-long damage such assaults inflicted, the shattered lives, the mental trauma, the vanished confidence, that was so often the victim's lot.

Some, like the Walkers' daughter, committed suicide. He could understand the women's anger, their determination to do something. He frequently felt the same way. That was the trouble.

But he knew he couldn't afford to show his weakness. These women were suspects in a murder case, and it would be as well for him to remember it. Now, thrusting aside his instinctive sympathies, he said bluntly, 'I'm aware of all this, Ms Kemp. But I'm only a policeman. I just try to catch villains. And whatever Maurice Smith did or didn't do, and whether I like it or not, I have the task of finding his killer. Now, perhaps you could tell me where you all were on the evening of Thursday the eighteenth of December, when we understand Maurice Smith was murdered.'

'Certainly. We were here. We were all here.'

'All evening?' She nodded.

As an alibi, it was far from convincing. Rafferty was beginning to think of them as the Three Musketeers – one for all and all for one. He'd made a bad mistake in speaking to them together like this. Next time he'd make sure he spoke to each of them alone; that way the wiser head of Ellen Kemp would be unable to restrain Sinead's hotter one.

'What about your daughter? Was she here too?'

Ellen Kemp's smile was ironic. 'No. As you saw, my daughter prefers ogling men to getting involved with her mother's campaigns. She spent that entire day at her friend Cindy's house and slept over. Check, if you like.' She supplied the address of her daughter's friend and sat back.

They were too much on their guard for Rafferty to imagine much more could be achieved today and, recognizing the futility of continuing the interview, he stood up to go. But he was more than ever convinced they were involved.

'They sent that letter,' he said to Llewellyn as they walked down the path. 'I'm sure of it. It would explain why they were outside his flat – probably scared he'd do a bunk so they were taking turns on guard duty. Making sure he didn't get a chance to escape whatever punishment they had decided on. We already know that from where they were positioned they would have had a good view of both entrances of Smith's place. They'd have seen anyone going in or out, especially as there are street lamps within a few yards of back and front. If they didn't kill Smith, the odds are they know who did, so let's work from there. Who, exactly, are Sinead Fay and her friends likely to try to protect?'

'Smith's young victims, obviously.'

'Not Stubbs and Thompson?'

'I can't see someone like Sinead Fay putting herself out to protect policemen, even ones who had supplied them with information. I'm sure, like the other women, they would have thought the two men more than capable of looking after themselves.'

'What about Frank Massey?'

100

Llewellyn hesitated. 'More difficult. He's what you might call a halfway-house as far as they're concerned. A victim of sorts, but, again, I think it likely they'd feel that as a grown man he would be capable of protecting himself; even more so as he's already had one spell in prison. Whereas Smith's victims proper are still very young, possibly naive.'

Rafferty nodded as they got in the car. 'That's what I thought. We'll have to check with the neighbours. Put Hanks on to it. It's possible the neighbours noticed any comings or goings from Fay's house during the evening.'

He didn't hold out much hope. The neighbours on one side were an elderly couple. It was another dull, dismal day and like many people they had their living-room light on. He had noticed them when he and Llewellyn had arrived. The television had been on and plates of brunch in their laps, already engrossed in the day's viewing that probably continued till they went to bed. Perhaps they'd have more luck with the people on the other side.

'Get Hanks to check out Ellen Kemp's garage at the same time,' he added. 'If, as she says, Sinead Fay's car was there last week, her own vehicle could well have been parked on the street. The neighbours would have noticed and remarked on it, if so. After all, who's going to leave their car outside these icy mornings and give themselves the chore of scraping the frost off the windscreen if they don't have to? Better get him to check that she was telling the truth about the daughter, too, though she seemed too confident about that to be lying.'

Llewellyn nodded, then added, 'I was thinking.' Rafferty waited. 'Mrs Penny, Smith's landlady, said she rarely goes out in the evening. Don't you think it's strange that she should go out on the night Smith was murdered?'

Rafferty glanced at him, pleased that he was ahead of his sergeant. It was unusual at this stage of an investigation. 'Perhaps you should put that the other way round? Strange that Smith should be murdered on the night she goes out. It's clear that whoever killed Smith knew the flat downstairs would be empty that evening and made use of the knowledge. Forensic found traces of blood on the fire stairs at the back of the building, and we found a navy thread, which presumably came from his tracksuit.' Although they were still waiting to learn whether the blood and tracksuit threads had been Smith's, Rafferty felt it probable. He also felt they had enough evidence to guess what had happened.

'Getting a body, even a light one like Smith's, down those fire stairs is unlikely to have been a silent operation, so whoever killed Smith would have been keen to know the downstairs flat was unoccupied that night. Go and see Mrs Penny later today, Dafyd. Find out who knew she'd be going out. Ask her when she mentioned it to Smith. You might also ask around and see if anyone noticed a strange car parked behind the house. We know the lock on the back gate was forced, recently, too, as the wood is still clean; all the evidence points to the body being taken out that way. I reckon whoever killed him backed on to the hardstanding, using the gate to conceal it. Then they walked round to the front, got the once-over from Smith via his spyhole, was let in, and killed him, bundling his body into a rubbish bag and down the back stairs.'

'Pretty cold-blooded.'

'Don't they say revenge is a dish best eaten cold?'

Llewellyn frowned, then reminded him, 'According to his landlady, Smith was very careful about opening his door to strangers. Understandable, of course; he'd had to move from his previous address when a sharp-eyed neighbour recognized him and caused trouble. With this outing threat, he'd have been even more cautious, especially when his friendly landlady was out for the evening. He must have felt he had nothing to fear from whoever he opened his door to. So, who would be likely to fall into such a category?'

Rafferty provided the obvious answer. 'Police, family,

old friends – if any exist. Though as Mrs Penny said he had no friends that just leaves the police and his own family.'

'Jes Bullock, you mean.'

Rafferty nodded. 'He'd certainly stand further questioning, though to be frank I can't see the ladies of the RSG protecting such a man. Still, something's eating at him, I'm sure of it. We'll go and see him again this evening, as soon as we're free,' Rafferty decided.

Thoughtfully, Llewellyn put forward another possibility. 'You said, other than his family, Smith would be most likely to open the door to a uniformed officer, like Thompson. If we take that together with Mrs Nye's information that she thought maverick policemen were supplying Sinead Fay and her friends with information on possible outing targets, Thompson may well have left a computer trail behind him.'

'Doubt it. No, if Thompson has been supplying the breakaway RSG women with information, either the information he obtained wasn't taken from a traceable source like a computer, or he got someone else to access it for him. That's another area to look into. You're the computer buff, can I leave you to check that out?'

Llewellyn nodded.

'Check with the Social as well. They might have Smith cross-referenced in their files under his original and his current names. It's possible they gave his address out to someone. Whoever's responsible for this local spate of outing threats is getting their information from official sources. Trouble is, it may be difficult to get to the bottom of it. Most of the coppers I've spoken to about the case were of the private opinion that whoever killed Smith did an excellent job. If one of them provided Thompson with Smith's whereabouts, he's unlikely to admit it.'

Rafferty was sure that if Thompson was guilty he and his informant would be likely to hang together, scared, as the saying went, that if they didn't they'd hang separately.

'Anyway,' he decided. 'After what we learned from Mrs Nye, we'd better make checking the alibis of Stubbs and Thompson a priority. If they were supplying information to those three women we need something to tie them together. All we've got at the moment is the fact that Smith opened his door willingly, tied to the probability that Sinead Fay's old Zephyr was parked outside his flat. What we need is some *proof.*'

He fastened his seat belt. 'Come on, let's get back to the station. Maybe, by now, Liz Green and Lilley will have turned up a nosey neighbour or two for us.'

Chapter Nine

They drove back to the station. The council workmen had finished the belated erection of the Christmas decorations in the town and were standing about admiring their handiwork as throngs of busy shoppers bustled past.

With a guilty pang Rafferty remembered he hadn't yet been to see Gemma as he'd intended. Hopefully, if nothing broke between now and Christmas, he'd be able to make time to get round there.

It wouldn't be today, though, he realized, when they entered the office. Although Liz Green and Lilley had yet to return to the station – with or without a few nosey neighbours in tow – there was plenty to keep them busy. On his desk, a pile of reports awaited attention, among them statements from householders near the woods, from motorists who had been in the vicinity and had come forward, as well as those routinely stopped and questioned.

Rafferty read through them swiftly and pounced on the several that reported seeing an old Zephyr on the road to the west of the wood. The time was about right, too, he realized excitedly. As he read them, he passed them to Llewellyn, waited impatiently for the Welshman to finish, and then said, 'First we had a Zephyr parked outside Smith's flat; now we've got a sighting of the same make of car by Dedman Wood at the appropriate time and not just by one witness, but by several. What would you say to us pulling Ms Fay and her friends in for further questioning?'

'I'd say it would be unwise, unless you're anxious for some bad publicity. It seems likely, given that Ms Fay and her friends seem able regularly to put forward their views and opinions in the media, that if we do, they must have several tame newspaper editors more than willing to supply damning front-page headlines. We've no more than circumstantial evidence to link them with Smith, no more than our own suspicions to say they had anything to do with his murder. A clever lawyer would tear such evidence apart in five seconds.'

Automatically straightening the reports that Rafferty had disordered, Llewellyn went on. 'You said yourself that what we need is proof. Don't you think it would be better to wait and see if WPC Green and Lilley come back with some? After all, we don't yet know if these three women were even acquainted with any of Smith's victims, so if they saw one of them dragging a suspicious-looking shape down the fire stairs, why should they interfere?'

It was a point Rafferty hadn't previously considered. 'You're right. We *don't* know if they even met or counselled Smith's victims. Maybe it's time we found out.'

He began hunting through his desk; bits of paper fluttered to the floor as he shifted and shunted the contents. 'What did I do with Mrs Nye's phone number?'

Llewellyn, to save Rafferty's desk from any more wanton trashing, produced his own notebook. 'I've got it here.'

Rafferty read the number and dialled. His call was answered almost immediately. He knew it was a policy of Mrs Nye's; as she warned her staff and volunteers, it might be a distraught young girl on the other end and an endlessly ringing telephone could be enough to put her off trying again. Once put through to Mrs Nye, Rafferty explained what he wanted.

'I'll have to go through my records for the other two, Inspector,' Mrs Nye told him, 'but I know Ellen Kemp did similar work in Burleigh, some years ago. I'm not sure exactly when, though.'

'Perhaps you could let me have the details of your opposite number in Burleigh and I'll check it out myself.'

Mrs Nye supplied the details with her usual efficiency and also checked on Sinead Fay and Zonie Anderson, ringing back with the information that neither had worked as a support volunteer ten years earlier. Zonie Anderson, could, anyway, have been no more than fifteen at the time – hardly old enough to counsel rape victims.

After thanking her and ringing off, Rafferty told Llewellyn what he'd learned. 'It would be a turn-up if Ellen Kemp *did* counsel one of Smith's victims. It would give us our link, and the *third* circumstantial connection.'

After some minutes' difficulty, he managed to decipher his scribbled notes and dialled the number for the Rape Support Group in Burleigh. But his hopes were dashed as quickly as they'd been raised. There was no link between any of the breakaway RSG women and Smith's victims. Ellen Kemp hadn't become a volunteer until nearly two years after the Smith case and had never counselled any of his victims. Rafferty scowled and as soon as Llewellyn set off to see Mrs Penny he bent his head back to the reports, hoping to find evidence that would satisfy even the Welshman's requirements.

Llewellyn was gone for more than an hour. When he returned, Rafferty pushed aside the paperwork with a frustrated sigh and asked, 'How did you get on?'

'Smith knew several weeks beforehand that Mrs Penny would be going out that night.'

'Time enough for him to confide the information to his loving family, then,' Rafferty concluded. 'Go on.'

'Apart from the local shopkeepers, Mrs Penny was certain she told no one else. She told me there *was* no one else for her to tell.'

'Mmm. Gives us a lead to Jes Bullock, if nothing else. What about the neighbours? Did any of them notice a strange car on Mrs Penny's hardstanding?'

'Unfortunately, that alleyway leads not only to the back gardens of the houses but also to a row of rented Council garages. One of the men who rents a garage there works as a mechanic in his spare time and uses it for his workshop, so there are often strange cars parked there; I gather he tends to park the overflow where he can fit them, though, for what it's worth, none of Mrs Penny's neighbours could remember seeing a strange car parked on her hardstanding that night. If there was one it wasn't there long.'

Rafferty was just digesting this when Liz Green and Lilley reported back. He was gratified to learn that one, at least, of his ideas had borne fruit.

Miss Primrose Partington *hadn't* been the only one of Smith's neighbours to notice the strange car parked on the street. With the single exception of the baker's, it was a residential road, the nearest parade of shops being half a mile away. So apart from the residents and their visitors, few strangers would have reason to park there, certainly not for longer than the time it would take to make their purchases at the baker's.

Lilley and Liz Green found several of Smith's neighbours who had noticed the strange car, and one, a man who worked as a commercial traveller, had even taken down the number as a prelude to ringing the police, but his wife had persuaded him against it. Only trouble was, he was back on the road and could be anywhere as he followed no particular schedule. But his wife said he rang in periodically while he was away.

Lilley said she expected a phone call from him that evening and had promised she would ask him about the car. Rafferty, not one to rely on such promises, told Lilley to go back early that evening and wait for the husband to call, adding that if the man didn't have the number on him he could at least tell them what he had done with it. He prayed it hadn't been lost or thrown away in the meantime.

More reports came in and Rafferty dismissed Lilley. The forensic teams that Rafferty had sent to Smith's flat and Dedman Wood had finished their on-site investigations. They had turned up little enough at the Wood; the ground had been too hard for tyre tracks. And so far, what they had been able to find out about the rope used in the second hanging and the few fibres left behind from the first was not helpful. Whoever had strung Smith up had used rope commonly available from marine stores supplying the yachties up and down the Essex coast and beyond. It sold in huge quantities in all coastal areas and it was doubtful if further investigations would turn up anything more.

Rafferty and Llewellyn had debated on the difficulty of suspending a body and whether one could do it alone or would need assistance. Forensic had confirmed that although the task would be made no easier by being done at night it was not impossible, particularly as Smith had been slight, weighing only eight and a half stone.

Of course, determination would provide extra strength if any were needed, Rafferty knew. And whoever had killed Smith and carted his body to Dedman Wood for his ritualistic hanging had been very determined. Pity they'd chosen the dead of winter for the deed. Pity too that the body had vanished after its first suspension. It meant they couldn't be sure that the rope used the second time had been the original. It could have been removed, like the wrist bindings and hood, and another substituted. Consequently they couldn't afford to let the type of knots used encourage them to jump to conclusions about the killer's identity; the professional-looking noose could easily be a deliberate red herring intended to lead them astray.

Of course, as Rafferty now remarked, whoever had strung him up the second time was unlikely to know that the police had already learned of the first hanging. They must have hoped to conceal the ritualistic aspect of his killing, maybe even the cause of death. If so, as Sam Dally had commented, it had been a forlorn hope. Were they blind, stupid or just panic-stricken?

Perplexed, he shook his head. But if the body-snatchers had merely hoped to sow doubt and uncertainty they had succeeded very well with him at least.

Obfuscation, Llewellyn had called it. Rafferty had merely nodded his head when Llewellyn had made this pronouncement and had taken the first opportunity to surreptitiously check up in the office dictionary. *To obfuscate*, he had read: *to obscure or darken; to perplex or bewilder*. That sounded about right, he agreed, though he wished Llewellyn would give up using long words when a short one would do. It was an irritating habit.

While Llewellyn had been with Mrs Penny, Rafferty had checked on local Zephyrs. There were only twelve within a twenty-mile radius and a check had revealed that nothing was on file against their owners. Of course, as Rafferty commented, that didn't mean another family member hadn't taken the keys and 'borrowed' it. That was the trouble, he mused. Every time you found a worthwhile area to investigate, it meant checking out all a person's friends and relations, which meant a reduced team to check out everything else. It was important that they pin down the Zephyr parked outside Smith's flat. If they could at least get as far as a *probable* on Sinead Fay's car, they'd have a little more to go on.

Trouble was, of course, it still wouldn't be *proof* and he decided to leave further checks on the Zephyr owners till Lilley had been able to speak to Smith's other neighbour.

The work of the forensic team had proved more fruitful at Smith's flat. Although the only fingerprints found in the room were those of Smith and his landlady, forensic had confirmed that the small patches of blood on the armchair and the fire escape stairs were Smith's. They had also confirmed that the threads found on the stairs had definitely belonged to the tracksuit in which Smith had been found.

110

Rafferty had discussed the matter with forensic and had been told that the knife must have been at least 10 inches long, as it had gone through the thin padding of the cheap armchair in which Smith had been sitting, before penetrating the flesh and piercing the heart.

A fluke? Rafferty wondered. Or a knowing thrust? They were aware of no one with any reason to kill Smith who had sufficient medical knowledge to pierce the correct spot knowingly; certainly not from behind and through a padded chair. Rafferty stared at the report with anxious eyes as the face of Stubbs danced before them. A policeman would have more opportunity than most to learn.

Archie – Archibald Stubbs; unhappily, Rafferty rolled the name around on his tongue. Although he was much older, grey, taciturn and given to cryptic observations, Rafferty felt that beneath the superficial differences, he and Stubbs weren't so dissimilar. They even had unfortunate names in common, though at least Ma hadn't saddled him with Aloysius as a first name.

Stubbs had been a good copper, a straight copper, everyone Rafferty had spoken to about him had agreed on that, though he had the unfortunate knack of rubbing his superiors up the wrong way; another similarity. Rafferty found himself smiling ruefully.

Before his premature retirement from the force, Archie Stubbs had been generally regarded as an honest, plain-speaking man, the sort who called a spade a bloody shovel. Again like me, was Rafferty's immediate response. But when it came to devious behaviour, he'd been no match for the politicos upstairs. No match at all.

Thompson, too, had paid the price for embarrassing the brass. Like Stubbs, he had decades of genuine service and successes under his belt, had passed his inspector's exams, and should have received promotion. Instead, because of one failed case – in which the decision to prosecute hadn't even rested with the police – he had been shunted sideways, back into uniform and his career had advanced no further.

Who could blame either of them, Rafferty thought, if their resentment had simmered over the years; Stubbs, in his arid, lonely bungalow, and Thompson, denied the rank he must feel he deserved as less experienced men were promoted over him. Smith had been the catalyst of their misfortunes. But, he wondered again, would they act *ten years* later?

Yes, he realized, they just might. If, as he and Llewellyn had discussed, another more recent occurrence could be traced back to Smith. Some tragedy or trauma that could be connected with him. Aware he had been putting off any further investigation into the police suspects, scared of what he might find, he knew he couldn't delay checking them out much longer.

But for the moment, he was able to thrust the thought aside as more reports came in.

The Australian police had got back to them. According to Hanks, the Walker family had checked out and were in the clear. None of them had made a surreptitious trip back to the old country. They had all been seen about their business in the normal way around the time Smith had died. So that was one lot of suspects out of the running. Which – apart from the police suspects – left them with the Masseys, the Figgs and the Dennington families, plus Sinead Fay and her friends.

The Dennington boys' regiment had cleared them. They had both been on duty during the relevant time, a fact verified by senior officers. And, with the father dead, that left only the victim herself and her mother.

Hanks also reported on his other assignment and Rafferty's forehead began to resemble a ploughed field as he learned that Ellen Kemp was either entirely innocent or had the luck of the devil. It turned out she had a double garage, a sizeable, old-fashioned affair that was built to house the larger cars of an earlier era – the Bentleys, Daimlers and Rollses – and had more than enough space to accommodate two cars as well as providing ample space to work on them.

Sinead Fay's neighbours had proved no help either. Hanks had checked and the neighbours on the other side of the RSG woman had been out on the evening of Maurice Smith's murder. They had left home by cab around seven that morning and hadn't returned till the early hours.

The elderly couple on the other side were no more helpful, even though Hanks said they seemed desperately eager to be so. His visit was, Hanks told Rafferty, obviously the most exciting thing that had happened to them in years. Rafferty sighed. And I thought *I* had a dull life. As he had guessed, the television had been on all evening and had drowned any sound from next door. What Ellen Kemp had told them about her daughter had also checked out.

Rafferty perked up when Lilley returned to the station and reported that he had spoken to Smith's other neighbour, but he deflated again when he learned that the wretched man was unable to remember what he'd done with the piece of paper on which he had scribbled the registration number. Worse, his wife now thought that she'd thrown it away after persuading her husband not to ring the police and report it.

'Isn't it just great?' he complained to Llewellyn after dismissing Lilley with the instruction to keep pushing the couple to find the elusive paper. 'Why did they have to be so damn reasonable that night of all nights? Any other time and half the street would have been behind the net curtains with their biros and scraps of paper, noting down strange men, strange cars and windscreens lacking the Road Fund Licence.'

Rafferty had hoped for a definite confirmation that the Zephyr had been Sinead Fay's. Now he was still in limbo-land and didn't know whether to accept that the piece of paper would never turn up and start checking out the other Zephyr-owners, their friends and relations, in order to eliminate them or whether he should delay such checks in the now faint hope that the piece of paper would still materialize. In the end, he decided to wait and see.

By the next morning they had received no more helpful news on the case and Rafferty knew he could no longer delay checking out Stubbs and Thompson. He turned to Llewellyn and opened his mouth to issue instructions, but his sergeant was far away in a world of his own, gazing out of the window with an anxious frown.

Rafferty could guess why. Llewellyn's mother had arrived already – Ma had never been one to put off till tomorrow what could be done yesterday. Rafferty guessed the tendency came from having had six kids to get up and out every morning. So, the extension of the invitation, the railroading of any excuses and arrival of guest had all occurred in little more than twenty-four hours.

Rafferty had given Llewellyn a few hours off to drive to London and collect his mother from the train. He was about to ask how she was settling in, and if she and Maureen had taken to one another, when Llewellyn's pensive expression caused him to think better of it. He wasn't sure he wanted to know the answer. Besides, he excused his moral cowardice, I've got enough on my plate at the moment without going out of my way to find other things to plague me.

He interrupted Llewellyn's doleful wool-gathering to say, 'I'm going to have to drive up to London tomorrow to check out Frank Massey and his ex-wife and daughter. They'll all have learned of Smith's death by now, so I imagine they'll be expecting to hear from us. Not,' he added quietly, 'that I imagine that will make it any easier. I want you to go and see the Dennington and Figg families. Ring first and warn them you're coming. They all still live in Burleigh. Take Liz Green with you. Lilley can keep pressing Smith's neighbour to find that registration number.' He paused, then added, 'Could you look into

Stubbs' and Thompson's movements as well? If you have time, that is.'

'Of course.'

Thankfully, Llewellyn came out of his reverie on being asked to carry out the delicate task of questioning the police officers. Of course, he knew that Rafferty felt more than a sneaking sympathy for Stubbs and Thompson.

They were busy the rest of that day keeping on top of the reports. It was late when Rafferty finally stretched, yawned and checked his watch. It had been another long day with little to show for it; the sort of day Rafferty found most tiring – nothing happening to give him an adrenalin rush, but masses of paperwork to be read and absorbed. Still, he decided, it wasn't too late for them to see the Bullocks again that evening and, reluctantly, he heaved himself from his comfortable chair. The office was warm and it was freezing outside, the window sporting icicles.

'It'll be interesting to find out what Bullock claims he was doing on Thursday evening that was important enough to make him late for his pint,' he remarked to Llewellyn on the way out. 'Spot of light dusting, perhaps. Though from the look of their flat, I doubt it.'

Although it was nine o'clock on an icy winter's night, young children were still out on the Bullocks' estate.

As Rafferty and Llewellyn got out of the car, one of the older boys yelled at them. 'Hey, copper. You wanted to know when Roger the Rapist was about last week.'

Rafferty turned. The youth was about fifteen, but he already had cold, watchful eyes and hardened features. 'That's right,' he said. 'Why? Can you help?'

The boy nodded. His name was Darren, he told them. 'He was 'ere last Thursday. I saw him leavin' from up on the balcony.'

Rafferty frowned. 'Thursday? You're sure about that? Sure it wasn't the Wednesday?'

'Nah.' Darren shook his head. '*EastEnders* had just

finished on the telly and I went to knock for me mate. While I was waiting for him to open the door I saw Roger the Rapist's car pullin' out of the car park.'

Rafferty was surprised that a lad like Darren should help the law. From the look in his eyes, so was Darren. 'You live here?'

'Yeah. Number fifty-eight.'

Rafferty felt a sudden doubt. How well could Darren have known Smith? After all, not only had Smith visited his family infrequently, he was far from outgoing and unlikely to pause to swap gossip with the local toughs. 'You're sure it was Maurice Smith?'

''Course I'm sure. I know everything that goes on in these flats. It's my place. Besides, 'ow could I mistake that miserable ferret face? It's been splashed over the newspapers enough lately.'

'I'm not saying I don't believe you, Darren. But you must realize that what you've told us is important. Can anyone corroborate what you say?'

'Do what?'

'Do you know if anyone else saw him at the same time?'

Darren's face cleared. 'Yeah. My mate's mum. Sharon Gates at number twenty-three. She'd be able to tell you. She opened the door to me just as he reversed his car out of the parkin' bay like a bleedin' maniac. She yelled at him over the balcony that he'd kill somebody, drivin' like that.'

His eyes narrowed. ''Course, she didn't actually see *him*, any more than I did. The angle was wrong. But we both recognized his car.' Darren's lip curled as he added, 'Boasted to my kid brother once that he was an Advanced Driver – passed the test, like. Lyin' bastard. The way he reversed out Thursday night, I shouldn't fink he's even got a licence. Thought old Bullockbrains, his dad, was a rotten driver, but he's worse.'

Darren was wrong, Rafferty knew. Maurice Smith *had*

116

passed the Advanced Driving Test. The searches through his flat had confirmed as much. It was Smith's one solid achievement in life. 'Might have been drunk,' Rafferty suggested.

'Nah. Not him. Never drank as far as I know. Kevin, his brother, told me once he hardly touches a drop.' This was said with the scorn of the experienced drinker. Darren's lips drew back over sharp teeth. 'Know why too, now, don't we? Must 'ave been scared he'd give away his real identity and let slip what he does to little girls. I mean, it's not somefing old Bullock would want him to boast about, is it? Not like 'avin' a bank robber in the family. Must be a bugger 'aving to live with such a thing, especially if people find out.'

Darren's sharp features suddenly became even more razor-edged. 'Here – maybe he *was* worried it was goin' to come out?'

'Why do you say that?' Rafferty asked.

'Jes Bullock was offering money in the pub to 'ave him duffed up late Thursday afternoon; a persuader to get him to move, he said. Why should he do that after all this time unless he had reason to think it was going to get out? Obviously, 'e was 'oping to scare him away from the area. Or else,' Darren added darkly, 'he changed his mind and decided to get rid permanent. I mean, Roger the Rapist *is* dead, isn't he? You can't get more permanent than that.'

Darren having declined to tell them if anyone in the pub had taken up Jes Bullock's offer, Rafferty decided not to press the matter and let Darren go off with one of his mates, leaving the two policemen to check his story with Sharon Gates, his friend's mother. She confirmed that Maurice Smith had been at the flats on Thursday evening.

'I told you Jes Bullock had a guilty secret,' Rafferty remarked smugly as they tramped back down the stairs. 'Do you think it was him driving the car that night and not Maurice Smith at all? He might not have been good at anything else, but you've got to be a first-rate driver to pass the Advanced Test. His stepfather's a big bloke. He could easily have overpowered Smith and taken him somewhere private so his mates could convince him it would be healthier for him if he left town. Or maybe Darren's right, and he decided to end the problem of his stepson once and for all. It's possible, especially if Maurice had told him about the "outing" threat.'

Llewellyn didn't agree. 'Why bring him back to Smith's flat, stab him, then take him all the way to Dedman Wood and string him up from the Hanging Tree? If there was one way to guarantee that Smith's picture appeared on the front page of every newspaper, that was it. Surely that would be the last thing Jes Bullock would want? Even if he did decide to rid himself permanently of his stepson, he would be certain to remove all traces of Smith's identity and dump the body far from home. That way the body would be just another John Doe, and Jes Bullock could tell anyone who asked that his stepson had moved away.'

Rafferty nodded. 'Maybe.' As Llewellyn made in the direction of the other staircase that would lead them to the Bullocks' landing, Rafferty stopped him. 'After what we've just learned, I think we should wait till Sam Dally's got a few more answers for us on those bruises before we tackle Bullock again. He surely can't be much longer, unless his Christmas rush has started, after all. Anyway, I want to check what Darren told us with the pub landlord. Let's get along there and see what we can find out.'

With a certain reluctance, Tim Hadley, the landlord of the Pig and Whistle confirmed Darren's story about Jes Bullock offering to pay someone to beat up his stepson. However, he added, as Bullock had the reputation of being a penniless scrounger, no one had taken him up on it as far as he knew.

'When my regulars just jeered at him and asked to see

the colour of his money, he shouted that he'd do the job himself, then stormed out of the bar. He was the worse for drink, of course.'

That had been around four on Thursday afternoon, they learned. Five and a half hours later, Mrs ffinch-Robinson had found Smith's body hanging in Dedman Wood.

'Remind me to bell Sam Dally in the morning before I go to London,' Rafferty remarked as they left the bar. 'I want to get in early before he gets busy and remind him I'm still waiting to hear about those bruises. If he has the results, and they confirm what I suspect, we might be able to lever a little more out of Bullock. Might even get a confession out of him.'

Llewellyn didn't seem to think it likely. 'Drunk or sober, I can't believe Bullock would be so stupid as to kill Smith after making such an announcement. If Smith had died accidentally from a blow, it would be different, but he didn't. He died from a single knife wound to the heart. Rather unlikely that could have happened accidentally. Even more unlikely that Bullock wouldn't have tried to cover his tracks.'

Rafferty had to admit that Llewellyn had a point. He scowled and commented tartly, 'It's just one damn obfuscation after another, isn't it?'

Llewellyn merely nodded, shot a quick glance at Rafferty, cleared his throat and murmured, 'Er, sir – Joseph—'

Oh God, thought Rafferty. Here it comes. Although he'd long ago asked Llewellyn to stop being so formal and call him by his first name, he rarely did. When *Joseph* came accompanied by throat-clearing it was a sure sign he was about to be told something he would rather not hear. For instance, that Mother Llewellyn's visit was already promising to be an unmitigated disaster. And that it was *his* fault. He took a deep breath and forced himself to ask, 'So what's on your mind?'

119

'It's just—' Llewellyn paused, looked doubtfully at him for a moment and then began immediately to backtrack. 'It's nothing. Really. Never mind.'

Rafferty, never being a believer in meeting problems halfway, didn't push it.

Chapter Ten

Rafferty was glad of the excuse to get away to London. It would give him a brief respite from the endless reports as well as from the increasingly hang-dog look that Llewellyn had worn since his mother's arrival.

Rafferty was convinced that his fears about the visit were coming true. Especially as, when in the office, Llewellyn had taken to spending a large part of his time uncharacteristically staring into space, and his face, long and lugubrious at the best of times, seemed now to be permanently creased by frowns.

Rafferty had already tried several times to find out the worst from his ma and sisters, but none of them returned his calls. Now, becoming paranoid, he decided they were making him sweat it out as punishment for inflicting Llewellyn's Welsh dragon mother on them. If it suited her, his ma was more than capable of forgetting that she was the one who had insisted Llewellyn's mother visit at Christmas.

As he stared at Llewellyn's long, lean profile, he asked himself why he had pushed him into this visit. It was obvious now that he hadn't been that keen. Grimly, he resolved never, ever again to get involved in someone else's love life. It was a fool's errand. God knew, it wasn't as if he had made a huge success of his own. It was hardly surprising that as Christmas Day and the big family dinner approached he felt more and more apprehensive.

Forcing his mind back to business, he asked Llewellyn,

'Have you managed to get anything on who might have been passing official information about Smith?'

Llewellyn dragged himself from his reverie and stared blankly at him. 'I'm sorry. What did you say?'

Rafferty repeated his question.

As though annoyed at his own inefficiency, Llewellyn's frown deepened. 'I meant to tell you. I haven't been able to find out anything on the police angle. Apart from us, nobody has accessed the computer for information on Smith, but an official at the Department of Social Security got back to me first thing this morning before you got in. He told me one of their young clerks had admitted giving out Smith's address.'

'Did this clerk remember anything about the person they spoke to?'

'Only that the voice sounded sufficiently authoritative to persuade her to part with the information and that it was a female voice.'

Rafferty nodded and Llewellyn once more lapsed into silence. Wary of Llewellyn's silences and what they might bring forth, Rafferty hastily got on the phone to Dally. Sam told him he still hadn't finished his tests on Smith's bruises, but he expected to have done so later that day.

Rafferty rang off. Pulling on his overcoat, nervous about the simmering undercurrents, he gave his instructions with unusual hesitancy. 'About Stubbs and Thompson,' he began. 'I know I don't have to warn you to be discreet, but—'

'Don't worry.' Llewellyn gave him a bleak smile. 'I shall be as discreet as if it were *you* I were investigating.'

Rafferty wasn't sure he liked the comparison, but at least he knew he could rely on Llewellyn; he was the most discreet copper he knew. 'I'll probably be away for most of the day. I'm taking Mary Carmody with me. These interviews with the families are going to be difficult enough without us flat-footed males making it worse.'

Usually, Llewellyn would have been sure to point out

that his comment was unfair; certainly as far as *he* was concerned. Convinced now that his sergeant had other things on his mind and worried that he might overcome his reluctance to confide with more success than he had managed the previous night, Rafferty made his escape to London.

Left alone, Llewellyn stared broodingly into space for another five minutes before, giving himself a mental shake, he picked up the phone and rang through to Liz Green. After telling her he'd be back to pick her up later for the interviews with the Dennington and Figg families, he made for the car park. He was glad of another busy day. It would keep his mind occupied.

Putting aside his unprofitable thoughts on personal matters, which he had, anyway, already gone through over and over again without forming any constructive conclusion as to what he should do, Llewellyn forced himself to concentrate on the task Rafferty had left with him. At least there he felt he had a reasonable chance of success.

He decided to begin the delicate task of investigating the two police suspects by first looking into Stubbs' movements. Of the two men, he felt the older man had been the most affected by the failure of the case. It was therefore logical to assume he would be the most likely of the two to take action. Llewellyn felt it wouldn't have been difficult for him to get hold of a police uniform; he might have managed to hold on to his old one from the time before he had joined the CID.

Llewellyn, having taken Rafferty's hints to heart, resolved to speak to Stubbs himself only if he could find out what he needed to know no other way. Stubbs, like Thompson, had devoted years of his life to the force and deserved a certain consideration – especially if he turned out to be innocent. He felt Rafferty had been right about that. Llewellyn was a little surprised to find himself agreeing with his inspector. It was a novel experience.

Settling on Stubbs' cheery neighbour as the obvious source of information, he parked the car round the corner from their street. Fortunately, he had only to wait half an hour before he saw Stubbs drive off towards town.

Llewellyn waited for a minute, drove round the corner and parked in front of Stubbs' bungalow. He got out of the car and, for the benefit of Stubbs' gnomelike neighbour who was standing at his front door chatting to the postman, he made a pantomime of disappointment at finding Stubbs' drive empty.

Things were falling into place nicely, Llewellyn reflected, with a tiny, self-mocking smile. If Stubbs' neighbour hadn't been standing at his own door, he would have had to knock, which would have robbed the visit of the casual air with which he had cloaked it.

The neighbour shouted hello and walked up the path as the postman resumed his deliveries. 'Aren't you one of those chaps who visited Mr Stubbs the other day?'

'That's right.' Llewellyn walked over to the gate.

'Thought I recognized you. I'm afraid you've missed him. What a pity. He gets so few visitors.' The gnome seemed a kindly man and was genuinely upset that Stubbs should have missed this one. But then he cheered up. 'He's only gone to get a bit of shopping. I don't suppose he'll be more than half an hour.'

Llewellyn made a play of consulting his watch. 'I can't wait, unfortunately, and I won't be able to return till Thursday evening. I suppose he'll be in then?'

'Thursday?' The gnome frowned. 'He's not often in on Thursday evenings. Usually he goes to visit a friend of his – a chap called Thompson. Perhaps you know him?'

'No, I'm afraid not.' Llewellyn hadn't expected it to be so easy. Now he knew where Stubbs was generally to be found on Thursday evenings, the next step was to try to find out if he and Thompson had actually been there last Thursday. Llewellyn gave the helpful gnome one of his rare smiles. 'Thank you. You've saved me another wasted journey.'

'Maybe I can give him a message for you?'

Llewellyn paused as if considering. 'No. I don't think so. It's nothing that can't wait. But thanks for the offer. I'll contact him myself another time.'

Llewellyn said goodbye and as he walked back down the path he could almost hear Rafferty's cryptic voice telling him he was a jammy devil. 'Simply a matter of finesse and delicacy, sir,' Llewellyn murmured under his breath as he got in the car. 'You should try it some time.' His shoulders slumped as he remembered that finesse and delicacy weren't working quite so well in other areas of his life.

He checked in his notebook for Thompson's exact address and set off, working out how best to repeat his success thus far. However, this repetition proved elusive as he soon discovered that Thompson *had* no neighbours. He got out of the car and walked round the perimeter of the cottage. There was not a sign of another house for half a mile in any direction. The loneliness of the location brought a return of the melancholy thoughts.

Too late, he realized he should never have let Rafferty talk him into agreeing to his mother coming for a visit while his relationship with Maureen was still so new. Of course Joseph Rafferty's enthusiasm for his own ideas had a way of carrying all before him. Besides, it had been a generous offer and it would have been churlish to turn him down.

Llewellyn felt sure of nothing but his own uncertainty. He'd never been in this situation before – a woman on either side pushing him – and he wished he could find the courage to act forcefully.

Briefly, he wondered how Rafferty would deal with a similar situation and his unhappy expression lightened momentarily as he realized that Rafferty would undoubtedly start shouting, slam out and go to the pub; a simple outlook, perhaps, but at least he would have done *something*, however pointless. Llewellyn felt incapable of doing anything at all. He longed for the boldness which he had always lacked in relationships, wished he could convince himself to act decisively, but too much thinking had always been his trouble.

He had already tried to ask Rafferty's advice once and had then thought better of it, but now he wondered whether he ought to try again? After all, the inspector had a reputation at the station as something of a ladies' man and if the canteen talk was true, he certainly had plenty of experience with women. There again, was it the *right* sort of experience?

Llewellyn's lips twisted at the thought that if he was truly considering asking Joseph Rafferty's advice about his love life he must be desperate; the inspector had a tendency to give advice first and think about its wisdom afterwards, if at all. Had he reached the point where he was desperate enough not just to ask for his advice but to take it?

Conscious that a decision was as far away as ever, he forced his thoughts back to work matters.

Reluctant to return to the station to report failure, he sat in the car for several more minutes, turning over what they already knew about Stubbs and Thompson.

Out of all his old colleagues, Stubbs had kept in contact with only Thompson, his right-hand man during the long-drawn-out rape investigation. Thompson had been transferred from Burleigh police station to Great Mannleigh after the collapse of the Smith trial and had remained there ever since.

Llewellyn wondered about the friendship between the two men. On the surface it was as unlikely a one as the growing bond between himself and Rafferty. Stubbs was very much the loner in every other respect but this one, self-contained and apparently self-sufficient, and Thompson, also a widower though a very recent one, was reported to be a much more outgoing character and was a regular at the police club in Great Mannleigh. The only tie likely to bring them together in such a friendship was their mutual bitterness over the Smith case.

Rafferty, with an ease Llewellyn couldn't help but envy, had tapped into the police grapevine with as little trouble as a bird tapping through the foil on a milk bottle. With a rude joke and the rough exchange of banter that Llewellyn knew he would never manage, Rafferty had learned that, as they had suspected, Thompson's desired advancement had been continually blocked. The taint of the Smith case and the embarrassment it had caused his superiors had effectively removed the career ladder from beneath Thompson's feet.

Such things happened, Llewellyn knew. It served no purpose to rage about their unfairness as Inspector Rafferty was inclined to do. They were both aware that a word here, a whisper there, were sufficient to bring a man's career to a standstill or to an abrupt end, like that of Stubbs.

Unconsciously, Llewellyn echoed Rafferty's unspoken question: Why, if they *had* killed Smith, should they act now? There was no reason, or none that he had been able to discover.

Thompson's wife had died in a road accident a few months ago certainly, but Smith hadn't been involved, they'd checked. Even the death of Stubbs' wife, which could be attributed indirectly to Smith, had happened years ago. So why act now?

Aware he was going round and round in circles, chasing his own tail in a way that Rafferty so often did, Llewellyn forced his mind to pause and consider. He remembered he had seen a pub a mile back along the road, presumably Thompson's local; he decided it might be worth paying a visit.

From the outside, the pub looked for all the world as if it was designed to repel strangers. Small and scruffy, it appeared strictly a neighbourhood pub, which indicated the locals would be familiar with one another's routines.

After parking the car, he opened the main door and

was pleased to find that, inside, the pub wore a far more welcoming air. It was a real old-fashioned place and had a smell all its own, made up of some aromatic tobacco in the pipe of one of the old men playing dominoes in the corner, hearty vegetable soup simmering its way to lunchtime from the kitchen behind the bar and the sharp tang of woodsmoke curling from the fire. Tense earlier, Llewellyn found himself relaxing into the ambience of the place.

The landlord was as welcoming as his pub, and put his paper away and gave Llewellyn a warm smile and a 'What can I get you?' as he perched on the well-polished oak bar stool. Llewellyn was beginning to understand something of Rafferty's inclination to head for the nearest pub when life was proving difficult.

Llewellyn hesitated. Although teetotal and relatively unacquainted with pub rituals, he had learned enough during his time with Rafferty to be certain that the purchase of his usual orange juice or tonic water would be insufficient to encourage the landlord to gossip. As he ordered a pint of Elgoods, he sent up a silent prayer that Inspector Rafferty didn't somehow get to hear of it. For a man of his age and rank, Rafferty could be extraordinarily childish and would be sure to tease him unmercifully if he learned of his broken non-drinking vow.

'Not seen you in here before, sir,' the landlord commented. 'Just passing through?'

'That's right.' Llewellyn took a sip of his beer, surprised to discover that *bitter* was a misnomer. It was actually rather sweet. 'Attractive countryside round here. It must be delightful in the spring.'

''Tis that.' One of the old men in the corner spoke up. 'Very popular with young couples is this area.'

'It certainly appeals to me. Actually,' catching Rafferty's habit, he crossed his fingers against fate's revenge, even though the bulk of what he said was true. 'I'm hoping to marry soon and I was by this way last Thursday evening and noticed a cottage I thought might be ideal for my girlfriend and me. There was no *for sale* sign, so I didn't knock and make enquiries – not that there were any lights visible. That's why I came back today, but there's still no one in. Perhaps you know it? It's about a mile up that way.' Llewellyn gestured with his thumb back the way he had come. 'It's set back from the road quite a way.'

'That'll be Harry Thompson's place,' the landlord told him. 'Doubt he'll sell, though. He'll not be there now. You should have knocked last time you passed it. He's generally at home on a Thursday night.' He turned to the old man who had spoken earlier. 'Doesn't he have that retired copper friend of his over on Thursday nights, Sid?'

'Ar. That's right. Three Thursdays out of the four, anyway. He's usually on duty one Thursday in the month.' Sid ambled over to the bar, stroking his unshaven chin. 'Though, now I come to think of it, the pair of them passed my place around eight last Thursday evening. Still weren't back when I walked by for me nightly pint at half-nine.' Sid sniggered. 'Maybe Harry fixed his mate up with a blind date.'

'Blind?' his friend in the corner echoed and commented, 'She'd need to be, and all. That mate of Harry's has a face on him that'd stop a clock. Miserable-looking bugger.' The other men laughed.

'Maybe you should try coming back another time if you're that taken with the place,' the landlord suggested. 'Though, as I said, I doubt Harry will sell. He lost his wife a few months back so I shouldn't think he'd want the upheaval of moving just yet.'

Llewellyn nodded, pleased he had learned so much with so little time and effort. It meant he now had ample time to return to the station, pick up WPC Green and drive to Burleigh. Altogether it was turning out to be a very successful day and he spared a thought for Rafferty. Interviewing Massey, his ex-wife and daughter would be difficult, requiring a tact and delicacy that Rafferty rarely displayed. Llewellyn hoped he didn't make a hash of it. Apart from any other consideration, having the inspector stomping about the office in a foul temper was the last thing he needed right now.

'Another in there, Sid?' the landlord asked.

The old man was still at the bar clutching his empty pint pot, and Llewellyn, although unused to pub traditions, was quick to guess what was expected of him. 'Allow me,' he said and put a five-pound note on the counter.

'Ta very much.' Sid smiled, exposing a mouth entirely innocent of teeth. 'Don't mind if I do.' He raised his replenished glass and saluted Llewellyn. 'You'll find the natives friendly hereabouts, young man, if you do move this way.'

'Aye.' The landlord laughed. 'Any man not afraid to put his hand in his pocket can be sure of a welcome from Sid at least.'

Reassured that there were still some areas of his life under his control, Llewellyn finished his drink, made his farewells to his new friends and returned to the station.

Liz Green was waiting for him and they wasted no time in heading for Burleigh and their interviews with the Dennington and Figg families. If only everything in life went as smoothly, was Llewellyn's thought as he drove north.

Chapter Eleven

Rafferty's morning, as Llewellyn had predicted, wasn't going quite so smoothly. Feeling Frank Massey would be more communicative if he questioned him alone, he had left Mary Carmody in the car. But, as it turned out, Massey seemed to have no inclination for talking whether it be to one person or twenty-one.

After Rafferty had explained the reason for his visit, a haunted look came into Massey's eyes. His body visibly trembled and Rafferty was afraid he'd collapse. But Massey managed to get himself together. He let go of the doorpost and, after staring at Rafferty with a mixture of fear and aggression, he turned abruptly on his heel and left Rafferty to follow or not, as he pleased.

Massey had not only gone down in the world in terms of money and social standing, Rafferty realized as he followed the man into the room and shut the door. He had also let himself go. Not altogether surprising, he acknowledged, sitting down on a hard wooden chair. From being a respected academic, a university lecturer, he was now unemployed and had exchanged a comfortable semi-detached house for a bedsitter, success for defeat; Rafferty could smell the sour odour of it in the damp walls, the unwashed body and rumpled, none-too-clean clothes. The fumes of strong lager and cigarette smoke added to the fetid atmosphere.

Rafferty knew Frank Massey wasn't yet forty, yet already he looked old. His hair, what remained of it, hung lank and greying over his shirt collar and his neck was thin and stringy with the wrinkles from age that were more commonly seen in a much older man. Even his fingers, long and slender like those of an artist, showed the decline and were stained with nicotine, the nails bitten to the quick.

All this Rafferty took in in a few seconds, conscious of a terrible feeling of pity. He could imagine what a man like Massey would have suffered in prison and his experiences would be unlikely to encourage him still to view the police and the judicial system with any confidence.

Rafferty couldn't blame him. The poor sap had been confident of justice and had instead brought that very justice down on his own head. Between them, the law and Maurice Smith had destroyed him; his marriage, his career, his entire life had been smashed to smithereens. Conscious of this, and aware that his sympathy was already heavily engaged in Massey's favour, he was careful how he proceeded.

'So what do you want?' Massey's voice was rough, scratchy from too many cigarettes, but underlying the harshness and the rough manner undoubtedly learned in prison for self-protection were the well modulated tones of an educated man.

The battered collection of books that Rafferty saw on the cheap shelving confirmed this; there were literally hundreds of them. He squinted and managed to read a few of the names. There was Dostoevsky's *Crime and Punishment* and *The House of the Dead*, Milton's *Paradise Lost*, and George Orwell's *Down and Out In Paris and London*. Rafferty hadn't read any of them, but he found it unsurprising that such titles should look the most thumbed of the lot.

Into Rafferty's mind flashed the thought that his own determination to advance further with his reading had come to a grinding halt because his motives were all wrong. A desire to top Llewellyn's aggravating partiality to literary allusion was proving an insufficient carrot, whereas Massey, as appropriate for a one-time university lecturer on literature, obviously loved books for their own sake. Another unwelcome thought immediately followed; that Llewellyn, who normally spouted superior quotes at him several times a day, had, since his mother's arrival, failed to produce one.

He turned back to Massey and said, 'I'm sorry about this, sir, but I have to ask you where you were last Thursday evening. In view of your, er, past association with Maurice Smith, we have to check. You must realize this.'

Massey's throat produced a strangled laugh. '*Only doing my job.* Is that what you're saying?'

Already finding his task as investigating officer repugnant, Rafferty shifted uncomfortably at Massey's taunt. Before he could attempt a reassuring reply, Massey asked, 'Have you got children?'

Rafferty shook his head, reluctant to admit another area for possible grievance. Aware he was letting Massey take control of the interview, he tried to regain it. 'Mr Massey, if you could just—'

But Massey was off on a different tack. 'Do you know, Mr Stubbs – the inspector in charge of Smith's case – told me I'd gone about getting my revenge all wrong. The attack on Smith, I mean. He told me I should have got myself an alibi organized, *then* beaten the shit out of him.' Broodingly Massey stared at the carpet, as though intent on consigning its faded pattern to memory. Then he gave a shuddering sigh and looked up, meeting Rafferty's eyes with a tortured gaze. 'He came and pleaded for me at my trial. Decent chap.'

As he listened to the strange mixture of prison slang and BBC English, Rafferty found himself agreeing with Stubbs' advice. In Massey's position, if revenge had been his intention, getting a decent alibi organized first was what he'd have done. He could, he knew, have relied on any of his family to lie with the determination of Pinocchio in such a good cause.

But what was the point in telling Massey that Stubbs'

advice had been sound? He was already embittered, why make him feel he had been foolishly naive as well? 'Look, Mr Massey,' he began again. 'All I want to know is where you were last Thursday evening and I'll go.'

Massey raised his head. His eyes looked haunted, but beneath that and the lager dullness Rafferty caught the gleam of intelligence. 'That's all you want, is it?' He shook his head. 'I doubt it. When it comes down to it, you're all looking for the big one that will give you promotion. If you think I'll provide you with it you won't let sympathy get in your way.'

Rafferty, aware that he was getting nowhere, broke in sharply. 'Have you got an alibi for last Thursday evening or not?'

He was immediately sorry as his sharp tone caused Massey's whole body to recommence its uncontrollable trembling and, as Rafferty stared, a tic started up beneath Massey's left eye. His face, already pale, now looked ashen. Rafferty, suspecting his aggressive tone had brought back ugly prison memories, immediately felt a complete heel. He was surprised when Massey managed to pull himself together sufficiently to frame a reply.

'As-as it happens, I have got an alibi.'

'So, where were you?' Rafferty deliberately kept his tone soft. 'Here?'

Massey shook his head, then winced. 'Have you got an aspirin?'

Rafferty, suspecting Massey was using delaying tactics while he sorted out his troubled mind, quickly fished a silver foil packet out of his pocket and handed two tablets over. Massey gulped them down and nodded his thanks. 'You were about to tell me where you were,' he reminded him.

'I-I went to see my daughter.'

'Well, if you were in London and she and your ex-wife can corrob—'

'They weren't in London. Alice and her mother were

134

at the coast for a short break. I went there, only we had a row and I left.'

'Where was this?'

'Place near Clacton, called Jaywick.'

Rafferty's interest stirred. The coast? In December? And barely more than ten miles from Elmhurst? If this was the best Massey could manage in the alibi line, it was little wonder he had been caught last time. Had the man learned nothing? 'What time was this?'

Massey shrugged. 'Must have been about half five when I left them.'

'So where did you go after that?'

'I just drove around for a couple of hours, then parked in a layby out Great Mannleigh way. I-I needed a drink.'

Rafferty stared at him. Was the man a complete fool? Great Mannleigh was ten miles from Elmhurst. A short enough drive for a man still looking for revenge.

He began to wonder just how friendly Massey had become with ex-Inspector Stubbs. Friendly enough for him or Thompson, who was still on the force, to tip him the wink on Smith's whereabouts? But if that were the case, surely this time he'd have the sense to take Stubbs' advice and get himself a decent alibi? Unless, Rafferty cautioned himself, unless Massey was being twice as clever as his police advisor and had figured that the police would expect him to have a good alibi this time – especially after his previous experience, especially if he *was* guilty.

Anyway, why would Stubbs or any other copper leave it till ten years after the case to help Massey get his revenge? The man had been out of prison for eight years. Long enough to trace Smith himself if he'd still been set on it. But, Rafferty reminded himself, Massey was broke. And even if he had managed to trace Smith, he had already nerved himself up to give him one beating; Smith would hardly have opened his door to him.

Massey may have got older, thinner and unkempt, but he hadn't changed so much that Smith would have been unable to recognize him through his spyhole. Massey, thin to the point of emaciation, looked as if he wouldn't have the strength to tear open a milk carton, yet from somewhere had found the strength of mind and muscle to beat Smith to a bloody pulp ten years earlier. You don't forget the face of the man who does that to you. 'Still drive the same car, Mr Massey?'

Massey's lashes, long, dark, girlishly beautiful, began to flutter above the still-frantic tic as he nodded. 'A white Cortina.' He looked at Rafferty, then quickly away before adding, 'Some of your boys picked me up and brought me to the station. That would have been around seven, seven-th-thirty Thursday night. I spent the rest of the night in a cell.' He stumbled to a halt.

Rafferty looked sharply at him. Massey wore an air half-hangdog and half-triumphant. He couldn't decide if Massey was lying or playing with him, deliberately holding back the alibi that would put him in the clear in order to get some sort of revenge.

Outwardly he didn't look capable of such tactics, but then Rafferty glanced again at the mass of well-used highbrow books and realized that the intelligence that read such heavy novels for pleasure was still there.

If Massey was telling the truth, he couldn't have killed Smith. They had the testimony of several witnesses, Smith's landlady among them, to say that Smith had certainly still been alive at seven-thirty that evening.

Rafferty stood up. 'Your story will be checked out, Mr Massey. If you were picked up by the police, it'll be on record.'

He let himself out and breathed the scarcely less malodorous air on the landing with relief. Poor bastard, he thought again. Poor stupid bastard. You should have got yourself that alibi all those years ago. But at least, Rafferty consoled his uneasy conscience, if his story checked out he was in the clear *this* time.

Mrs Massey and her daughter lived in the London house

the family had moved to from Burleigh. After stopping for a bite to eat, Rafferty pulled up in the quiet suburban street. Aware that the next half-hour was likely to be even more trying than the last, he lingered in the car for a few minutes, steeling himself for the interview with a short review of the facts.

Alice, Massey's daughter, was only eighteen now, but she had been through a lot; the rape, the trial and Smith's release, her father's trial and imprisonment, and then the divorce. He was worried about her likely reaction to being questioned about Smith's death. He had left Detective Sergeant Mary Carmody in the car during Massey's interview, but he knew he would need her moral support for this one. He turned to her and asked, 'Ready?'

Mary nodded. Suddenly, Rafferty was even more relieved he had brought her. At thirty-four, she had a motherly air, as well as considerable experience with rape victims. Rafferty had telephoned Mrs Massey the day before, so they were expected. In the circumstances, he felt it was a necessary courtesy. It gave her a chance to get a friend to be with her.

Alice Massey let them in. She was small, slender, and looked much younger than her eighteen years. But, given her dreadful experiences, she seemed remarkably composed, self-contained, if reserved. Her clothes were dowdy, mouse-brown and dingy khaki and came nearly to her ankles at one end and just under her chin at the other as though she was determined to make herself as unattractive to men as possible.

After inviting them into the living room, she offered tea or coffee and, after calling her mother, served it very efficiently.

Alice and Mrs Massey seemed to have exchanged roles, Rafferty noted with surprise. It was extraordinary, but Alice treated her middle-aged mother as if she were a child, explaining who they were and mopping her up and calming her down when she spilled her coffee and became upset.

'I'm afraid my mother hasn't been well for some time, Inspector.' Alice quietly explained her mother's clumsiness, easy tears and general air of not quite being with them. 'I had hoped to keep this business from her.'

Relieved that Alice hadn't dissolved into hysterics as he had half feared, Rafferty saw no reason why they couldn't at least spare her mother the upset of questioning. All he needed to do was check a few facts and Alice could supply answers for both of them. He told her this and suggested her mother might like to return to whatever she had been doing before their arrival.

As though she feared he might change his mind, Alice had her mother on her feet straight away and steered her firmly through the door, shutting it gently behind them.

'Poor girl,' Rafferty commented when he and Sergeant Carmody were alone. 'Don't you think her mother ought to be in a nursing home where they have the facilities to treat her?'

Mary Carmody shook her head. 'I imagine looking after her mother is the only thing that's keeping young Alice together. I think she'd go to pieces if her mother was taken away. She probably blames herself for everything, from the rape through to her parents' divorce; rape victims often do. Can't you see how brittle, how unnatural that calm manner of hers is? It's as if she's got such a tight hold on herself because she's frightened of what might happen if she were to let go.' Sergeant Carmody glanced carefully at Rafferty. 'I think it might be a good idea if I questioned her.'

Alice came back into the room. 'We can talk now,' she told them. The unnatural stiffness of her smile convinced Rafferty that Mary Carmody was right. Alice was stretched as taut as a bow-string that might break free at any moment. She sat as far away from him as possible, perching on a hard chair against the wall rather than sharing the sofa with him. He gave Sergeant Carmody the nod to begin. He listened hard as she began to question Alice.

Alice told them she and her mother had taken a planned trip to the east coast the previous Thursday, when her father had turned up on their holiday doorstep unexpectedly. 'He upset Mother. He always does. He gets so angry.' For the first time, there were signs of anger in Alice's face. Two pink spots of colour brightened her cheeks, making her appear more alive than at any time since their arrival.

'I suppose he gets upset, too, Alice,' Mary Carmody told her gently. 'I'm sure he must be concerned about you.'

'He's only concerned about himself.' Alice's voice was cold. 'He feels what-what happened to me reflects on him. It makes him feel weak, unmanly. His ego can't take that.' Her gaze hard, her expression scornful, she looked utterly unforgiving. In a girl so young, it was quite chilling. 'But he couldn't even protect himself. He was stupid. That's why he got caught when he attacked the-the man. The policeman told him what he should have done.'

'I'm sorry he upset you.'

'He didn't upset me. I told you. It was Mother he upset by bringing it all back again.' She seemed determined to make herself appear calm, as though such untidy things as human emotions had nothing to do with her. It merely emphasized all the more how unnatural her behaviour was. 'I asked him to leave. Things got a bit heated.'

Rafferty had taken it for granted that when Frank Massey had said he'd had a row and left, he'd meant he had rowed with *Mrs* Massey, not Alice. It was interesting that she didn't always cling to her emotionless stance.

'So, where did you go, you and your mother? You said you went to the seaside?' He might as well get confirmation of where they had been while he was here, he thought.

'We went to Jaywick, along the coast from Clacton. A

quiet place.' And no distance at all from Elmhurst, Rafferty thought again as he met Mary Carmody's eye. 'We stayed in a boarding house.'

'Bit chilly at this time of the year,' Mary remarked with a bright smile. 'Or are you one of these hardy types who swim in winter?'

Alice didn't return the smile. Her face gut-wrenchingly solemn for such a young girl, she told them, 'I never swim. Not since the man.' She paused and when she went on her voice was less like that of an automaton and more that of a young woman. 'Mother had been sleeping badly here at home. If we can afford it, I always try to take her to the coast when she has a spell like that. She seems to sleep so much better beside the ocean. Sometimes, I can hardly get her to wake the next morning.'

They left shortly after. They didn't trouble Alice for the name of the boarding house. As she had said, Jaywick was a small place. It should be easy enough to trace.

Rafferty was half afraid of what they might discover. Alice looked a lot younger than her years, small and slenderly made, unthreatening. Smith might easily have opened the door to her. But Rafferty was certain that her outward composure concealed more emotions than she had wanted them to see. He had sensed her anger; she was full of it. An anger that only the cork of determination kept bottled. Had something shaken her up so the cork had briefly popped? If so, he felt certain her rage would be all the more powerful once it escaped that unnatural hold she kept on it.

'I'd like you to go along to Jaywick when we get back,' Rafferty said to Mary Carmody when they were in the car and pulling away. 'Check out her story. There can't be much bed and breakfast business in Jaywick in December, so if Alice and her mother were there, they would likely be remembered.'

Mary Carmody nodded and glanced across at him. 'Do you think she might have killed Smith?'

Rafferty prevaricated. 'Do you?'

She didn't answer and Rafferty reluctantly admitted, 'She's a possible. She admits she was in the general area. Of course, she didn't have any transport but I've one or two ideas about that and it would have been easy enough for her to dose her mother with something to keep her quiet so she could slip out.'

As though determined to push him to examine the evidence against Alice, she asked, 'But how would she know where to find him?'

'If ex-Inspector Stubbs or Thompson became friendly enough with Frank Massey, as, at least to a certain degree, Stubbs must have done to offer to stand as a character witness at his trial, he may well have tipped Massey off about Maurice Smith's address on the quiet. Easy enough for her to get it out of her father when he was on one of his drinking binges.'

'Even if she managed to gain access to his flat and kill him, how would she get him from his flat to the woods? She doesn't have a car. Can't even drive, as far as we know.'

'All right,' Rafferty snapped. 'So she had help.' He jammed his lips tight together, aware he was being unprofessional and feeling doubly annoyed because of it. Why was it, he asked himself, that when other people tried to manipulate him into facing up to unpleasant possibilities, he reacted so unreasonably?

Conscious he could evade the issue no longer, he saved Mary Carmody the trouble of dragging the rest of his conjectures out of him. 'Sinead Fay and her friends were watching Smith – parked outside his flat in a car. To my mind, there's damn all doubt about that, even though we're still waiting for proof of it. From where they were parked on the other corner, they had a clear view front and back. They could have seen anyone using the fire stairs at the back of Smith's flat. There was a full moon that night and there's a street lamp right on the corner, so they'd have had no trouble seeing her. I reckon they'd have been only too delighted to help her.'

'But I understood that they didn't know her,' Mary Carmody objected. 'Why should they help her? Why should they even care what she did?' Rafferty was cheered a little at the reminder. 'Sergeant Llewellyn told me that none of them had ever counselled her, so how would they, ten years later, recognize her as one of Smith's victims?'

Unfortunately, Rafferty's brain raced ahead of her and reluctantly he added, 'Even if they consider men far from being the greatest thing since sliced bread, I don't suppose they elect to remain in purdah. I imagine they visit other Rape Support Groups from time to time. For all we know or are likely to be able to find out after all this time, one of them met her on a visit to Burleigh and befriended her. Ellen Kemp's the most likely. She's the right age to have done so. And even if they didn't help her, there's always her father. He has a car.'

'But according to you, by that time he'd been picked up by the police.'

'According to *Massey* he'd been picked up by then. We've yet to check it out. But did you notice he's got a mobile phone? I saw it on his bedside table. God knows why or how he affords it. But there's a phone box on the corner of Smith's road; maybe, *if* she killed Smith, she contacted her father from there and told him what she'd done. Do you really think her own father would have left her to take the consequences? Especially after he'd made such a hash of things ten years ago. He'd have helped her get rid of the body.'

Mary Carmody called a halt to her questioning for long enough to filter her way on to the M25. It was busy. The rush hour started earlier and earlier, particularly in the lead-up to Christmas. Rafferty was thankful to have a respite from her prodding questions. But the respite didn't last long and five minutes later they resumed.

'So who moved the body from the wood?'

'Who else but Sinead Fay and her friends? We know

142

full well where their sympathies lie – certainly not with the police. They'd have been only too happy to muddy the waters of the police investigation into Smith's death. Even if they didn't help Alice herself they must have seen it all, as it's pretty certain that it *was* them watching Smith's flat. They were probably hoping to make sure he didn't do a bunk after he received their "outing" threat and elude their punishment. If Frank Massey helped his daughter shift the body to the wood, those women would have followed and removed it.'

'So why would they – presuming it *was* them – string it up again?'

'Because they'd acted on impulse, hadn't really thought through the consequences. Then cold, hard common sense set in and they got scared.' Rafferty, aware his thoughts were still muddled, fought for answers. 'It would only be later that they would have been likely to appreciate what they had done; that they had a corpse on their hands, or rather in Sinead Fay's car boot. They could hardly leave it there. As Smith *was* strung up again, I imagine they decided that Massey and his daughter had had the right idea in the first place. Smith was dead. They might as well get some useful publicity from his death. Hiding his body served no purpose so they decided to put it back where they found it. They just took the precaution of removing his wrist ties and the hood in an attempt to confuse us and protect his killer.

'Unfortunately for them, they didn't realize we already had a description of how the body had originally been left. Though even if we hadn't known, the cord on his wrists had left recognizable marks. I don't suppose they noticed those as they must have done the necessary in a great panic. I doubt they even looked at him much. Easy to miss such a giveaway in the circumstances. Easy, too, to miss the fact that he was stabbed, as most of the bleeding was internal and his tracksuit, being dark, would have meant the blood wouldn't have shown up too well.'

143

He glanced quickly across at her. 'Shame we've no proof one way or the other; no prints, no nothing. Smith's visitor didn't even shed a hair, according to forensic.'

Carmody glanced quickly back at him. 'But Alice doesn't necessarily know that.'

Rafferty stared at her as her quiet comment penetrated. 'Are you suggesting we deliberately try to entrap a young girl into admitting she was there, that she killed him? After what he did to her?' He frowned. 'Hardly seems sporting.'

'But we're not involved in a friendly soccer match, sir,' she reminded him. 'Admittedly, it wouldn't make you the most popular boy in the school, but the question is, do you want to catch Smith's killer or not?'

Rafferty didn't answer her question. Unfortunately it was one he had already asked himself several times. And even though, during the course of the slow, stop-start journey, he had plenty of time to think about it, he still didn't have an answer when they finally reached Elmhurst.

Chapter Twelve

Liz Green and Llewellyn had not returned by the time Rafferty and Mary Carmody got back to the station. After a quick refreshments break in the canteen, Sergeant Carmody set off for Jaywick to check out what Alice Massey had told them.

Rafferty, left alone with his troubling thoughts, tried to keep busy. He got on the phone to Great Mannleigh station to corroborate Frank Massey's statement but the two officers who had picked him up were off duty and the Custody Sergeant to whom he was put through was interrupted by wild, drunken shouting before he could check his records. Yelling down the line, 'I'll get back to you!' the officer slammed down the receiver.

Rafferty sighed, rubbed his ringing ear and glanced at the clock. He'd chosen a bad time to call. Christmas drinking started early and, like Elmhurst, Great Mannleigh charge room would be cluttered with the human detritus of pub brawls and domestic violence, their numbers swelled by the seasonal revellers. He sighed again as he realized it might be some time before the Mannleigh Custody Sergeant was able to get back to him.

He reached in his pocket for the bag of boiled sweets that had earlier that year taken the place of the habitual cigarettes. The bag was empty. Aware that if his urge for lemon sherbets wasn't quickly appeased the older habit might resurface, he pulled on his coat and headed for the sweet shop round the corner from the High Street.

It was a still afternoon, the air crisp with the bite of a wild animal at the back of the throat and, after buying a fresh supply of tooth-rot, Rafferty was anxious to get back to his warm office. He'd only walked a few yards when he heard music coming from the High Street. Curious, he retraced his steps and turned the corner.

A Salvation Army band had struck up beside the Christmas tree and, in spite of the icy greyness of the weather, a crowd had gathered. Illuminated by the lights of the tree, the breath of each rose like a little phantom and seemed, as it mingled with the rest, to encourage a warm camaraderie to which Rafferty's current low spirits were drawn.

The crowd, encouraged by the band's enthusiasm and probably a tot or two of something even warmer, were soon singing along to the carols with gusto. When the band struck up with 'God Rest Ye Merry Gentlemen', Rafferty, who loved a good singsong as much as most bad singers, forgot his problems for long enough to join in, belting out the words in his off-key voice. It was only when the opening bars of 'Mary's Boy Child, Jesus Christ' gentled the mood that he recollected himself.

What the hell are you doing, Rafferty? his conscience demanded, as it reminded him, *You're in the middle of a murder investigation. You've no business to be singing carols.* He crept away, hoping no one had recognized him.

When he got back to the station he tried to concentrate on reading the reports that had accumulated in his absence. But, apart from noting that no one had come forward to say they had seen what time Smith had arrived at the Bullocks' flat last Thursday evening and that Sam Dally had rung back to confirm that some of Smith's bruising *had* occurred ante-mortem, he took little in.

Try as he might to stop it, his mind kept returning to what Mary Carmody had said. Was he committed to finding Smith's killer? he asked himself again. Or would he prefer just to go through the motions and report a failure at the end of it? Part of him couldn't help feeling that bringing Smith's wretched life to an end was the best thing for all concerned, Smith included. Yet, the other half of him chimed in, is anyone, no matter what the provocation, entitled to act as judge, jury and executioner?

Backwards and forwards his internal arguments went. No final answer presented itself, but one thing he was sure of was that if he couldn't put himself heart and soul to the task of catching Smith's killer, he should consider asking to be taken off the case.

But before he took such a step he needed advice. To ask the opinion of any of his family would be worse than useless. Their own petty foibles apart, the Raffertys were staunch members of the 'hang 'em and flog 'em' brigade. They would think that Smith had got what he deserved and that he shouldn't strain himself to catch his killer.

The only other person he felt he could ask for advice was Llewellyn. He wondered what the Welshman would say if he went to Bradley and asked to be taken off the case. But there was no comfortable answer there, either. He didn't have to ponder the question for long before concluding that Llewellyn, although understanding of human frailties, was also a staunch believer in right and wrong, the rule of law and personal responsibility, and he would think he was trying to avoid his own responsibility. He would be sure to remind Rafferty that a policeman's job didn't just consist of catching vicious killers but also the perpetrators of the less clear-cut, more grey-shaded crimes, like this one. And whether black, white or any shade in between, Llewellyn would believe their duty as policemen was clear. Rafferty wished he found it easy to separate the instinctive, human reactions from those of the law enforcer in the way that the Welshman seemed able to.

Although still niggled by Mary Carmody's question when Llewellyn returned, to his surprise his dour sergeant provided a little light relief. Even better, it seemed that something had dragged the Welshman's mind from the gloomy contemplation of his love life, for now Llewellyn's long and generally lugubrious face quivered with something close to outrage.

'That family!' Llewellyn never swore, but the way he ground the words out from between clenched teeth was the closest he was likely to get. 'They shouldn't have charge of a cat, never mind a child. Yet they seem to have a dozen or more of each roaming around that yard and cats and children both look hungry and neglected.'

Rafferty gaped at him. He'd never heard Llewellyn go in for such sweeping judgementalism; that was more *his* style. 'I take it you're talking about the fruitful Figg family?'

Llewellyn nodded. 'Do you know what one of Tracey Figg's uncles said to me?' he demanded. 'At least,' he frowned, 'I presume from his age and the family likeness that he's one of her uncles. He said that if Smith hadn't *broken her in* – his words – someone else would have. He even suggested she must have taken to *rough loving* – his words again – as she always got herself *knocked up*, made pregnant, by her more violent boyfriends. It never seemed to occur to him that the early assault and subsequent feelings of worthlessness might go a long way to explaining her choice of boyfriends.' Llewellyn threw up his hands. 'What do you do with such people?'

'Not a lot you can do,' Rafferty told him. 'Though if it'll make you feel any better you can take your frustration out on my expensive new chair. Giving it a good kicking always does the trick for me.'

Superintendent Bradley had ordered the new furniture. Since being made Great High Wallah Wallah in the Masons, his self-importance knew no bounds. And although the cost had strained Long-Pocket's natural parsimony, pride had dictated that the GHWW and his acolytes must be suitably seated. Frankly, even though they whizzed about with a far more satisfying vigour than most of the force, Rafferty doubted the chairs would catch many criminals.

'Families like that are sent to try policemen, Dafyd,' he soothed, when Llewellyn had calmed down a little. 'They just don't think in the same way as you or me. I doubt if *thinking* as such occupies much of their time at all. In my experience, such people operate on a different level altogether; one of instinct and appetite.'

'You make them sound like so many wild animals.'

Rafferty shrugged. 'They're human enough. Maybe I should say they haven't *evolved* – too much in-breeding perhaps accounts for it; you've only got to look at some of our so-called aristocracy to see the problems *that* can cause. Anyway, with people like the Figgs the usual civilizing influences seem to pass them by. How do you instil a sense of responsibility, morality even, in people who have no real understanding of either?'

Unwillingly reminded of his earlier brooding on where his own responsibilities lay, Rafferty leant back in his chair and determinedly concentrated his thoughts on the Figgs. 'I remember when I was young, there were two or three families on our Council estate like the Figgs. They all left school – when they went at all – without having learned much that employers would regard as useful. Yet they were all canny enough. The men could all figure out, without benefit of pen, paper or adding machine, what their winnings should be from a four-way accumulator. And the women were all adept at bamboozling whatever petty official the Council sent to enquire why the rent hadn't been paid.'

He grinned. He couldn't help it. Part of him admired people who managed to get the better of authority. He suspected he shared something of the Figg outlook himself. 'I bet, if I asked any of the current breeding stock, they could all tell me exactly what they were entitled to from the Social, whether it's a new cooker or a cage

149

for the budgie.' He paused consideringly. 'So, apart from learning that compassion is their middle name, what else did you discover?'

'That's just it.' Llewellyn slumped in his chair – a less grand version of Rafferty's, but still impressive. 'I learned absolutely nothing. The men, those who didn't just sidle out as soon as we arrived, all seemed to be called either Jack or Jason. And the women all called themselves Mrs Figg, whether they wore a wedding ring or not. The Jack who elected himself as spokesman insisted they were all at home on Thursday evening, watching videos on their enormous television. Though I'd have thought, given the size of the screen, the quantity of Figgs and the smallness of the room, there would scarcely be space for half of them. WPC Green was of the opinion they'd need to eat, sleep and watch television in relays.'

'What about the daughter, Tracey? Did you manage to see her?'

Llewellyn scowled as he was forced to admit, 'I've no idea. She might have been there – there were several young women around the right age, but it was impossible to ask them anything. They all seemed to have numerous toddlers and babies scrambling all over them and half of the offspring were screaming. And the smell!' Llewellyn gave a fastidious shudder.

Rafferty had known it was a mistake to send the band-box-fresh Llewellyn to see the Figg family. He'd have been so busy stopping sticky fingers pawing at his beautiful suit that he'd have been only too glad to leave; even the high-moral-ground Welshman had his weak points. 'Never mind. We'll go and see them together tomorrow.'

Like a bloodhound on downers, Llewellyn's whole face seemed to droop at the news. Rafferty was just about to remind him that it was all part of a policeman's lot, that he'd said himself that they had to take the rough with the smooth, when, just in time, he remembered that Llewellyn had had no part in his earlier internal monologue on duty and responsibility. Still, the family had to be investigated and he was damned if he was going to be the only one the babies were encouraged to throw up over when the Figgs tired of being questioned.

'It might be a good idea to borrow someone from Burleigh nick next time. Most of the Figgs are, I gather, regular customers there. If nothing else, they'll be able to tell us who's who.' Rafferty paused. 'What about the Denningtons? Any joy there?'

With every appearance of relief, Llewellyn turned to the other family. 'They seem to be out of it. Mother and daughter were both at a pantomime in London that evening. The neighbourhood got up a coach party and most of the street went. The coach didn't get back to Burleigh till after midnight. I checked and they were both on the coach back from London and their neighbours vouched for their presence all evening. So they had no opportunity to kill Smith.'

Rafferty nodded. Llewellyn's outburst had made him forget to ask about Stubbs and Thompson. 'Any joy on the policeman front?'

Llewellyn met his eyes steadily. 'Depends on your point of view,' he told him. His words indicated that he had guessed some of Rafferty's inner battle. 'Stubbs goes over to his friend Thompson's house regularly once a week, usually on a Thursday, though it depends what shift his relief is on.'

'I take it he went there on Thursday last week?'

Llewellyn nodded. 'Though according to a witness I spoke to, neither man remained there. They went out in Thompson's car around eight that evening – the neighbour saw them go past his house and they hadn't returned by nine-thirty.'

'Mmm.' Rafferty pulled thoughtfully at his ear. 'You didn't alert Stubbs or Thompson to our interest in them?'

Llewellyn shook his head. 'All Stubbs will find out is that I called to see him again, which is something he must

151

have been expecting anyway. And I doubt he'll even give the chap I spoke to the chance to tell him that much, as he seems to keep the neighbours at arm's length. As for Thompson, all he's likely to learn is that a stranger admired his house and was told it was unlikely to be open to offers.'

'Good. If they're innocent I don't want to make things difficult for them. Thompson is still in the force, after all. But now we know they're still in the running we're going to have to question both of them more thoroughly. We've given them every consideration so far, but it's time to take the gloves off. I want to know where they went that night and why, and police officers or no, they'll answer.' He paused and gave Llewellyn a faint grin. 'Working with you might not have given me the wisdom of a Solomon, Daff, but you must admit my grammar's improving.'

Llewellyn made no comment and Rafferty's grin faded. 'Let's hope ex-Inspector Stubbs appreciates the grammatical quality of my English when I question him again.'

Quickly, Rafferty related what he had learned in London and added, 'I'm waiting for Great Mannleigh nick to get back to me.'

Mary Carmody put her head round the door. 'I've just got back from Jaywick, guv. Alice Massey and her mother were there all right, from Thursday afternoon to the Sunday morning. They were staying at a guest house called "Sunnyside". Mrs Johns, the owner, confirmed Frank Massey's visit and the times he arrived and left, though she couldn't swear to it that neither Alice nor her mother didn't slip out later without her noticing.

'It's only a half-hour walk to Clacton along the seafront. They could have got a train from there to Elmhurst. There's also a bus service from both Jaywick and Clacton to Elmhurst. I asked the staff on duty at both the train station and the bus depot, but no one recognized my descriptions of Alice or her mother. I'll check again when the shifts are due to change.'

152

Rafferty nodded.

'DC Lilley's in the canteen waiting to see you, guv. Shall I send him in?'

'Only if he's got good news,' Rafferty told her glumly. He hated this stage of a case when all the ends still seemed to be dangling, with various suspects with poor or non-existent alibis. He was beginning to feel like a juggler with too many balls in the air and too few hands; constantly in danger of dropping one of them.

Lilley's news turned out to be neither good nor bad, only more of the same. Smith's neighbour had still not found the piece of paper with the registration number of the Zephyr.

Rafferty decided he could no longer delay checking out the other Zephyr owners and he told Llewellyn to get it organized. 'Though it'll probably be a waste of time.' He stuffed a sherbet lemon in his mouth and crunched. 'Kids tend to borrow their parents' cars without bothering to ask or even mentioning it afterwards. And if they find out that Mr Plod the policeman is investigating Daddy's Zephyr they'll keep stum for sure.'

The phone rang and Rafferty broke off his complaints. After listening for a while he asked a few questions, then replaced the receiver and looked at Llewellyn. 'That was Great Mannleigh. They confirm they picked up Frank Massey last Thursday. Though at *nine*-thirty, not seven-thirty as Massey claimed. He was drunk as a lord and kept shouting something about proving he was a man after all.'

Llewellyn raised an eyebrow. 'He didn't say what form this machismo test took, I suppose?'

'No, worst luck. Unfortunately, he threw up all over the arresting officer's boots before he could confide in him further. He went rather quiet after that. Could be something, could be nothing. Maybe no more than that he's got lucky with a woman. Still, at least now we know he had ample time to kill Smith.'

153

Llewellyn nodded and made the same observation that Rafferty had made in London. 'Great Mannleigh is only ten miles from Elmhurst. Certainly a short enough drive for a man looking to prove his manhood.'

Rafferty repeated the thought that had already teased him several times. 'Makes you wonder just how friendly Massey became with Stubbs and Thompson, doesn't it? We already know that Smith had received an "outing" letter. They'd be aware any attempt to use the police computer to locate Smith could be traced back to them, so they'd need to use other means of finding him.

'Could be they got a sympathetic female friend to ring the Social and persuade that young clerk to part with Smith's address and then passed it on to the breakaway Rape Support Group. Why would either of them draw the line at passing the same information to Massey? Especially as Massey was already a friend, and a hard-done-by friend at that. Especially as, like Stubbs and Thompson, the case concerned him so intimately.'

'If Stubbs and Thompson were involved and had used Thompson's official uniform to gain Massey entrance to Smith's flat, they would hardly have left him to cover up his own tracks,' Llewellyn objected. 'His stupid lie would seem to indicate that if he did kill Smith he didn't have police help to do it.'

'That's true.' Rafferty felt relieved when Llewellyn pointed out the obvious. He didn't relish the prospect of arresting either Stubbs or Thompson.

Trouble was, he wasn't overkeen on proving *anyone* guilty. 'So whose help did he have?' he demanded. 'Smith's door was undamaged, remember. Yet if Massey had been alone he'd have had to break his way in. Smith certainly wouldn't have opened the door to him.'

As he'd mentioned to Llewellyn, Massey was an intelligent man. He'd been out of prison for eight years; if he'd been determined on it, he could have traced Smith long ago. So why hadn't he? Against that, he came back to the

154

fact that Massey *had* lied to them. Why else would he do that?

Round and round went Rafferty's thoughts, when, into the middle of them popped the words *Maybe he was protecting someone.* Which led him back to the earlier reluctant suspicions that Mary Carmody had forced him to confront. Into his mind came a picture of Massey's daughter, Alice: petite, young-looking for her age, and with all that pent-up emotion waiting to be released. He tried to push the picture of her out of his mind.

'I wondered earlier whether Massey might have gone in for the double-bluff of again failing to provide himself with an alibi, but, thinking about it, I really don't believe – even after his prison education – that the man has the type of mind for such deviousness. Which means either that he's innocent – or guilty but unconcerned about getting caught.'

'The latter's unlikely, I would have thought,' Llewellyn commented. 'Could he take another prison sentence?'

'Maybe.' Reluctantly, Rafferty confided his suspicions concerning Alice Massey. '*If* he felt that by doing so he was protecting someone even less likely than himself to survive in prison – his daughter, for instance. You haven't met Alice Massey, but Mary Carmody will confirm that she seems such a mass of bottled-up rage she could easily go looking for revenge on her own account. If she did, I think Frank Massey would sacrifice himself in order to protect her.'

He shoved another sweet in his mouth and sucked fiercely. 'Let's face it, she would have had a much greater chance of getting Smith to open his door than Massey would. She's small, dainty – just the way Smith liked 'em. And she looks much younger than eighteen. Maybe she sweet-talked him into opening the door and he was so flattered he let her in.'

For a change, Llewellyn didn't immediately apply his usual cutting logic to shoot Rafferty's theory down in flames. All he said was, Do you want them both picked up for questioning?'

Rafferty juggled with his conscience. Duty won, but only just. However, still squeamish, he postponed its application. 'It's a bit late to drive up to town. Massey'll keep till morning.'

'And the daughter?'

Rafferty struggled a bit more before deciding. 'Just Massey. He's the one we've found out in a lie. If we get nothing from him we can speak to his daughter. Mary Carmody and Hanks can pick him up.' He consulted his watch and got up from his comfortable chair. 'And while it may be too late to journey to the great metropolis, it's still early enough to take a little drive to see Jes Bullock. Even if he didn't kill Smith, he's certainly hiding some guilty secret. And now that we've got Sam Dally's report on Smith's bruises we might be able to use it to lever it out of him.' The thought was a satisfying one.

Chapter Thirteen

Glad of something to get his teeth into at last, Rafferty set off happily. He didn't like Jes Bullock and he was relieved this case had thrown up one suspect who didn't make him feel like the rope in a tug of war contest.

When they reached Bullock's flat he didn't shilly-shally but came straight to the point. 'Why did you lie to us, Mr Bullock?'

Jes Bullock stared blankly at him. 'I don't know what you're talking—'

'I'll explain it to you. You told us your stepson visited you on the Wednesday before he died. Strange that you should forget that, whatever he did on Wednesday, he certainly visited you on the Thursday. He was seen by two witnesses.'

'Well, *I* didn't see him.' Bullock thrust a belligerent face inches from Rafferty's. 'Who told you I did? Some lying little toe-rags, was it? Tell me their names and I'll—'

He'd been drinking. Rafferty could smell the sour lager on his breath and hoped it might make the man more incautious than even nature had intended.

'You'll what?' Rafferty broke in. 'Arrange to have them beaten up like you tried to do with your stepson?'

Bullock's lips clamped shut and he backed away, but Rafferty was relentless. Aware that he was taking his other frustrations out on Bullock he was, nevertheless, unable to stop himself. 'We know you offered to pay someone to beat up your stepson, so you needn't trouble to deny it.'

Bullock shouted back at him, 'All right, so what if I did? If you know that, you also know that no one took me up on it.' His heavy features, thrust forward aggressively, challenged them to contradict him.

'Was that when you decided to do it yourself?' Bullock said nothing and Rafferty went on. 'We know you stormed out of the pub, shouting you'd do the job yourself. We also know from the pathology report that your stepson had sustained a number of bruises before death and—'

'What does that prove?' Bullock broke in. 'He bruised easy and he was always awkward. As a young 'un he'd trip over a matchstick, likely as not. Even now, old as he is – was – he was as likely to bump into the furniture as avoid it. Ask anyone.'

Rafferty's lips tightened. Damn the man. He knew as well as they did that Maurice Smith's anti-social lifestyle provided few, if any, witnesses to contradict his assertion.

He signalled to Llewellyn to take over the questioning.

'We understand you were later than usual arriving at the public house the evening your stepson died, Mr Bullock,' Llewellyn began quietly. 'Perhaps you could tell us what delayed you?'

Suddenly, Bullock lost his temper. Rafferty guessed it would be an unstable element in the man's personality at the best of times.

'I'm telling you nothing!' he roared. 'I didn't kill him and that's all you need to know. You should try hounding that bunch of mad bitches he had on his tail instead of trying to—' Abruptly, Bullock clammed up.

Rafferty and Llewellyn exchanged glances. So, the glance said, in spite of his previous denials Bullock *had* known about the 'outing' letter.

Rafferty silently reviewed what they had so far learned about the letter. The Document Examiner's report had told them that while inevitably the envelope had many prints as it passed through the postal system, the 'outing' letter itself had only Smith's prints on it.

158

Other checks had revealed no saliva on either the seal or the stamp on the envelope, indicating that it had been sent by someone knowledgeable about DNA and the dangers inherent in leaving bodily fluids behind.

Taken together with the stencilled address, which negated handwriting identification while ensuring the envelope arrived at its destination without drawing too much attention to itself, it pointed pretty conclusively to the probability that this had, in fact, been the envelope in which the 'outing' letter had arrived. And, according to their information, Maurice Smith hadn't received it till after he returned from the Bullocks' on Wednesday evening, as Mrs Penny had taken it in with her own post that morning and forgotten about it till Smith's return.

So, Rafferty now mused, if, as Bullock claimed, he hadn't seen Smith at all on the Thursday, how had he known about the 'outing' letter? Smith hadn't gone out again on the Wednesday night, according to his landlady. She had told them that she often slept badly and that night had been no exception. She had said she had heard Smith pacing about till the early hours.

Now, Rafferty asked, 'Do you have a phone, Mr Bullock?'

Bullock didn't answer straight away, but as the matter could easily be checked he finally admitted that the flat had no phone.

'Your stepson didn't receive this 'outing' letter till the Wednesday evening after he returned from his visit to you, so perhaps you can explain how you knew about it?'

Rafferty could almost see the metaphoric clunking and whirring taking place inside Bullock's brain as he sought to provide an answer that didn't implicate him further. He had already admitted that his stepson's notoriety had caused him and his son a lot of difficulties in the past. Once he had learned of the 'outing' threat had he decided enough was enough? He had certainly uttered threats in the pub. Had he gone one further and carried them

through himself? After all, as young Darren had said –
Maurice *was* dead.

Bullock's brow unfurrowed. His air became quite
jaunty. 'He dropped a note through the door, didn't he?
Some time last Thursday, mentioning this threat he'd
received. Of course I'm only guessing that it was women
behind it. Maurice didn't say either way. But I do read
the papers, and to my mind this has got man-hating bitch
written all over it, just the same as those other cases I've
read about. It's the sort of thing these bloody feminists
would go in for. Anyway, he asked my advice as to what
he should do.'

Aware he had been snookered, Rafferty tried to put a
brave face on it and continued to stare Bullock down. 'So
where is it, this note?'

'Threw it away, didn't I? What would I keep it for? Not
my problem.'

'What about your son?' Llewellyn broke in. 'Did he
see it? Surely you mentioned it to him.'

Bullock transferred his truculent stare to Llewellyn.
'Why would I do that? Not his problem either, was it?
He never saw it and I never mentioned it to him. Saw no
reason to.'

Rafferty took over again. 'When did you find this note?
Morning? Afternoon?'

Bullock shrugged. 'Afternoon. Found it on the mat
when I got in.'

'Was this before or after your threats in the pub?'
Rafferty questioned.

Bullock ignored him and went on with his explanation
as if Rafferty had never interrupted.

'Screwed it up and threw it over the balcony when I'd
read it. Nothing to do with me.'

'Oh, come on!' Rafferty countered. 'Nothing to do with
you? If you felt that why did you try to get him beaten
up that very day?'

Bullock's lips drew back, but he still had sufficient wit
to say nothing.

'He asked for your advice,' Llewellyn pointed out reasonably into the sudden silence. 'Are you saying you never contacted him?'

'Why should I contact him? Told you, it was his problem. Nothing to do with me.'

'Apart from any other considerations, you *were* his stepfather.'

Bullock scowled and slumped in a chair. 'Hardly my fault. I married his mother – I got him as well. Doesn't make me responsible for him for life.'

Presumably exhausted at successfully answering so many ticklish questions, Bullock now tried for the sympathy vote as if hoping to waylay any more. 'If you'd known what it was like for us in the past you'd understand why I didn't want to know.'

He reached for another can of lager and sucked on it for comfort, like a baby with a dummy. 'Couldn't even send my lad to school when Maurice was arrested. Killed the missis, of course. Killed her stone dead, the shame and worry of it. Nobody thinks about the families, do they? Nobody thought what it would be like for us when they let him go.'

Although Rafferty was reluctant to sympathize with the man, grudgingly he found himself nodding. But sympathy didn't stop him saying, 'You realize I'll need an alibi from you for Thursday evening? It's up to you, of course, but you must understand that it would be better from your point of view to admit that you beat him up earlier that evening and give us the names and addresses of anyone who can give you an alibi for later, than be suspected of anything worse.'

A crafty look came into Bullock's eye as if he realized Rafferty had deliberately not pointed out the other alternative.

'Beat him up? My own stepson? Not me, Inspector.' He finished the can of lager, dropped it on the floor and opened another. He seemed to realize that this late declaration of paternal affection was unbelievable, because he added, 'I admit I shouted my mouth off a bit in the pub. But I was upset at the thought that all the trouble was going to start up again. I didn't really mean it. 'Course I didn't. I've barely laid a hand on him since he was fifteen. As a matter of fact, I met a few mates to talk business that evening. We're thinking of buying a dog – a greyhound.' He mentioned two names and where they were likely to be found.

Damn the man, thought Rafferty again. He thought he'd got him rattled enough not to realize he had a get-out. He so much wanted Bullock – rather than anyone else – to be guilty of Smith's murder, he'd been over-eager.

'You ask my mates,' Bullock continued. 'They'll confirm I was with them last Thursday. And none of us saw Maurice. If he came round here that night, as you say, I never saw him. I wasn't in. He must have gone home again.'

Rafferty's lips clamped shut and he fought to get his own temper under control.

Although Mrs Penny, Smith's landlady, had told them Smith had been at home at seven-thirty that evening, it was only a few minutes' drive from his flat to the Bullocks' place. Darren had only said he had seen Smith leave; he hadn't mentioned seeing him arrive. And, so far, no one else on the estate who had been questioned had admitted seeing Smith arrive either. It could have been as Bullock claimed and that Smith had turned up at the flat only a few minutes before eight and, finding no one home, had left immediately. And unless and until they found some-one to say otherwise Bullock was off the hook.

Brusquely, Rafferty thanked him for his time, turned on his heel and left, trailed by Llewellyn.

It was only when they turned into the station car park that Rafferty finally remembered who it was that Bullock senior reminded him of. It was Dobson, Fatty Dobson, his old junior school headmaster, and as ardent a sadist as Rafferty had ever encountered.

162

Dobson and Bullock both shared that truculent, aggressive air, the menace not far below the surface, though Dobson's had been smoothed off by education. Instinctively, Rafferty sensed they also shared a pleasure in the infliction of pain and he wondered how many beatings Maurice Smith had taken at his stepfather's hands.

Rafferty, one of the back-row rebels as a schoolboy, remembered the sting from his buttocks after he had paid yet another of his frequent trips to the headmaster's study.

About to remark to Llewellyn on the similarity between Dobson and Bullock, he wisely kept silent. Llewellyn wouldn't understand his feeling that Bullock was a thoroughly nasty piece of work, certainly a liar and a bully and probably worse. He doubted the Welshman had ever been on the receiving end of a vicious caning; he'd have been the school swot, at the front of the class, first with his hand in the air and first with the answers. He wouldn't understand Rafferty's instinctive dislike of Bullock at all.

Rafferty recalled the aftermath of another beating he had suffered at Dobson's hands. It had been the last. The headmaster had never touched him again. The evening of the beating, he had been in the tin bath in front of the fire trying to soothe his wounds. This had been before they had been allocated the Council flat with its proper bathroom and he had been at that self-conscious age that demands privacy. The younger children were in bed, his father was up the pub and his mother, after he had insisted that he was old enough to bathe himself, had been banished to the scullery. He had been climbing out of the tub when Ma had bustled in in her usual busy manner, his request for privacy either forgotten or suspected as a ruse to avoid clean-ear inspection. Of course, she had seen the scarlet stripes criss-crossing his buttocks. He'd never forgotten what followed.

The next morning she had marched him to the school, his brothers and sisters running behind in an awed silence, and straight into the headmaster's study.

Before Rafferty had realized her intentions, she had grabbed the thinnest, most venomous of Dobson's instruments of torture and set about the headmaster with it, lambasting him across his back, across his legs, across his quivering, jelly-buttocks. Dobson hadn't shown his face in the school for a week.

Rafferty chuckled. His ma had been lucky he hadn't sued her for assault.

'What's the joke?' Llewellyn asked, as he finished his careful parking manoeuvres.

Rafferty glanced at him and his chuckles subsided. 'Nothing. I was just remembering an incident from my schooldays, that's all. You wouldn't appreciate the joke if I told you.'

Llewellyn shrugged and climbed out of the car without further comment.

The last of Rafferty's amusement vanished at the thought that, for Maurice Smith, there had been no Ma to stand up for him. According to what Records had on the family, the mother had been a weak, not overbright woman and had been as much a victim of Bullock as her son. Bullock could have beaten him black and blue if he'd chosen to and no one would have tried to stop him. And, Rafferty reminded himself, Smith's body *had* been black and blue, some of the bruising certainly occurring before death. And not long before his death, either. Such a beating would explain why Darren had said Smith had driven like a maniac. After a beating at the hands of a man like Bullock, it would be surprising if Smith was able to drive at all.

Rafferty found himself wondering who was the real criminal in all this; Smith, or the stepfather who had treated him little better than a despised cur.

The worst thing was, he realized as he followed Llewellyn into the back entrance to the station, that Bullock would get away with it. And it was *his* fault. He'd handled the interview badly. He should have brought

Bullock to the station to question him. It was too late now. If he had been lying he'd have already phoned his mates from the nearest public phone box and primed them with what they were to say.

Although he was beginning to share Llewellyn's feeling that it was unlikely that Bullock had actually killed his stepson or had any involvement in subsequent events, Rafferty felt it could be said that Bullock had effected a killing of sorts – a slow, long-drawn-out killing of whatever spirit Smith had had – and in so doing he had created another monster.

Rejected by society, rejected and beaten by the nearest thing he had to a family, Maurice Smith had still clung on, desperately seeking a sense of belonging. Had that desperation encouraged him to open his door willingly to his murderer? Massey, for instance? Hoping a plea for forgiveness, for understanding, would be heard, had he instead been forced to plead for life itself?

Perhaps, Rafferty thought, as he climbed the stairs to his office and the endless paper mountain that always awaited his return, he'd find out tomorrow when they questioned Massey again.

Chapter Fourteen

The next morning, while Mary Carmody and Hanks drove up to London to see Frank Massey, Rafferty checked out Jes Bullock's alibi.

He wasn't surprised when Bullock's friends confirmed his story. According to them, they had all been at the flat of Mick Coffey, another of Bullock's cronies, from about seven-forty till just before nine-thirty on Thursday night, when Bullock had left for his usual drink.

Rafferty was disinclined to believe them, but he couldn't prove they were lying. Still keen to give Bullock his comeuppance, he had despatched Llewellyn and Lilley to question Coffey's neighbours. But again, as with their enquiries about Smith, the icy weather had kept most people indoors, so their questioning was fruitless. No one had seen Bullock either arrive at the flat or leave it. Nor had anyone seen or heard his car, even though it was a sad and rusty Ford, and, according to Bullock's own neighbours, had an engine as wheezy as an asthmatic's chest.

Undeterred, Rafferty sent Lilley out to try again on their return.

'You don't want me to go with him?' Llewellyn asked.

'No. I've got another little job for you,' Rafferty told him. He nodded to Lilley and the young officer went out. 'You're coming with me to see Stubbs and Thompson to find out what alibis they come up with.'

'I thought we'd already concluded that they hadn't—'

'I know we've managed to talk ourselves out of suspecting that they helped Massey,' Rafferty broke in. 'But we haven't done the same if the scenario changes to them acting *without* Massey. He's not the only one still under suspicion, not by a long chalk.'

'He's the only one to be caught out in a lie,' Llewellyn reminded him.

'Exactly. The only one to be *caught*. But if the liars and thieves in the population only consisted of those caught out, what a wonderful place the world would be. Come on. Let's get it over with.'

However, it wasn't so easy to catch Stubbs and Thompson out in lies. Prompted either by innocence or canniness, they claimed to have recently discovered a mutual interest in angling and that they had gone night fishing the previous Thursday evening. Although they had no other witnesses but each other to back up their story, instead of telling tall fishermen's tales to add verisimilitude, each was smart enough to say they had caught nothing, thus ensuring that freezers empty of fish didn't weaken their lies.

If they *were* lies, Llewellyn had felt obliged to put in as they left Thompson's home after he had backed Stubbs' story.

'Bit of a coincidence that they should both take up such an uncomfortable hobby recently,' Rafferty retorted. Although far more favourably disposed towards them than to Bullock, Rafferty couldn't persuade himself to believe *them* either.

Frustrated by stalemate on several fronts, Rafferty hoped their visit to the Figg family might produce something more than yet another exercise in futility. But, even with the assistance of 'Curly' Hughes, one of Burleigh's most experienced officers, they were unable to get the Figgs to shift from their previous dogged stance.

Of course, as Rafferty was aware, families like the Figgs knew how to use the law to their advantage; they'd had plenty of practice at it if what Hughes had told them was anything to go by.

They had, at least, managed to speak to Tracey Figg. She turned out to be timid, and, as Rafferty had feared, not only looked to her father for the answer to each question, but, in general, appeared so cowed that she would have made a hopeless witness even if they succeeded in getting anything valuable out of her. But her parrot-like repetitions of her father's promptings was all they got and, like a cow chewing the cud in a favourite part of the field, she couldn't be shifted from it.

Only nineteen, she already had three children – all with different fathers if the range of skin tones was anything to go by. She had a collection of bruises, too, which to judge by their coloration, were fairly recent. Of course, in a family like the Figgs, who were likely to hit first and ask questions after, if at all, violence was probably a way of life; the bruises didn't necessarily indicate that she had been persuaded to collude in the concealment of murder.

The interviews, like Llewellyn's previous efforts, were conducted in the noisy squalor of a family's living room. And, as Rafferty had prophesied, one of the children had thrown up over Llewellyn's trousers just as Tracey had made her first stumble in the obviously rehearsed tale. And when the nauseous toddler had started up an unearthly wailing which set his siblings and cousins off in sympathy, they had beaten a hasty retreat to the relative peace and freshness of the yard.

Rafferty had paused to check if any of the vehicles differed from those which Llewellyn had noted on his previous visit. They didn't. And none of them had been noticed as being parked near Smith's flat on the evening of his murder, either. Not that that proved anything, of course. That was the trouble, Rafferty fretted. Proof – of anything – was in very short supply.

'I did warn you what they were like,' Llewellyn muttered in aggrieved tones as he dabbed ineffectually at his trousers with a wad of tissues. 'I wouldn't be surprised if they coached those children to vomit to order.'

'Very likely. You must admit it's an effective ploy. That and the bawling got rid of us pretty sharpish.'

Hughes, brought along as the local expert on the Figgs and their tricks, and reduced to red-faced fury when he had proved inadequate to the task, suggested hauling them into the station one by one. After mopping his gleaming bald head, he said, 'We should be able to get 'em for something. If nothing else, those dogs of theirs look vicious. They're sure to have bitten someone.'

Like Llewellyn, Rafferty had had enough of the Figgs. Anyway, doubting they'd get anyone to come forward, he vetoed the plan. 'Didn't you say the sons have a reputation for being handy with knives?' Curly Hughes nodded. 'Would *you* like to get on the wrong side of such a tribe? If I was one of their neighbours I'm damn sure *I* wouldn't. No. Thanks for the offer, but we'll leave it and concentrate on the Elmhurst end. At least if the Figgs are involved any witnesses we turn up there are unlikely to know them or their reputation and would be less likely to be shy at coming forward.'

After dropping Curly Hughes off they made their way back to Elmhurst. At the station, Llewellyn disappeared into the toilets to wash the Figgs from his trousers. Rafferty's rumbling stomach beckoned him to the canteen for a bacon sandwich and a consoling mug of tea. It was there that Llewellyn found him twenty minutes later.

'Carmody just phoned,' he said. 'Bad news, I'm afraid.'

Rafferty grunted, 'That makes a change,' and carried on sipping his tea.

'Frank Massey's gone missing.'

Rafferty's tea slopped over the canteen's chipped table. He'd been complaining that the case had come to a standstill and he wanted something to break, he reflected. But this wasn't quite what he had had in mind.

Llewellyn's choice of words penetrated and he demanded sharply. 'You said "missing". You don't mean . . .?'

'No. He's just missing. An entirely voluntary disappearing act, according to Sergeant Carmody. When he didn't answer her knock, she persuaded his landlady to let her and Hanks into his room. His passport's gone and so have most of his clothes. His car is also missing. No one seems to have seen him since about eight last night when his landlady saw him drive off.'

Rafferty was relieved to learn that even if he'd despatched Carmody and Hanks to collect Massey when they first got the truth from Great Mannleigh nick, it wouldn't have made any difference. Now, at least, he realized why Massey had told them such a stupid, easily disproved lie. It had given him time; time to get away. And that was all he had wanted.

'What about his books?'

'Books?' Llewellyn frowned. 'She made no mention of books. Is it important? If so, I can get her on the radio.'

'It'll keep. It's just that he was a book-lover, like you. They were his escape from reality, if you like. Or, perhaps,' Rafferty corrected, as he recalled some of their titles, 'they were a form of hair-shirt – a constant reminder of the past and his own failures. And if he's left them all behind, maybe it's because he no longer has a need for them in that way.'

'They're symbolic, you mean? That the failures are a thing of the past, not the present.'

'Could be.' Rafferty swallowed the rest of his tea at a gulp and strode back to his office. 'It's now one o'clock in the afternoon,' he commented as he glanced at the clock on the wall. 'If Massey left yesterday evening he's had hours to make good his escape. He could be anywhere. Still, at least his doing a bunk would seem to let his daughter out of the running, wouldn't you say? He'd hardly skedaddle and leave her to face the music alone if she was the one to kill Smith.'

Llewellyn nodded. 'Sergeant Carmody said she spoke to Alice Massey again when they found her father was missing and she now believes she had nothing to do with

170

Smith's murder. The girl's mother says they spent that evening playing Scrabble and that Alice certainly didn't slip out at all. She was extremely shocked when she realized the reason for Carmody's questions.

'Another point in the girl's favour is that when Sergeant Carmody went back first thing this morning to check the bus and train staff again, no one recognized the descriptions of Alice or her mother. They all swore they didn't see either of them travelling to Elmhurst on Thursday evening, at least. Jaywick's a small place and out-of-season strangers would be likely to be noticed and remembered.'

Rafferty nodded. Mary Carmody was a good judge. And, even without Frank Massey's disappearance, if she was now convinced that Alice had had nothing to do with the murder, he was inclined to believe her. Another point against Alice's involvement, he now realized, was her anger. If she had either killed Smith herself or known that her father had finally avenged her, that anger would surely have subsided. It hadn't. It was still bottled up inside her. One less ball to juggle, Rafferty told himself.

'Do we have any idea how much money Massey had with him?' he now asked.

'Carmody's checking that now.' Llewellyn paused. 'She did learn one thing that might be significant. According to Massey's ex-wife, he and Elizabeth Probyn used to be very close at one time. They were all three at college together, I gather, though in different years. She claims her ex-husband and Elizabeth Probyn had an affair then. The implication being that Ms Probyn might have helped him get away.'

Rafferty frowned. 'I can't see Elizabeth Probyn risking her precious career because of some ancient sentimental attachment between her and Frank Massey.'

'Not so ancient, according to Mrs Massey. She seems to think that her ex-husband and Ms Probyn might recently have become friendly again. If it's true he might have confided his intentions to her.'

Rafferty thought it unlikely and said so. 'Still.' He

tapped his pen against his lips. 'We've got to cover all avenues, though I can't say I relish the prospect of questioning our esteemed prosecutor about her love life. How the hell do you tactfully ask her if she's into aiding and abetting murder suspects to do a bunk?'

Llewellyn said, delicately, 'Perhaps I should—'

'No.' Rafferty shook his head. As he explained to Llewellyn, he felt he owed her the courtesy of questioning her himself. 'Not that she's likely to appreciate it. What about Mrs Massey herself? I don't suppose she had any idea where he might have gone? Or the daughter?'

'None. Massey said nothing to either of them. And though Mrs Massey didn't have any idea where he might be, according to Carmody she did express the hope that it was somewhere very warm.'

Rafferty grinned and joked, 'Love, that many splendoured thing, hey? Where does it all go? Sounds like she shared my old man's views on holy wedlock; that two hours before you die is time enough to get hitched—' He stopped abruptly, appalled to find himself talking about love with Llewellyn. It was not a sensible move. Llewellyn's next words confirmed it.

'Clever trick to manage,' Llewellyn muttered and added, half to himself, 'Maybe I should bear it in mind.'

'No,' Rafferty hastily answered. 'The two-hours-before-you-die philosophy is only for cynics like my old man and worn-down women like Mrs Massey. You're too young and innocent to follow such a creed. Anyway,' he finished with a forced cheerfulness, 'it's too late. Ma's bought her hat.'

Fortunately, Llewellyn didn't take the opportunity to confide any other thoughts he might have on love, splendoured or otherwise. And Rafferty, already hung about with an uneasy feeling that his well intentioned nose-poking had dragged a divisive Mrs Llewellyn too early into the lovers' embrace, hastily broke the silence before it encouraged such confidences.

172

'To get back to the task in hand, I want the number of Massey's car circulated. If he's left the country as seems likely, it may be dumped at one of the air or sea ports. Get on to them, Daff. You know the drill. We need to know if Massey *has* left the country, and if so where he's headed for. Does he speak any foreign languages, do you know?'

'Only a smattering of schoolboy French, according to his ex-wife.'

'What about family or friends? Any contacts abroad?'

'None. Unless Elizabeth Probyn knows of any. There are the Walkers, of course – the family who emigrated to Australia after their daughter killed herself. Might be worth getting in touch with them, or at least with their local police. Their daughter was an even more tragic victim than the rest. It could create a bond.'

'I'd rather not trouble the Walkers at this stage. They've been through enough. For the moment just let their local police know the situation. Send them a description of Massey and ask them to keep an eye out for any sudden visitors to the house. It's long shot. I doubt that Massey would be able to find the money to travel to the other side of the world, especially at Christmas, when it's high summer and the most expensive time of the year to get there.'

'Unless Elizabeth Probyn helped him.'

Rafferty's eyes narrowed. 'You've changed your tune. Just a few days ago you thought the sun shone out of her—'

'No,' Llewellyn corrected. 'I merely pointed out that she's not the ogre you seem to think her. It's called being impartial.'

'You can call it what you like,' Rafferty butted in. 'I've got another name for it altogether.'

Llewellyn's thin lips became thinner and Rafferty, regretting his taunt, didn't clarify his statement. Instead he muttered, 'If you'll stop putting the temptation to be

173

otherwise in my path, I'll *try* to be impartial.'

I'll even try to keep my cool when I question her, he added silently to himself. Though, considering the delicacy of the questions he had to put to her and her likely reaction, he didn't hold out much hope of succeeding.

After flicking through his desk diary and checking Elizabeth Probyn's office number, he dialled and spoke to her secretary. The secretary told him her boss had taken a few days' leave. He shared the news with Llewellyn, adding, 'The secretary suggested I try her at home. She even gave me the number. Funny, I'd have sworn I was on the black list.'

But Elizabeth Probyn wasn't at home, either. Rafferty cocked a hopeful eyebrow at Llewellyn. 'Maybe she's done a bunk with Massey.'

Llewellyn didn't need to point out that Rafferty's impartiality had died a quick death; his expression said it for him. However, he did say he thought it unlikely.

So did Rafferty, but, try as he might, he found it impossible entirely to abandon the fantasy that the ever-so-correct Elizabeth Probyn had finally blotted her copybook and eloped with one of the criminals she seemed so fond of.

'Didn't her cleaning lady say her daughter's in hospital? She'd hardly take off, if so.'

'I'd forgotten that.' With a regretful sigh, Rafferty put the tattered rags of his fantasy behind him. 'I bet she's at the hospital now.'

He picked up the telephone directory and flicked through till he got to St Saviour's, Elmhurst's general hospital. After fighting his way past the switchboard, he got through to Admissions. But they had no record of a Miss Probyn as a patient.

'Probably at some fancy private clinic,' he muttered, as he replaced the receiver. 'I suppose it will wait till she returns home.'

Anyway, he realized, the likelihood of her having any

involvement in Massey's disappearance was slim at best, and huge quantities of wishful thinking were unlikely to fatten it.

Putting Elizabeth Probyn to the back of his mind, he busied himself with overseeing their enquiries into Massey's whereabouts, checking out the usual mistaken identifications of car and man that such a search always brought.

It was after eight before he gave Elizabeth Probyn another thought. But when he tried her number again, there was still no answer. 'Maybe she's run off with Massey, after all,' he muttered to himself.

But, true to form, Llewellyn immediately robbed him of such a self-indulgent thought. 'I've just remembered,' he said. 'She's appearing in the "Scottish play" at the church hall. If you recall, she gave me two tickets. I imagine you'll find her there.'

Rafferty nodded. He'd forgotten. Llewellyn had tossed the tickets to him, evidently of the opinion that Rafferty was in greater need of exposure to culture than himself. What had he done with them? He rummaged in his pockets, finally finding them in the lining where they had fallen through a hole and been idly screwed into a ball by fidgety fingers. He smoothed them out. 'Bingo. It's the last night. I'll get along there, then.'

He glanced at the clock. With any luck he'd catch her in the interval. He hoped so, anyway. He didn't relish having to sit through a great dollop of Shakespeare in order to question her.

Llewellyn, ever keen to encourage Rafferty's limited interest in the arts, suggested he did just that. 'Although they're only an amateur group, they're very good. I saw them last year in their production of *A Midsummer Night's Dream*. It's only for a few hours and if Massey turns up you can be back here in a matter of minutes. It's not as if anything else is breaking.'

'You know I'd like nothing better, Daff,' Rafferty hastily assured him. 'But, as Ma says, life shouldn't be given over entirely to the pursuit of pleasure. Duty must come first.'

To forestall any acerbic comment from Llewellyn concerning this previously unsuspected rectitude, Rafferty picked up the mobile phone from his desk, stuffed it in his torn pocket and headed for the door. 'You can contact me on this if anything comes up.'

As Rafferty drove off, he thought about Frank Massey. Things looked black for him, all right. The man was a fool to do a bunk; but was he a *guilty* fool? The question occupied him all the way to the church hall, which took some time as he hit every red light on the way.

To his annoyance he arrived too late for the interval and the doorman, a self-important jobsworth, refused to let him wait backstage.

'Can't do that,' he was told, as, with arms folded over the brown overall, Jobsworth's tiny, piggy-pink eyes subjected him to a top-to-toe examination. He realized he'd failed the test when Jobsworth told him tartly, 'Get too many so-called theatre-lovers back here already. Light-fingered, the lot of them. Now I don't let nobody back here unless they're vouched for. More than my job's worth. You got anybody to vouch for you?'

Rafferty rallied and whipped out his warrant card. 'Only the Essex Police Service.'

Jobsworth nodded sagely, as if he'd suspected as much. It soon became clear he had no higher opinion of police honesty than he did of the theatre-lovers'.

'Had some of your lot in here last week,' he informed Rafferty. 'Unruly bunch. Discovered my spare uniform cap was missing when they left. You can be sure I'll do my best to make certain they can never hire *this* hall again.'

Rafferty gave up and conceded victory to Jobsworth. Resigned to either waiting in the car or sitting to watch the play, he realized that if he didn't want to risk missing

176

Elizabeth Probyn altogether, he'd have to do the latter.

The hall was packed. He spotted one empty seat half-way down a row on the right-hand side. Accompanied by tuts from the theatre-lovers, he crept towards his seat, throwing apologies left and right as he stumbled over feet. Subsiding into his chair with a sigh of relief, he squinted at his neighbour's programme.

As Llewellyn had reminded him, they were doing *Macbeth* and he stifled another sigh. For although he had never seen the play, he'd heard enough about it to know that it contained plenty of blood and gore; just what he needed in the middle of a murder enquiry.

He gazed up at the stage, but under the actors' wigs, costumes and stage make-up, he couldn't pick out Elizabeth Probyn. Eventually, after another sideways sneak at his neighbour's programme, he twigged that she was playing Lady Macbeth, whose character had already committed suicide. Thank God for that, anyway, Rafferty thought. Steeling himself for further tuts and muttered 'Well, reallys!' he got up and made for the door, dispensing more apologies as he went.

Luckily, Jobsworth had taken himself off to be obnoxious elsewhere and Rafferty had no trouble finding the dressing room of the female members of the cast. He knocked on the door and Elizabeth Probyn opened it. Surprisingly, she was alone. Unsurprisingly, she didn't seem pleased to see him.

'I didn't have you down as a theatre-lover, Inspector,' she coolly commented as she turned back to the mirror and sat down. 'Did Sergeant Llewellyn bring you?'

'No.' Irritated by the implication, especially as it was true, that he'd have to be *brought* to culture like a horse to water, he instantly bridled and then checked himself. 'He gave me the tickets, though. He knows I'm a sucker for culture.'

'Really?'

Too late, he realized he had laid himself open to an

enquiry as to why such a self-proclaimed culture-vulture would voluntarily abandon the last part of the play. Fortunately, if she had the impulse to ask such an awkward question she managed to control it and simply resumed collecting various tubes and creams and packing them away in a bag.

'You're here on an autograph hunt, perhaps?' she drily suggested. 'Or did you just want to congratulate me on my performance?'

'What?' Rafferty stared at her. 'Oh. Yes. Sorry.' Not having actually witnessed her performance, he judged it tactful to lie and hope she wouldn't question him. 'You were very good. Actually,' he began, 'I wanted to speak to you about another matter.' He paused, unsure how to go on, and only too aware, given the subject matter, that this meeting was even more likely to follow the usual dismal course than most of their previous ones.

'Another matter?' she encouraged.

'Er, yes.' Maybe I should have let Llewellyn tackle this one after all, he thought, and be blowed to professional courtesy. But it was too late now, so, taking a deep breath, he blundered on. 'We've just heard that Frank Massey, one of the suspects in the Smith murder case, has done a runner.'

In the mirror, her eyebrows raised and Rafferty deduced from her expression that she had guessed why he was here and wasn't going to make it easy for him. 'So? What has that to do with me?'

'His ex-wife told us you and Massey had been quite close at one time and had recently become reacquainted. I wondered—'

She didn't give him time to finish. 'You wondered whether I might know where he had gone? Really, Inspector, the implication of that leaves me quite breathless. Let me assure you that I remember my position and the responsibilities it carries even if you do not.'

'I'm sorry. But you must see that I had to ask?'

She dropped the make-up bag and turned to face him. 'Why? In case I still carried a torch for my first love, you mean?' The idea seemed to amuse her, for she gave a twisted smile. 'What a romantic heart you must have, Inspector Rafferty. I'd never have guessed. I wish I could help you, but I have no idea where Frank Massey is. He didn't confide in me. He certainly didn't ask for my help.' She turned back to the mirror and consulted the watch sitting on the table. 'Now, is that all? Because I'm due to take the curtain call with the rest of the cast.'

He had little choice but to accept his dismissal. Anyway, he was inclined to believe she was telling the truth. What would a woman like Elizabeth Probyn want with a wreck like Massey? She would, he told himself, probably despise him even more than she does me.

Still, he had a feeling she was keeping something back, something that perhaps she didn't consider important enough or sufficiently relevant to mention. The trouble was, he doubted she would be co-operative if he were to question her further now. Pausing at the door, he nevertheless made a tentative attempt to encourage her confidences.

'If you should happen to think of anything, anything at all that might help us, I'd be grateful. Whether it concerns Frank Massey's long-forgotten haunts, friends in foreign places, or anything else.'

She inclined her head imperiously, as though she were still in the role of Lady Macbeth. 'As I said before, Inspector, I wish I could help you. I really do. Naturally, if anything occurs to me, I'll contact you.'

She adjusted her queenly headdress and softly added, 'What a pity the police didn't do their job properly all those years ago. I know that, inexperienced as I was, ex-Inspector Stubbs thought he could lay all the blame at my door for the failure to secure a conviction. He certainly tried his best to do so.

'But if he hadn't botched Smith's interview in the first

place he wouldn't have had to look round for a scapegoat in an attempt to salvage his career, and he'd have saved everyone a lot of grief into the bargain: the victims who came forward as well as the one who didn't; Frank Massey, who wouldn't now be on the run; you, who would avoid the embarrassment of asking me insulting questions; and me, who'd be saved the indignity of answering them.'

Touché, thought Rafferty. The ringing of his mobile phone saved him from ignominious dismissal and gave him the excuse he was looking for to make a more digni-fied escape. Waving the ringing phone at her stiff, mirrored face, he decamped into the corridor only to find Jobsworth bearing down on him.

It was Llewellyn on the phone. They'd found Massey's car. It had been abandoned in Harwich.

'Harwich,' Rafferty muttered, frowning as he strained to hear Llewellyn as he headed for his car, over Jobs-worth's loud reproaches. 'Whose ferries operate from there?'

'I've checked,' Llewellyn told him. 'Sealink and Scandi-navian Ferries both run services from there; Sealink to the Hook of Holland and the Scandinavian line to Esbjerg and Göthenburg.'

'Could be he's headed somewhere else altogether. Left the car at Harwich to fool us and took a train to Ports-mouth, Dover, Newhaven, Felixstowe or some other sea- or airport. He could still be just about anywhere.'

'I gather Ms Probyn wasn't able to help you, then?'

Rafferty grimaced. His answer was brief and to the point. 'I'll be back in five minutes. You've spoken to the ferry staff?'

Llewellyn confirmed it. 'None of those we've so far been able to question noticed a single man fitting Mas-sey's description. Of course, they're busy at this time of the year and I don't imagine they had time to notice individuals, anyway.'

'All we can do is keep plugging.' He paused and tried to wave Jobsworth away. Apart from the oddness of Smith letting Massey into his flat at all, there was still another question he remembered that had yet to be answered. He asked it hopefully. 'I don't suppose that neighbour of Smith's has found the note with the registration number of that Zephyr yet?'

He supposed right.

'No. I rang him earlier. A party was obviously in full swing, though, so I doubt either he or his wife have tried too hard.'

Rafferty swore. 'What's the matter with the bloody man? Surely he realizes how important that piece of paper could be? Get on to him again, Dafyd. Put the fear of God into him if you have to, but make him promise to have a thorough look for it first thing tomorrow morning.'

Llewellyn said he'd try and with that Rafferty had to be content, though putting the fear of God into anyone wasn't exactly the Welshman's strong suit.

He broke the connection, put his face close up against the still expostulating Jobsworth and muttered a few choice Anglo-Saxon expletives before he strode out to the car park and got in this car, his only satisfaction the fact that he'd managed to miss the bulk of the wretched play.

Chapter Fifteen

Christmas Eve dawned with a hard frost and when Rafferty went out to start his car he found he'd not only neglected to cover the windscreen but had also used the last of his de-icer. Cursing, he set to scraping the glass, bruising his knuckles in the process. Few of his neighbours had stirred, he noticed. Lucky devils had probably already started their holiday.

The thought made him realize that they probably wouldn't be the only ones putting their feet up. The search for Frank Massey might as well go on hold, he thought, for all the chance they'd have of finding him over the Christmas period. Policemen, too, liked to put their feet up; somehow he doubted his continental opposite numbers would stir out of their warm stations in any number for anything less than a full-scale riot.

Anyway, he reminded himself, just because Frank Massey had lied to them and then taken off, it didn't automatically make him guilty of murder; stupidity, yes, blind panic, yes, murder – not necessarily.

Massey had not done his time at an open prison; his had not been a white-collar crime and the cushy billets were mostly reserved for crooked accountants, bent City whizz-kids and the like. Instead, cultured, sensitive Frank Massey had spent his time with the violent criminals, rapists, murderers, pimps and pushers.

Rafferty needed to do no more than recall the haunted look in Massey's eyes when he'd introduced himself and revealed the reason for his visit to know what he must have suffered. Even eight years had evidently not been long enough to dim the memory. He'd have been picked out as a soft target practically on his arrival; a natural victim.

Rafferty found it hard to believe that Massey would be willing to risk a repeat of the experience. Earlier, he'd concluded that the only thing that would make him take the risk would be if his daughter had pleaded for his help; then, he might be prepared to sacrifice himself. But they were pretty sure now that she had had nothing to do with Smith's murder.

When his car had finally slid its way to the office, he was reminded by Llewellyn that whether Massey was a murderer or just a fool, they still had other suspects to keep them busy while the hunt for Massey continued.

'True,' Rafferty admitted. 'And no leads from any of them.' He shoved his hands in his trouser pockets. Something rustled in the left-hand one and idly he pulled out the piece of paper.

It was Mrs ffinch-Robinson's list of poachers, he discovered, and a guilty dart pricked his conscience. Like Llewellyn's unwanted and unasked-for tickets for Shakespeare, he had appeased Mrs ffinch-Robinson by the simple expedient of shoving her list in his pocket and forgetting about it.

'What's that?' Llewellyn enquired. 'Your Christmas list?'

'Bit late for that, if so. No. It's a list of local poachers, courtesy of Mrs ffinch-Robinson. She seemed to think it might be useful.'

Llewellyn reached for it. 'She could have a point.' He pointed a bony finger to the name at the top of the list. 'This chap, Fred Skeggs, lives right by Dedman Wood.'

'He'll have already been checked out by the house-to-house teams,' Rafferty pointed out. 'And, presumably, had nothing to tell them.' He remembered, a lifetime ago it seemed now, reassuring Mrs ffinch-Robinson that her poachers would be checked out. It hadn't been a lie, but they perhaps hadn't been interviewed in depth, as she had undoubtedly expected.

'Still,' Llewellyn persisted, 'a personal visit might prove rewarding. And at least we'll be doing something.'

Rafferty shrugged. Most of his irritation at Mrs ffinch-Robinson's high-handed ways had now faded. Although she still rang up regularly to enquire into the progress of the case, Rafferty had left orders that she wasn't to be put through to *him*. Now that he had been reminded of the list, though, he decided he might as well look into it, to appease his conscience if nothing else.

Fred Skeggs looked about a hundred though he was probably no more than seventy. Small and wizened, his eyes were as sharp and full of mischief as the nanny goat who had chased them up the path to Skeggs' isolated cottage.

'So, Mr Policeman.' Fred fixed Rafferty with a gimlet eye. 'What makes you think I can help you?' he asked, after Rafferty had explained why they had called. 'Sit, sit.' He waved his hands at them. 'You're making my kitchen look untidy.'

Rafferty couldn't imagine that their presence could make the tiny room look any more like a rag-and-bone merchants than it did already, stuffed to the rafters as it was with verminous-looking clothing, rusting enamel basins, bait boxes and discarded tobacco tins, but he looked around for a chair. There was only one; a stout, wooden affair that was clearly the old man's. Glad he had put on his oldest, darkest suit that morning, Rafferty sat on a pile of dusty sacks and gestured Llewellyn to do likewise. There was nothing else but a pile of dog-eared and grubby copies of *Farmers Weekly* – an ancient job lot that had been obtained at a sale, by the look of them.

Llewellyn's face was a study as, with a cloud of dust wafting around him, he perched his expensive, pale-grey suited posterior on the precariously balanced edifice.

Rafferty choked back a grin, but Fred Skeggs, obviously less inhibited, sniggered and flashed his toothless gums at them. 'You'll take a cup of tea with me? Not often I entertain peelers. Usually, it's t'other way about.'

'Tea would be very welcome,' Rafferty thanked him, ignoring Llewellyn's quick shake of the head. 'We're trying to find anyone who might have been in Dedman Wood last Thursday night between, say, eight and nine-thirty.'

Fred turned his head sharply away from the blackened stove. 'What would I be doing in the woods at that time of night?' Rafferty went to break in but the old man forestalled him. 'Given up the poachin', Mr Policeman, iffen that's what you're gettin' at. Too old for such larks now.'

Rafferty doubted this. For his age, Fred Skeggs seemed pretty sprightly. Rafferty kept his eyes averted from the outhouse, where, even through the begrimed windows, he could make out what looked suspiciously like the small bodies of hare and wood-pigeon hanging from the roof. Instead he nodded at the stringy mutt who hogged the opposite side of the hearth to that occupied by his master's chair. 'I wasn't implying you might have been in the woods poaching, Mr Skeggs.' Not much. 'No, I thought maybe you walked your dog there as it's right on your doorstep.'

'Old Growler?' Fred scratched under his filthy cap as though considering Rafferty's readily provided excuse. But just then Old Growler staggered to his feet, wobbled his mangy body around on arthritic legs, then slumped again with a weary old-age sigh to toast the other side at the fire, and Fred abandoned the idea.

'Takes himself for a walk iffen he wants one. Not that he bothers much now. Goes no further than the back garden to do his business.' He turned back to the stove and made the tea, handing them theirs before he hitched up his baggy string-belted trousers and sat down.

The mugs were cracked, badly stained, handleless; the tea dark brown and scaldingly hot. Although he kept a nanny goat, Skeggs evidently didn't believe in wasting its produce on policemen. Rafferty quickly found a space on the cluttered table and put the hot mug down before it stripped the skin off his palms. He noticed Fred seemed impervious to heat. His first proffered excuse being rejected, Rafferty tried another. 'What about you, Mr Skeggs? You look as if you'd still enjoy a stroll in the moonlight on a crisp night?'

Skeggs looked startled at this suggestion. Rafferty had often noted that most countrymen were unsentimental about nature's beauties. Skeggs was no different and gave the impression that the only interest he had in nature was for the bits of it that he could kill and eat. But he seemed prepared to consider the idea that he was a closet nature-lover and Rafferty nodded encouragement. If Fred had seen or heard something on Thursday night, he wanted to know about it. He was prepared to turn a blind eye to a little light poaching.

'Thursday night, you say?'

Rafferty gave another encouraging nod and Fred rubbed his whiskery chin thoughtfully. Rafferty half expected the desiccated skin to crumble away like the dried-up leaves it so resembled.

However, Fred's face stayed intact and suddenly he barked at Llewellyn, who, unable to stretch across to place the mug on the table in case he tumbled from his precariously balanced paper throne, had been passing the piping-hot brew from hand to hand. 'Are you going to drink that tea or play with it, young feller? Made it special, I did.'

Llewellyn, obliged to humour the old man if they wanted to get anything out of him screwed up his eyes in the manner of one taking a particularly nasty medicine and obeyed, his Adam's apple shuddering with each swallow, as though attempting to jump aside from the molten brown stream as it gushed past. Scarlet and breathless, Llewellyn lowered the empty mug, only to have Fred leap from his chair, his gums bared with a peculiarly malevolent humour as he snatched the mug. 'Can see you enjoyed that. I'll make you another.'

Llewellyn looked aghast and Rafferty frowned him to silence. It was too late, anyway, as Fred thrust another piping hot tea at him. Rafferty buried his grin in his own mug. Fred's crockery must offend against every hygiene regulation known to man, not to mention the extra ones that only the hygiene-obsessed Llewellyns of this world knew about. Llewellyn would have to comfort his Virgo-pure soul with the thought that the mug's plentiful germs would be killed by the boiling water. Most of them, anyway. Rafferty turned his attention back to Fred Skeggs.

'We were talking about last Thursday,' he reminded him. 'And whether you might have enjoyed a stroll in the woods that night.'

Fred nodded and confided artlessly. 'As it happens, I *do* like a bit of a stroll.' He sat down again and sipped his tea, slapping his sunken lips together in obvious enjoyment. 'And, as you say, the wood's right on me doorstep. Shame not to make use of it.'

'That's what I thought.'

'Mind, as I told them other young fellers you sent, I'm not sayin' I was there. Not for certain. Might not have been Thursday.' He studied Rafferty through the steam rising from his mug. 'Might have been another night. Mebbe you can jog me memory?'

Rafferty had anticipated that a bit of memory-jogging might be required and had brought the necessary. He pulled a five-pound note from his pocket and placed it on the table.

Faster than any professional conjuror, Fred made it disappear, before taking another sip of tea and confiding,

'It *were* Thursday night, now I think about it. Funny how it comes back to you. Mind,' he added, as though reluctant to get Rafferty's hopes up, 'I can't tell you what the time were. A light in the wood, it was, that drew me attention. Someone had a torch and I could see a car parked right on the verge near the old Hanging Tree. Thought it were the sneakin' old bugger Jenkins at first, and though I were only enjoyin' the moonlight, like you said, I were about to scarper.'

Jenkins was the official warden of the nature reserve. An unctuous, humourless man, Rafferty had found him, and one who would, without doubt, insist on prosecuting poachers, so he could understand Fred's concern.

'Then I 'ear this woman muttering under her breath. Pretty rum. Don't get many wimmin in the woods at night, certainly not alone. Not nowadays, with so many of these 'ere crim'nals about. Anyways, I creeps forward and takes a look. She were just gettin' in her car by the time I got close.'

'Would you recognize her again?' Rafferty asked quickly, eager for a firm description.

Fred looked at him as if he were mad. 'She were just a woman,' he told him, in tones that made Rafferty realize that to a solitary man like Fred Skeggs women, like Chinamen to a Little Englander, were probably all alike. 'Mind, she had a big arse.' He cackled, drawing his lips over his gums. 'I remember thinking that fat rump'd make many a fine meal.'

'What about the car?' Llewellyn asked in a strangled voice as his scalded throat recovered, determinedly wiping his hands and mouth with a pristine white handkerchief as though he felt he would never feel clean again. 'Were you able to make out what style of car it was or to get the registration number?'

Fred spared him an even more scornful look; he seemed to have a vast store of such expressions. 'Are ye daft, man? The moon had gone in and it were black as my old dad's fingernails under the trees. Besides, I don't take my reading glasses with me. Not when I'm strolling in the woods, enjoyin' the moonlight. And cars is all the same to me.'

Like wimmin, Rafferty muttered under his breath. Needless to say, Fred hadn't noticed whether Smith's corpse had been hanging from the tree either. Rafferty was surprised that the old man hadn't simply supplied them with a steady stream of made-up information in exchange for more fivers. But it seemed Fred Skeggs had a moral code of sorts. He'd told them all he knew, which was that one unidentifiable woman, in an unidentifiable car, had driven away from Dedman Wood on Thursday night at an unidentifiable time. He was really glad he'd come.

To Llewellyn's obvious relief, they were able to avoid any more of Fred's determined hospitality, though on the way out the goat proved to have an even more mischievous character than her owner. Having missed making their acquaintance on their arrival, she made sure she didn't miss the pleasure on their departure. Llewellyn had a hell of a job to shake her off when she took a fancy to his trouser leg. He was still complaining bitterly about the trouble this case was causing his wardrobe as they got in the car and pulled away; it was all Rafferty could do to keep them on the road for stifled laughter.

'I think we should contact Sinead Fay and the other women again,' he commented, when Llewellyn climbed back in the car after insisting they stop at his flat so he could change his clothes. 'See what they have to say for themselves. One of them might let something slip. If one or more of them didn't kill Smith, it's becoming obvious that they followed the person who did to Dedman Wood, and know their identity.'

'And if they refuse to admit it, what could we do?' Llewellyn asked shortly, as usual putting his finger on the nub of the matter. 'We would have shown our hand and be forced to back down. After all, what have we got? A Zephyr parked near Smith's flat that might or might not be the one belonging to Ms Fay; a car that *might* be the same one seen on the road near the woods and Fred Skeggs, who, I might add, is scarcely the most reliable witness, who saw an unknown car and an unknown woman in the woods at an unknown time. As I've already pointed out, we wouldn't have them in the station more than five minutes before the merest journeyman solicitor would have them out again. You're a gambling man, I would have thought you would realize the dangers of showing your hand prematurely.'

Deflated, Rafferty asked, 'What do you suggest we do, then – ignore it and them and hope something breaks?'

'Something already has – Massey. I have a feeling it won't be long before he's caught. From what you said, it doesn't seem likely he's equipped for a life on the run. I doubt he's equipped either to withstand determined questioning. Once we've got him, and if he's aware of the involvement of Sinead Fay and her friends, he'll certainly implicate them – if they're involved, that is. So, yes, I do think we should do nothing. At least until then.'

Rafferty considered. Llewellyn was right, of course, as usual. All the evidence they had against the breakaway Rape Support Group women was circumstantial. Although Rafferty had finally made the decision to investigate the other Zephyr owners more deeply, little had been turned up.

Out of the twelve, three were rust heaps which the neighbours had assured them hadn't gone for months. Of the others, the families all seemed respectable enough – not that that proved anything, Rafferty told himself. His own family looked respectable enough but thought nothing of breaking laws they regarded as minor.

The checks into the Zephyr-owners were continuing, but Rafferty was convinced it would lead nowhere. He was still certain that Sinead Fay's car was the one that had been parked outside Smith's flat. The only thing was, it was looking increasingly likely that he'd never be able to prove it.

Frustrated by the desire to be doing something – *any-thing* – he turned the engine back on, rammed the gear lever into first, and as he pulled away from the kerb said, 'All right, we'll leave them alone for now. But if Frank Massey isn't caught soon, we may have to think again. You know what the Super's like. He wants results and it's up to us to give them to him.'

He consulted his watch. It was almost lunchtime. 'You might as well get off. No point in the two of us sitting in the office twiddling our thumbs. Your mum's seen hardly anything of you. I'll drop you at Ma's.'

Llewellyn glanced at him. 'Why don't you take a few hours off yourself and meet her?'

Rafferty, suspecting that Llewellyn was looking for moral support, took the coward's way out. 'Better not. I'm already taking most of tomorrow off. And even though nothing's breaking, I should be there, on the spot. Besides, you never know, if I sit quiet something might occur to me to get this case back on the road.' He pulled up as close to his ma's house as he could get and dropped Llewellyn off.

'You've got the mobile phone,' Llewellyn reminded him. 'Don't hesitate to contact me if anything breaks in the meantime.'

Llewellyn seemed reluctant to leave. Several times he began to say something, then broke off. Rafferty found it unnerving. Convinced Llewellyn had finally geared him-self up for an uncharacteristic emotional outpouring, he did his best to sidestep it by saying firmly, 'I'll see you tomorrow.'

Tomorrow, he thought. The nose-poker's day of reckon-ing. If, as he suspected, the visit of Llewellyn's mother had driven a wedge between him and Maureen, the next day would be soon enough to discover it. Soon enough, too, if Llewellyn and Maureen's romance was teetering on the brink of destruction, to face the fact that it would be largely *his* fault.

Chapter Sixteen

Rafferty came into the office bright and early on Christmas morning, through streets that, overnight, had been clothed in a light sprinkling of snow. The air was hushed, expectant and even though he was usually caustic about what he regarded as sentimental religious mush, he was forced to acknowledge a sense almost of awe.

Nothing to do with babies in mangers or any similar tosh he had been force-fed as a child, he insisted to himself. It was something to do with the rare peace and beauty of the December day; like the pavements, the roads were practically empty and, with most of the populace still at home, the snow retained a purity of look and texture that brought magic even to the meanest street. It would be spoiled soon enough as the Great British Public indulged the annual humbug of family togetherness which the rising divorce statistics put in perspective.

The pleasure in the morning vanished as he remembered he would soon form part of the visiting hordes himself, and he turned glumly away from admiring the lacy patterns on his office window, sat down and tried to concentrate on the latest reports. There were few enough of them and as they brought nothing in the way of new areas of investigation, his mind was soon free to return to the problem of Llewellyn.

Why did I ever suggest this visit? he asked himself for the umpteenth time.

He put off leaving for as long as he could, but eventually could procrastinate no longer. His ma had already had him on the phone several times asking when he could be expected as she'd put the dinner back twice and if he didn't get a move on it would surely be spoilt.

Slowly, like a man going to his execution, Rafferty put on his coat, quietly shutting the office door behind him.

Rafferty had imagined Llewellyn's mother, when he had found the courage to think of her at all, as being as long and thin and forbidding as those tall black hats Welsh women traditionally wore. So, when he finally met her, he was prepared for the worst. Although surprised to find that Mrs Llewellyn was a rather elegant woman, tall, small-featured and, at fifty-five, still pretty, he had more than half-expected her to have a sharp tongue and decidedly old-fashioned attitudes. And, with the introductions barely over, she didn't disappoint him, though the attack came from an angle he hadn't expected.

Tapping him on the arm, she said, 'I understand you've been introducing my son to the local public houses. He's told me all about it and I have to say I'm surprised. I never thought to live to see the day when he entered what his father always called *dens of iniquity*.'

Rafferty threw an accusatory look at Llewellyn, who was sitting on the sofa with Maureen, before he attempted to defend himself. 'I'm sorry if you don't approve, Mrs Llewellyn,' he began, looking desperately round his family for some moral support. But they all seemed to find his predicament fascinating. Conversations died and everywhere he looked he met bright eyes and elbow nudges. They were enjoying his discomfiture, he realized indignantly. Taking a deep breath, he attempted to defend himself. 'I didn't mean—' he began. 'That is, I can assure you he didn't—'

A howl of laughter went up round the room as she tapped him on the arm again and said simply, 'I hope you'll take me, too, while I'm here, if you can find the

194

time. Dafyd might have taken a vow of abstinence to please his father . . .' For the first time, Rafferty noted the laughter in her eyes, as she added, '. . . but I didn't. I imagine he knew I was a lost cause as far as that went.'

Another howl of laughter went up. Even young Gemma, whey-faced and unnaturally quiet in the corner of the room, managed a tiny smile.

'Your face, Joe. It's a picture.' Maggie, the eldest of his three sisters and the one he had always felt closest to, teased him before she took pity on him and explained. 'Gloria was a dancer before she met Dafyd's father. Case of opposites attracting, you might say.'

Gloria. Rafferty repeated the name and realized it was the first time he'd heard Mrs Llewellyn's forename. Pity he hadn't heard it before, he reflected, then his imagination mightn't have worked overtime turning her into a monster. He'd know a few Glorias in his time and they'd all known how to enjoy life.

'Dafyd takes after his father, apparently,' Maggie advised him.

'Who'd have guessed it?' Rafferty muttered. Obviously Dafyd's likeness to his father was in character, not looks, for he and his mother were both dark and remarkably similar, superficially at least. But, as Rafferty began to discover, where he was all long-faced lugubriousness, she was lightness and laughter. She smiled often and obviously enjoyed a good joke as much as any of the other Glorias he had known. And not only did she and his ma appear to have reached a remarkable level of understanding and friendship, but Maureen and her prospective mother-in-law also seemed delighted with one another. There was no trace of the imagined breach. It had all been in his mind. But *something* had put it there, he reasoned. And that something had undoubtedly been Llewellyn. He resolved to have a quiet word with his sergeant as soon as he got a chance.

'I don't know quite what he expected when he saw you,

Gloria,' Kitty Rafferty commented mischievously. 'Some kind of fire-breathing dragon, I dare say.'

Rafferty managed a sheepish grin. 'Not at all,' he insisted. 'Take no notice of Ma,' he advised. 'She's always had this tendency to exaggerate.'

As the conversation in the rest of the room returned to its previous volume, he turned back to Gloria and confided, 'Though Ma's right. I was a bit apprehensive about meeting you. Especially as your visit was my idea and I was more or less responsible for getting Dafyd and Maureen together in the first place. I was afraid—' He paused, reluctant to admit just what he had been afraid of.

Gloria continued for him. 'You were afraid that, as Dafyd's my only son, I'd come between them.'

Rafferty nodded. 'It's just that Dafyd's talk of his childhood coloured my expectations, especially when he mentioned that you didn't even have a television. I suppose I thought—'

'He thought you must be a terribly dour, humourless woman, Gloria,' Ma chipped in. 'And isn't he ashamed of himself now?' She darted a glance at Gemma before confiding, 'Gloria's been that sympathetic, Joseph. Her visit and good sense has made us all feel so much better about the baby.'

'Anyway.' She got to her feet. 'I must dish up. No, you stay there, Gloria,' she insisted when Mrs Llewellyn went to get up and help. 'Perhaps you can persuade Joseph that he's too old to be still playing the field. Maybe, if you tell him it's time he settled down, he'd listen.'

Gloria smiled at him when his ma had bustled off to the kitchen. 'Don't worry. I wouldn't dream of telling you any such thing. And, actually, I *do* have a television set. Just don't tell Dafyd. He adored his father and even now he would be upset if he thought I wasn't living up to his father's high-minded principles. I'd rather he didn't realize I'm just a weak human being like everybody else, so, whenever I know Dafyd's coming for a visit, I hide the

TV. It's only a small portable, so it's easily enough done. That and the radio go under my bed.'

Her gaze strayed to the upright figure of her son as he sat chatting to Maureen and Maggie and she added softly, 'His father was killed by a hit-and-run driver – drunk, the police thought. The man was never caught. I think it was that which prompted him to join the police. He never actually said, but I think he wanted to try to make sure that other people received the justice that we were denied. Promise me you won't tell him my secret?' Rafferty promised.

Just then his ma carried the turkey in. It was the plumpest turkey he had ever seen and as the aroma of the well-stuffed bird wafted past his nostrils his mouth watered, making more speech impossible. His sisters followed on with dishes piled high with vegetables and everyone came to the table.

There were eighteen for dinner this year; it was fortunate that his sister, Maggie, lived only a few doors away and had cooked a second turkey and all the trimmings. Fortunate, too, that Ma had had the two downstairs rooms knocked into one. As it was, the younger children were seated round a painter's board and trestle. It was covered with a large white linen sheet and made as festive as the table proper with crackers and tinsel garlands and snow-sprayed pine cones that marched across the cloth, stuck down with double-sided sellotape.

Rafferty smiled. Ma always went to town at Christmas and the tables were a glorious riot of over-the-topness.

As soon as Ma had said grace everyone set to with a will. Even Maureen's mother, no doubt given the jollop of something as Ma had threatened, soon became as lively as any of the drunks overnighting in Elmhurst's nick, and began teasing an embarrassed Maureen and recounting such tales of her own courtship days that she had Rafferty's 'Uncle' Pat blushing for shame.

The party was still going strong at midnight, the tables

pushed back against the wall and the ancient radiogram by now piled with romantic ballads for the close-dancing couples. Ma and Gloria, both widowed for many years, were both up dancing with a couple of Ma's gentleman neighbours who had popped in and Rafferty and young Gemma were the only wallflowers.

Even in the now-dimmed lighting he could see that her pretty face was still as unhappy and strained as it had been for most of the day. She had been the first grandchild in the family and had been a bit spoiled by them all. Rafferty, a couple of years out of his teens when she had been born, had fussed over her as much as anyone. Of course, as the rest of the grandchildren arrived, the novelty had worn off. But Gemma remained special to him.

He sighed. And now she was going to be a mother herself. His attempts during the day to cheer her up hadn't succeeded. How could they? What did a single, childless man of thirty-eight say to a young girl of sixteen who was soon to be responsible for a new life? But she looked so wretched that he knew he had to have another try and he made his way through the crush of bodies.

'All right, Moppet?' he asked.

She shrugged.

It was apparent she didn't want to talk. She'd probably listened to enough advice and admonishment to last through a dozen pregnancies as the women of the family thrashed out her future. Instead, he said, 'What do you say we take a twirl and show these shufflers how it should be done?'

That brought a smile as he'd known it would. Gemma had been dance-mad until just lately; ballroom, Latin-American, jive: every time Rafferty had seen her she'd inveigled him into partnering her, till he'd become pretty adept a dancer himself.

Now, before she could refuse him, he grabbed her hand, shouted, 'Make way for the champions,' and after putting one of Ma's livelier records under the needle led her into the much-practised jive that cleared the floor and brought a welcome sparkle to Gemma's eyes. 'See,' he whispered in her ear, 'being a single parent is not the end of the world. You can bring up kids alone and still find time to enjoy yourself. I mean – look at Ma.'

Kitty Rafferty, mother of six, grandmother to twelve, and soon to be a great-grandmother, was now ensconced on the middle of the settee, a gentleman friend on either side of her and flirting like mad with both of them.

Gemma giggled. It was the first time she had giggled all day. Relieved, Rafferty whirled her around, turned her with a flourish that Nureyev in his heyday would have died for and set off back up the room.

It was much later when Rafferty sought Llewellyn out. By now, emboldened by his success with Gemma and more than his share of Jameson's whiskey, he was ready to put the rest of the world to rights and he followed Llewellyn to the bathroom and demanded a few answers. After all he had been put through, he felt he deserved them.

Fixing Llewellyn with bleary-eyed stare, he said, 'I don't get it. Your mum's come down, met Maureen, they get on like a house on fire, so why have you been looking as miserable as a doctored poodle all week?'

'Surely you can guess?'

'I wouldn't ask if I could. Come on, out with it.'

'It's Maureen. She's *your* cousin. So tell me, how would you go about asking "Daisy" the cow if she'll consent to your putting a ring through her nose?'

Rafferty gave a shout of laughter, but quickly sobered when he saw Llewellyn was serious. 'You mean you haven't even asked her yet? What the hell have you been doing all this time?'

'Trying to pluck up the courage,' Llewellyn finally confessed. 'A task not made any easier by the fact that both your mother and mine seem to assume that asking her is a mere formality. I even tried seeking your advice several times,' he admitted, 'but each time I tried you seemed to cut me off.' Rafferty shuffled his feet guiltily. 'You know Maureen. She's a woman with very modern, feminist ideas. She may not even *want* to get married.'

'You must at least have pinned her down to a general opinion on the subject?'

Llewellyn shook his head. 'Not exactly.'

Exasperated, Rafferty exclaimed, 'For God's sake, man, why ever not? Perhaps if you and Maureen had socked old Socrates and his mates into touch once in a while and discussed the basics, you might know where you stood. Maureen's not stupid. Do you think she doesn't know that both your mother and mine have got you married off already? Especially when Ma hasn't stopped teasing the poor girl about wedding bells all day. And then when *her* mother chimed in about keeping the guest list small and *select*' – which he guessed meant as few Raffertys as possible – 'I wouldn't have thought she could have much doubt of the way the wind's blowing.'

'I realize that,' Llewellyn retorted. 'But even you must have noticed she looked more embarrassed then pleased about it and immediately changed the subject. What does that tell you?'

'What does that tell me?' Rafferty repeated incredulously, as through his mind, in swift succession, were paraded all the tortures he'd suffered because of Llewellyn's wimpish wooing. That they'd stemmed almost entirely from his own over-active imagination he disregarded.

'I'll tell you what it tells me.' He realized he was shouting and lowered his voice. 'Has it not occurred to that over-sized intellectual brain of yours that the poor girl was embarrassed not, as you seem to think, because she doesn't *want* to marry you, but because you haven't bloody asked her!'

He again dragged his voice down to a loud whisper and demanded, 'What else do you expect her to be when she must think you don't want to marry her? I'd be bloody mortified in her position.'

While Llewellyn absorbed this, Rafferty thrust his advice home with the poke of an index finger in his chest. 'Do everyone a favour, find the courage of your convictions and *ask* her.' Rafferty's eyes narrowed. 'Or do you expect Maureen to do it? Let me tell you something, Mo might be a modern sort of girl with plenty to say for herself on other matters, but on this subject she's likely to be as traditional as my ma. Besides, it's hardly good for a girl's ego to have to confess to her friends, her workmates, her snotty-nosed *mother*, for God's sake, that she had to do the asking.'

Rafferty paused for breath, then went on. 'Do you think that mother of hers wouldn't rub her nose in it every time they had a falling out? And Maureen would blame you. *Ask* her. That's my last word on the subject. Now.' Rafferty removed his body from its doorframe prop, staggered a little and aimed himself at the front door. 'I'm going home.'

As Rafferty drifted off to sleep, Gemma's face kept passing in and out of his dreams, each time gazing pensively at him from the frame of a photograph. It was as if, in his dream, she was trying to tell him something.

The dream moved on, became tangled up in the lives of the other young girls involved in the case, their emotions, their vulnerabilities. Perhaps it was the combination of those things that set his mind on the correct path at last. But, all at once, in his sleeping state, anyway, he had the answer.

Of course it had faded by morning, but certainly, when the phone woke him at seven and groggily he surfaced from an alcoholic sleep, stretched out a hand and sent the bedside lamp clattering to the floor, he was aware of a vague sense of having dredged up something vital. He shook his head to clear it, winced, finally found the phone and said, 'Ugh?'

He sat up pretty quickly when he absorbed what the voice was saying in his ear. When his head had stopped spinning, he said, 'They're sure it's Massey?'

He listened for a while, asked a few more questions, then hung up. Rubbing his hands over his face, he tried to think. Phone Llewellyn, his brain instructed.

Llewellyn was already up, that much was obvious. He heard Maureen's voice in the background and despite his throbbing head he managed a grin. 'Been keeping a welcome in that there hillside?' he asked. 'Guess what. The station's just been on. Massey's turned up – only trouble is, he's dead. Hanged himself in some Dutch barn.'

'*Hanged*, you say?'

It was obvious that the method of suicide Massey had chosen had stirred up Llewellyn's suspicions.

Rafferty paused to accommodate them, then continued. 'According to the Dutch police, he's been living rough for the last couple of days. The farmer said he saw this wild man in the woods near his place and reported it, but the police took their own sweet time in looking into the matter. Unfortunately, in the meantime Massey must have made up his mind to end it all. The farmer found him early this morning hanging from the beam in his barn.'

'So apart from the usual mopping-up operations, the investigation's over?'

'What?' Something went click in Rafferty's brain and the dream of the night returned in its entirety. 'No,' he said. 'The poor bastard didn't do it. Massey isn't the one who killed Smith.' That was another poor b— entirely, he thought, and I'm the poor sap who has to make the arrest.

Already depressed in body by alcohol, the thought depressed his spirit and he wondered again if he was really cut out for police work. 'I think the poor sod was just terrified of being on the receiving end of another piece of injustice. After all, he had no reason to think the law would get it right this time any more than they did last time.

'No,' he repeated, 'Massey didn't do it. I've finally fig-ured out who did.' He paused and crossed his fingers. 'At least I think I have. I've got a few things to check out first. I'll see you at the station in forty minutes and I'll explain then.'

Rafferty replaced the receiver before Llewellyn could ask any more questions and slumped on the bed. Was it *his* fault that Massey had killed himself? Had he driven an innocent man to suicide? Maybe if he'd been smarter, quicker to work out the clues that had been there all the time, the poor bastard might still be alive.

Slowly, his hand reached out again for the phone.

Chapter Seventeen

The Elmhurst Private Sanatorium might now be called 'Greenlawns' and be under different ownership, but as Llewellyn drove through the gates, Rafferty saw that the place looked much the same as he remembered from when it had been the scene of an earlier murder.

The hushed air that in a noisy modern world only the wealthy could afford still hovered over the manicured lawns, their well-nourished lushness emphasized by the light dressing of December snow.

Even the gate-porter to whom they had shown their identification was the same. Rafferty searched his memory for his name. Then it came to him. Gilbert – that was it. From what he knew of the man, he was surprised he still had his job.

After enquiring at the reception desk they were directed down a thickly carpeted corridor to the rear of the Georgian house which accommodated the administrative offices and into the much more recently added wings which contained the private rooms.

Elizabeth Probyn didn't look up when the door opened, but simply went on spooning the breakfast cereal into the girl's mouth, tenderly, carefully, making sure none was spilt. She didn't turn her head when he called her name, but continued to deliver spoon from bowl to mouth as though it were the most important thing in the world to her. It probably was, Rafferty reflected.

A silence took hold, which Rafferty forced himself to

break with a careful warning. 'I feel I ought to tell you, Ms Probyn, that we know pretty well everything now.'

Still she said nothing.

Rafferty had never had occasion to caution a Chief Crown Prosecutor before, though there had been plenty of times when he'd wanted to, particularly this one. That desire had faded. He'd disliked, resented her, for so long that the feeling of pity that had replaced such emotions didn't sit comfortably. Still, it was strong and threatened to unman him. He wished he could forget what he knew, what his phone calls had confirmed, sweep it under some wide, grey carpet out of sight of man's justice. But he couldn't. He reminded himself that he had fantasized about arresting this woman. And now . . . now it was the hardest, most gut-wrenching thing he had ever had to do.

He found his voice again. 'This is your daughter?'

She nodded. 'How did you find out?'

'It was the pictures that led me to the rest.'

'Pictures?'

'The photographs of your daughter in your home. It suddenly struck me you only had pictures of her as a newborn baby and as a young woman, with nothing in between, no photographic tracing of all the stages from toddler to school photographs in her uniform. I wondered why. Then it came to me. You only had early pictures and more recent ones because you hadn't *seen* her in between. Had no idea what had happened to her in between because she'd been adopted. Only then, when she reached eighteen, she traced you. And you found out what had happened to her; that she'd been Smith's fifth victim.

'Suddenly, it all made sense; most of it, anyway – the security you had installed and why, your daughter's 'woman's trouble', emotional and mental rather than physical, the fact that Smith had no qualms about letting you into his flat, and the ritual stringing up of his body.'

Her head swivelled and she glanced briefly at him, before turning back to the girl. 'I underestimated you,

Inspector; you seem to have worked it out very well.'

'Frank Massey was the father?'

Her bowed head acknowledged it. 'He wanted me to have an abortion. We rowed about it and I didn't see him again till my delayed return to college after the long summer holidays, after the birth, after the adoption. I told him I'd had the abortion he'd been pressing for.' She faltered, went on. 'He still doesn't know he had another daughter.'

Rafferty's breath suddenly quickened as he remembered she didn't know he was dead, that now he'd never know about his other daughter.

'I doubt I would ever have told him about her, but then Sheena – my daughter – traced me, wanted to know who her father was, to meet him. Only before I could bring myself to confess the truth to Frank, Sheena met Maurice Smith again. God knows, she was a nervy enough girl before that, distraught whenever I had to leave her alone in the house. I hadn't known he had moved to Elmhurst. There was no reason I should, of course, but if I *had* known I could have saved her from the trauma of meeting him again. I'd persuaded her to go shopping with the daughter of a friend of mine.'

She took a shaky breath and continued. 'She bumped into Maurice Smith, the beast who raped her when she was a little girl. Sheena became hysterical and ran home. I was at work, of course. She was alone for hours; refused to answer my friend's pleas to open the front door. So my friend rang me and I came home. She'd locked herself in the bathroom and we had to break the door down.'

Gently, she pushed the dark hair off her daughter's forehead. 'We found her much as she is now. It was only later, after the doctor had been and sedated her, that I got the full story of what had happened from my friend's daughter.'

She clutched the now-empty bowl and gazed at Sheena, who sat cradling a Raggedy-Ann doll in her lap, whispering to it in a lisping childlike voice.

'The doctors say she relapsed into childhood. She seems . . . happier there.'

Rafferty cautioned her again before she said any more. But she ignored the caution. She seemed to have a need to talk, to make them understand.

'She's my only child. I'd been told after her birth that it was unlikely I could have another baby, so you can imagine my joy when she traced me. Imagine, too, my horror when, shortly after our reunion, she broke down and told me she had been another of Smith's victims. I'd had no idea till then that he'd attacked a fifth young girl.' She raised her eyes to Rafferty's. 'How did you know there had been a fifth victim? I thought no one knew.'

'Stubbs mentioned it. He and Thompson went to see Smith after the trial. Smith told them then. Of course, even he had no idea who the girl was – she was just some little girl with a fiddle. Neither she nor her parents had come forward, there was nothing Stubbs could do. There was no point in mentioning it to anyone, including you. He confirmed when I rang him this morning that you hadn't been told.'

She nodded. 'Yet I knew there had been a fifth victim.' Suddenly she smiled. 'She's inherited my love of music. Piano's her thing now, rather than the violin, so I bought her the best instrument I could find. I-I hoped we could practise together.' Her voice stumbled and the smile faded. 'I doubt we'll ever do that now.'

Tenderly, she again smoothed her daughter's dark hair from her forehead. 'She told me she was coming out of her music lesson when Smith accosted her.'

She faltered for a moment and as she went on her voice hardened. 'Her adoptive parents reacted in the worst possible way when she told them what had happened to her. At first they refused to believe her, told her she was wicked to tell such lies. Even when she recognized his face in the newspapers when he was charged with the rape of the other little girls and they finally accepted she hadn't been lying they refused to come forward, refused

207

to let her speak of it even. She was made to feel it had been her fault. She said they had told her she was never to tell anyone about it because it was so shameful. Hardly surprising she never got over it.'

Silence descended again. The only sound was Sheena's voice chattering to her doll. Now, in the silence, Rafferty could make out what she was saying and he wondered how Elizabeth Probyn could bear it as Sheena whispered the same words over and over again. 'Naughty girl to tell such lies. You must be punished. Naughty girl to tell such lies. You must be punished. Naughty girl—'

'Frank Massey went missing,' he burst out, unable to stand the dreadful repetition. He wanted to get it over with, all of it, and get out of this room with its claustrophobia, its misery. 'You remember I told you?'

'Yes.'

He hesitated, then it came out in a rush. 'I'm afraid I've bad news. We found him – or, rather, a Dutch farmer found him in his barn.' Again he hesitated, but then forced himself to go on. 'He'd hanged himself.'

She didn't seem surprised. 'Poor Frank. Ironic when you think about it. He wanted me to kill our baby, instead my actions have resulted in his death.' Sighing, she added, 'He wasn't strong either mentally or emotionally.' Her gaze rested sadly on the girl. 'I'm afraid Sheena takes after him. He couldn't take prison. I know he had some kind of breakdown. Archie Stubbs made sure I knew that; I suppose he still wanted to punish me.

'Thankfully, he was unaware of our earlier affair. After he learned that Smith had been murdered Frank was terrified that he might be found guilty, might end up in prison again, especially as he had no alibi. He rang me, wanted my reassurance. I did my best to convince him he was safe, that the police would believe him, that no one would think he had anything to do with it. Obviously he didn't believe me. Perhaps I didn't try hard enough.' Her eyes shadowed. 'Maybe I still wanted to punish *him* for his weakness when I was young, pregnant and frightened.'

Quickly now, as though she wanted to get it over, she told them the rest. Ellen Kemp, the eldest of the three breakaway RSG women had given birth to her daughter, Jenny, at the same time as the young Elizabeth Osbourne had had Sheena. They'd been in adjoining beds and had kept in touch ever since. She told them that, by following Ellen Kemp's daughter's progress, she felt she was following that of her own daughter; the first words, the first steps, the first venture into the wider world.

When Sheena had traced her and told her what had happened to her, she had contacted Ellen Kemp for advice, in the hope that her professional counselling might help her daughter. But for Sheena it had been too late, the damage had gone too deep.

'It was then that she and her friends sent Smith the outing letter?' Rafferty questioned.

She nodded. 'Though I only learned about that later. I didn't realize they were watching his flat to make sure he didn't escape the punishment she and her friends had decided upon. Ellen was the one watching the flat when I went there that night. She saw me go in, saw me come out again, down the fire escape stairs, and guessed that it was Smith's body I was struggling to get down the stairs. I'd bought rubbish sacks to cover him; fitting, I thought.

'Anyway, I learned afterwards that she had assumed I had simply stunned Smith and she followed me, hoping to prevent me doing anything worse. She was too late, of course. I'd already killed him at the flat. The stringing up afterwards was something, like the rubbish sacks, I just felt fitting. By the time she reached Dedman Wood, I had already driven off.

'She took the body down and put it in the boot of her car; instinctively she told me she felt she had to hide it. Only, of course, it wasn't her car. It belonged to one of the other women. And when she told them what she had done, they persuaded her to put the body back, without

209

the hood or wrist binding. They panicked, I think, hoped it would be thought he had killed himself. Of course, they didn't realize that I had stabbed him. I can't imagine they examined him too closely and his dark clothes would have hidden any bloodstains.'

Rafferty nodded. He had been right. The RSG women had acted exactly as he had outlined to Mary Carmody. The realization brought little satisfaction. He had been right, too, in the supposition that it had been one of Smith's victims they had helped. Elizabeth Probyn, Ellen Kemp's friend for eighteen years and her daughter's 'Aunt Beth', had been as much Smith's victim as any of the raped girls.

Llewellyn's throat-clearing broke the silence. 'There is one thing, no, two, I don't understand.' She waited expectantly. 'Why he opened the door to you and how you knew his landlady would be out that night.'

'As for the latter, surely you haven't forgotten my "treasure"? I learned of the reunion from her. Her mother was going, she told me. She also told me, not once but a dozen times, the names of her acquaintances who were also to attend the reunion. Mrs Chadden likes to talk. It gives her a perfect excuse to avoid doing any work. And of course by then I'd found out where Smith lived, the name of his landlady and as much about him and his habits as possible. I knew that Thursday would be perfect.'

'It was you who rang the Social and got his address?' Llewellyn asked and when she nodded he reminded her of his other query.

'I was a representative of the law, Sergeant. He didn't see me as a threat. He remembered me from the trial: I still had my old security pass in my maiden name. I showed him that, told him I was researching for a book about men like himself and the raw deal he and other victims of justice had had.

'He swallowed it whole, was pathetically eager to talk.

210

He told me that his stepfather had beaten him up that very evening when he'd gone over there to see him. He was feeling sorry for himself and wanted a sympathetic ear. I did my best to oblige.'

Rafferty, glad to learn that he had been right about that, too, was only sorry that it was hearsay evidence and inadmissible.

'So, as I said, I was sympathetic, did my best to gain his trust, just as he had set out to gain my daughter's trust and the trust of those other little girls. It helped that I'm well spoken. I don't suppose he imagined that a woman with a correct BBC accent would be capable of violence. He got quite chatty. Of course, I couldn't afford to let his self-pitying rambling go on too long. I had to get back to the church hall before I was missed. I only had the interval and the last act of the play to accomplish my plan. I couldn't afford to waste time, though I had to let him talk for a few minutes to gain his confidence. I'd brought a tape-recorder with me and set it up on the table in front of his armchair.

'After a little while he seemed happy just to chat into the microphone, telling me about his grievances, while I wandered round the room. It was how I was able to get behind him. He had no suspicions. None at all. My one regret is that he died too quickly, happily pouring out his complaints into the tape-recorder.'

Her gaze was steady as she met Rafferty's. 'I had to do it, Inspector, you of all people must realize that. You were right. I know that now.'

Her voice was bitter, full of a passion Rafferty had never before heard in her voice. He hadn't believed her capable of such a depth of emotion.

'The law wouldn't give my daughter justice, I knew that. Maurice Smith destroyed her and by that act he also destroyed my belief in the law. Worse, under it all, I was conscious that *I* was the one who had helped him destroy her, I the one who had failed her. First at her birth, when

I was too weak, too scared to stand up to my parents when they insisted on adoption. Then at Smith's trial, when by my own eagerness to make a name for myself I not only deprived those other little girls of justice but also, unknowingly, convinced my own daughter that her adoptive parents had been right all along. In her mind, if Smith was innocent the rape *had* been her fault. I knew I had to avenge her. No one else would.'

Rafferty placed a hand on her shoulder. 'I'm sorry.' The words were, he knew, woefully inadequate.

She made no reply, just sat, gazing at her daughter. She seemed beyond pain now; like her daughter, she had retreated from the real world. Who could blame her?

Quickly, he told Llewellyn to summon a nurse. He didn't want to leave her daughter alone. He wanted to reassure her mother that Sheena would be looked after, but they both knew that this place cost a fortune. Once Elizabeth Probyn's money was gone, her daughter would be moved from this quiet sanctuary.

He took refuge in silence. When the nurse came, Rafferty took Elizabeth Probyn's arm. Surprisingly, she didn't resist, just kissed her daughter, once, on the forehead, and allowed herself to be led away. Of course, she knew that if she resisted, if she cried or struggled, she would only upset the girl.

She had done her duty as she saw it and in so doing had destroyed herself. Rafferty had long ago lost belief in the infallibility of the law. But she had believed in it, he knew, believed in it implicitly, even after the Smith case. But when she had discovered that her own daughter had been one of Smith's victims the foundations had been torn out of her world. She looked empty, anchorless, beyond reach. He had no choice. He had come this far, he had to go on. As he spoke the words of the caution, he had never hated his job more.

He may have done his policeman's duty, but in his heart he still felt he had perpetuated an injustice. What made it worse was that his arrest of Elizabeth Probyn would, after all the sensational coverage Smith's murder had received in the media, mean that the investigation would get a thorough raking over from his large family. He knew they would feel he'd have done better to ignore the clues and let natural justice prevail. He couldn't help thinking they had a point. What, after all, would Elizabeth Probyn's arrest achieve apart from more misery?

Predictably, he could hear Llewellyn's answer echoing in his head: it removed the stain of suspicion from others involved in the case. He supposed he'd have to be satisfied with that.

Chapter Eighteen

It was much later that day, after Ellen Kemp and her friends had been brought to the station and charged, when they were getting ready to go home, that the phone rang. Rafferty had been prepared to let it ring, but Llewellyn, never one to ignore duty's call, picked it up. The conversation didn't take long.

'Guess who that was,' he invited Rafferty when it was over.

Rafferty shrugged.

'Remember our travelling salesman who noted and lost the registration number of the Zephyr?'

Rafferty nodded.

'He's finally found the piece of paper and, surprise, surprise—'

'It's the same as that on Sinead Fey's car,' Rafferty finished for him. Llewellyn nodded. 'Pity he didn't manage to find it before.'

'If he had we may well have concentrated our attention more strongly on them and never got beyond the fact of their involvement. If Frank Massey hadn't begun to feel he was our number one suspect and gone missing, we might never have learned about his and Elizabeth Probyn's youthful liaison, you would never have begun to wonder about that liaison, and about the strange limit to the photographs of the daughter that no one seemed to know anything about and what exactly was the matter with her and why.'

Rafferty wasn't sure he wouldn't have preferred it that way. But he kept the opinion to himself. It wasn't the sort of thing a police inspector should bruit about.

At least the telephone call had succeeded in breaking the melancholy silence that the discovery of the truth and Elizabeth Probyn's painful confession had brought, because Llewellyn went on, 'By the way, thanks for the advice.'

'Advice?' Rafferty's head began to thump as his hangover returned. Oh God, he thought, I haven't been dishing out more of the stuff, have I?

He could hardly believe it after all the anxieties the last lot had caused him. Trouble was, he couldn't remember. Half suspicious, half wary, he stared at his sergeant, trying to discern the emotions behind the impassive countenance, never an easy task at the best of times, especially when Llewellyn was indulging his love of irony at his expense. And, in the past, Rafferty's unasked for and carelessly handed out pearls of wisdom had had a painful boomerang tendency that had only served to encourage the Welshman's withering wit. 'All right,' he muttered, 'out with it. What have I done this time?'

'You advised me to pop the question.'

Rafferty took a deep breath and asked, 'So what happened?'

'It was such a beautiful night, still and silent, made for poetry, for declarations of love and—'

'For God's sake, will you just tell me what happened!'

Llewellyn's long face actually split into a grin. 'I asked her. She said yes.'

Thank God for that, Rafferty thought and breathed a sigh of relief. The next minute, qualms forgotten, he clapped Llewellyn on the back. 'There – what did I tell you? Trust your old Agony Uncle Joseph to know what's what. Now you can start worrying about how much it's all going to cost. First it'll be the engagement ring, then—'

Llewellyn shook his head. 'Maureen doesn't believe in such things. She—'

215

Rafferty held up his hands. 'Don't tell me. She thinks engagement rings are symbols of male oppression, right?' A ring through the nose of 'Daisy' the cow, Rafferty repeated irreverently to himself.

Llewellyn nodded.

'Jammy devil. Mind, I wouldn't bet on such luck lasting. Wait till that mother of hers gets to work on her. That woman's got to have something to boast about. Bet you a fiver you end up paying for a stone that Liz Taylor would envy.' Rafferty thrust his chair back and pulled on his coat. 'Anyway, you can worry about that later. Now, I think it's time you bought the matchmaker a drink. We'll pop into the Green Man. It's not every day my sergeant gets himself engaged, with or without the ring.' It wasn't every day you arrested a Chief Crown Prosecutor either, he reminded himself. He wasn't sure whether the drink would be a celebratory one or a drowning of sorrows.

'So when's the happy day?' he asked as they walked out to the car.

'Not for some time. It doesn't do to rush these things. Though,' Llewellyn gave a faint smile, 'as your mother has bought her hat and has also found me the most wonderful new suit, I don't think we ought to disappoint her too long.'

'A new suit?' Rafferty queried, as an uneasy memory stirred.

'Yes, your mother showed it to me after you left last night.' He frowned. 'I forgot, she asked me not to mention it to you as she only had the one. Pity she didn't have one to fit you, though. It's of a marvellous quality and surprisingly reasonable. Your mother really has got an eye for a bargain.'

Rafferty gave him a sickly smile. 'Hasn't she, though?'